Tethered

A.K. Chatham

TABLE OF CONTENTS

CHAPTER ONE

Stable No More

What makes up an individual? Genetic factors linked with world experience? Nature versus nurture? Although social influence and financial status are known to significantly alter one's capabilities in life. To be or not to be, that is the question, right? However, to be what is the real question? Do you choose to be different from the parents who raised you? Do you alter your path due to the influence of others? Do you purposely strive to meet the goals that have been set for you by those who think they know what is best for you?

She was born ready. Life experiences had made her that way. Paige Peterson had lived and breathed the school since her admission, nearly two years ago. The Academy was a military ROTC driven academy for pupils in their sophomore year that rendered the Armed Forces well-qualified officers every year at graduation. Living with a distant father and a distracted mother, Paige left home at 16 on an early admission program to the Academy. The Academy was offered to her as an alternative to traditional public school. She had had a record of multiple absences and late days since her freshman year that had resulted in failing grades. The summer prior to her admission, she worked and stayed with friends, mostly to avoid home. She left behind parents who had led selfish, destructive lives, and she felt lucky to have gotten out when she did. She had gotten into the Academy either by the skin of her teeth or pity, which one she didn't know and she didn't care.

At first, her transition was difficult. She didn't enjoy the early morning wake-ups, strict requirements, or loss of freedom, but over time she had adjusted well. The program was challenging both physically and mentally. When Paige felt like giving up, she thought about the life she would have to return to, and that motivated her to push herself to succeed. Soon after she left home for the Academy, she received a letter from her mother informing her that her parents had separated. This confirmed, yet again, the state of their instability and gave her even more enthusiasm to start a new life. The school gave her boundaries she had never had before. She excelled and gained self-confidence, along with a sense of belonging she had never known. At the Academy, she wasn't the daughter of deadbeat drug-head parents, but her own person. She was well-liked in her cohort and had many acquaintances, and was especially close to her friends Jude and Natilee. Paige had received financial aid the first semester; but, she was forced to get student loans for the second semester and the current year. She worked as a library assistant three days a week, and that seemed to get her by without signing for another loan. Scholarships or loans, Paige wasn't willing to go back and live with her parents. That wasn't an option. She had freedom, and nothing would change that come hell or high water.

On the weekends, she either worked the morning hours or got coffee with her friends, Jude and Natilee. They spend time with each other every day, as a rule where you saw one you would see the other. On this particular Saturday, Paige had coffee with Natilee and was doing her laundry when she received a text from her Dorm Chief. The text stated she had a phone call on the landline in the dormitory office. Thinking this odd, she responded with a question mark and received an "IDK" response. Paige went downstairs to the phone. It was the secretary of the chancellor's office informing Paige they had been contacted by State of Virginia authorities, and they had requested her presence at 1330 that day. Paige had an uneasy feeling. The hairs sticking up on her arms were sticking up, and the walls of her stomach tensed.

"Do you know what this is about?" she asks the person on the other end of the phone. The voice on the phone was of no help, just repeated what she already had been told. Immediately, Paige's thoughts revert back to her past, to her parents, and her family issues. The sickening feeling worsened. She wanted to run, although that wasn't a realistic option. Paige called Natilee and quickly described the phone call and request she had received just minutes prior.

"Maybe it is just some kinda mix-up about your credentials or a placement offer for after you graduate." Natilee attempted to calm Paige, but the words she said did not penetrate through. All Paige was hearing were sounds from her past. She flashed back to a time when she was standing in the rain with her book bag and wet sneakers waiting on a bus. In the memory, she boarded the bus, then silently slouched down in her seat with her head laden heavy against the window.

"Paige, Paige, listen to me. I will come with you. I can be there in a few minutes," Natalie said, waking her up.

"No, it's ok. I will call you as I leave. Where is Jude? Tell him what is going on. This feels like some sketchy crap." Paige said to Natilee. Natilee agreed to fill Jude in on the situation and to wait on Paige's call. Paige hung up the phone, pulled on her academy sweater, jeans, converse sneakers. She threw her thick auburn hair into a loose messy bun. Not sure what to take, she grabbed her phone and dorm key before she left. As she walked, she couldn't help but fear that her stable world would return to chaos and uncertainty and her life would return to a state of survival.

When she arrived at the office, it was quiet. She had never entered this building before, and frankly, she had no idea what normally occurred here. There was a receptionist at the desk, so she checked in and was told to have a seat. Alone in the office waiting area, she began to become even more anxious. Paige could feel her heart pounding in her chest. Her mouth was dry. The door opened, and a man in a suit approached her. He introduced himself as the Academy liaison and seemed to be somewhat nervous himself. As she walked into the room, she noticed another man in a suit and a middle-aged woman there, who had a distinguished look about her. Paige was seated at a table with all three people facing her. She automatically assumed she was in some sort of trouble and began thinking hard, attempting to recall what she could have done. The liaison introduced Mr. Daniels, who was an attorney representing the State of Virginia, then he introduced Mrs. Diane Stewart. Paige couldn't help but display a look of confusion on her face.

The liaison asks, "How have you enjoyed the program you are in? Do you play any sports?"

Clearly, these questions were distracting and only stalling the actual topic of conversation; this only annoyed her.

She responded with, "I am fine, and I don't play sports." Paige quickly asked, "Why did you call me here?"

"Ok, we will get right to it," Daniels said. "Your mother has died. She suffered from an unfortunate illness, and given her poor health and multiple comorbidities, she did not survive." Mr. Daniels paused, waiting on Paige's reaction.

This news was not surprising to Paige. She had known her mother's habits of drugs and alcohol would eventually get her.

After a long pause, Paige felt pressured to speak. Not knowing what to say, she simply said, "Ok."

The attorney then looked at Mrs. Stewart, and silence fell in the room. Paige looked to Mr. Daniels then to Mrs. Stewart. She didn't understand why the attorney was staring at this strange woman. Mrs. Stewart nodded at Mr. Daniels, and he continued.

"It was revealed upon your mother's death while searching her medical records and history that Mrs. Peterson was not your biological mother," the attorney explained.

Paige was shocked. She just sat there, apparently confused, shaking her head and looking at the floor. As if she had woken up from a drunken stupor, she said.

"What the hell are you talking about?"

Mr. Daniels went on to explain, "Your, well Mrs. Peterson, had been found, by a passer-by, deathly ill. She was admitted to the hospital. Unfortunately, they discovered she required a kidney transplant to live. However, with your mother's, err Mrs. Peterson's, poor health, she was not a candidate for the United donor list, and the doctors were searching for a donor amongst her family and children."

"How long ago was this?" Paige asked.

"Your mother passed away two weeks ago," he explained.

"Ok, and it took you this long to track me down? It couldn't have been that difficult," Paige said.

"Please let me finish. This is very important," he stated, and Paige shut up. "When searching the records, it was confirmed, with a comparison of blood analysis and DNA, that Mrs. Peterson could not biologically be the mother of her stated daughter Paige Peterson, you," he explained.

Paige just stared at him.

"Mrs. Peterson's DNA structure and yours do not match. In fact, they are incompatible. Also, miss, it was determined that if, in fact, you had been her daughter, you should be 11 months older than your current age."

No longer able to maintain her composure, Paige, revealing her anxiety and frustration, stood and, raising her hands, asked loudly, "What the hell does all this mean?"

"Please sit, Ms. Peterson, and try to be patient," Mr. Daniels said. Paige grunted.

Not happy with someone telling her what to do, she plopped down heavy on her chair and crossed her arms. The attorney continued to explain that neither her mother nor father were her biological parents. In fact, Mr. Peterson had been sentenced to prison for multiple drug charges, armed robbery and was now being charged with kidnapping.

"So, you are telling me I lived with two people, who were not my parents all my life, basically. And now you don't know who the hell I am?" Paige asked, clearly agitated and getting worse.

"Paige, you seem upset. Would you like to talk to your father, I mean Mr. Peterson? I mean, about your mother, Susan's death. You must be shocked." stammered the attorney.

Paige looked at him like he was stupid. "Oh, do I seem upset?" Paige scoffed. "No, you idiot, I do not want to talk to him. I know him. He doesn't give two shits about me." Paige said like her statement was an obvious fact. "He is a druggy, and I don't doubt the robbery, but who did he kidnap?" Paige questioned the attorney, totally oblivious to the truth.

He then turned his head to the lady in the room again, seemingly looking for direction. The lady stared at him, offering no help. "What? Spit it out. Why are you looking at her?" Paige asked persistently. Mrs. Stewart looked to be getting agitated herself. She gave Mr. Daniels a stern look.

"We will discuss those details later," the attorney said, trying to change her affect. Paige looked at him and thought, this man has no balls or is an idiot.

Paige accepted his answer. She was afraid the staring lady was going to throttle him. "Do you feel that you need to talk to someone about Mrs. Peterson's death?" the attorney asked, trying to pull her emotions. This was not a good move. Paige looked at him like he was a fool and spoke.

"No, I am fine. She was in poor health. I have not spoken to her in almost two years. We were estranged. She made many poor choices." Paige responded without much emotion, putting up a block wall around her.

No one asked what choices she had made or what type of life Paige had growing up. It was clear Paige wasn't giving up any details voluntarily either.

"Are there forms or something I need to sign to establish I am not their child? I mean, am I done. I want to go." Paige said as she stood up, ready to leave.

"No, that is not all we need to discuss. You may want to have a seat." the attorney said. "Mrs. Stewart may I speak to you outside?" the attorney asked.

Mrs. Stewart nodded and stood as the attorney opened the door, following her into the hallway. "Mrs. Stewart, are you sure you want to go through with this? She seems to be rather. rough around the edges." he asked, looking nervous.

"Yes, of course, I do. She is my niece. Her parents have searched for her for the past 17 years." Mrs. Stewart said.

"Yes but are you sure they will want... what they have found," he asked boldly.

"How dare you ask me that. Yes, she is rough around the edges. She has had to be that way to survive. She was raised by incompetent fools. I believe she has done well to survive the circumstances she has been given thus far. It is my duty to take her home to her parents, so we can give her the life she deserves. Now stop wasting time and get on with it." Mrs. Stewart said sternly and turned to go back into the office, leaving him standing in the hallway alone.

"So?" Paige asked after she saw both parties rejoin the table. "Is this about school or funding or something?" She was eager to leave.

"Ms. Peterson, please be patient? This is a lengthy presentation of facts. You are not being expelled." Mr. Daniels clarified.

"Ok, then what is the big deal? I don't have parents. I have never really had parents. This is no real change for me. Send the rest of the details to my email? I have things to do." Paige said, then stood up to leave with an arrogant heir about her. She turned to open the door behind her and had her hand on the knob when she heard.

"Stop." Mrs. Stewart said as she slapped the wooden table. Paige turned around to see Mrs. Stewart now standing, leaning toward her side of the table. "You are not going anywhere. Sit down." Mrs. Stewart said loudly in a British accent.

Up until this point, she had not spoken. But she now had Paige's attention. Paige looked directly at her and blurted out before she could stop herself, "Who the hell are you?" Surprised at herself, Paige blinked but didn't lose eye contact with the lady. The attorney and liaison looked away, and Paige had a feeling she had done something wrong.

The lady stood up straight, meeting Paige's height, and stared directly at her and said, "I am Diane Stewart, your guardian."

"What?" Paige asked, puzzled and absent of words.

"That is what he is trying to explain. Sit down, now." Diane said, pointing at the chair.

Paige turned around and sat down in the chair, crossed her arms, and slumped back in the chair. She felt confused and like a child who had been scolded. She grasped her hands together and stared at Mr. Daniels, not engaged, but cooperative at least for the moment. Mr. Daniels, the attorney, continued.

"Paige, you are not an orphan. In fact, you have been missing since your birth, seventeen years ago. Your legal and given name is Anastasia Danielle Hutchinson, and you were born on September 7th, 2001 in eastern North Carolina."

Paige looked confused. "You were kidnapped, taken two days after birth. At the time, all evidence presented stated that an unknown female, impersonating an employee, had stolen Anastasia Hutchinson from the hospital. The location of your birth and dates of Mrs. Peterson's hospital admission correlates with the kidnapping. Mrs. Peterson had been discharged from the psychiatric floor that same day. The parents of Anastasia Hutchinson have been searching for her since her birth. When your DNA and blood didn't match Peterson's, the location, blood type, and birth date were found in a customized query. Once your medical profile was obtained from the Academy, it was compared to that of Andrea and Phillip Hutchinson's and was a perfect match," Mr. Daniels explained. Paige listened, linking up all the pieces in her head like some NCIS case she had seen on T.V.

"Miss, are you listening?" he asked her. She nodded yes and stared at the yellow papers on his desk.

"Ma'am, your biological parents were identified as Phillip and Andrea Hutchinson. Paige, you are Anastasia Hutchinson. You have a family who has been looking for you for seventeen years," he said, trying to help her understand. Paige didn't respond. She just glared at them.

"Do you understand?" asked Mr. Daniels. Paige heard him but didn't respond. She just felt empty and void. "Mrs. Peterson, do you understand?" he asked again.

Paige then responded, "yeah," so softly they could hardly hear her. Silently thought to herself, who am I, who are these people, and what does all this mean? Paige sat there still and silent.

"This is your guardian. She is here to take you to your new home and your family," Mr. Daniel's said.

The words "take you" stuck out, and Paige heard only that. "Seriously, you gotta be freaking kidding me, right?" she said.

"No, this is a good thing," Mr. Daniels said. Suddenly, it occurred to Paige that this would impact her far more than she was comfortable with.

"A good thing? Will I get to finish school? Where do these people live? I don't wanna move away. What does this mean for me? I don't know what the hell is going on." Paige responded, raising her voice again.

"You will not be continuing your studies here," Mrs. Stewart said.

"Why?" Paige asked warily.

The liaison joined in the conversation, "You will be dismissed from your program because you no longer meet the criteria. The program admission was given to Paige Peterson, and that person does not exist, so you are no longer eligible."

Paige responded rapidly, "Ok, that sucks and is not my fault. I am the same person, just a different name. And I am 18, an adult. I will reapply. I have to finish school."

"You are Anastasia Hutchinson. Your life has been changed. You…" started the attorney.

But, Paige interrupted, bursting out, "Stop saying that! That is not my name! I can do what I want to. I am an adult, and this is a free country. I am in the USA, for God's sake, where are my rights? Where is my freedom? What if she is lying? What if you are all lying?" Paige said, standing again, getting agitated. Mrs. Stewart pointed at the chair. Paige looked at her like she was crazy but still sat.

The attorney cut in, "We have done all the research. This information has been thoroughly reviewed, and there is no mistake."

"Am I really expected to just drop my life and play family reunion with people I don't even know? I am not a child." Paige said, getting more irritated and emotional.

"You are Anastasia Danielle Hutchinson, whose mother and father have been looking for her for 17 years. You are not going to finish school here. You are leaving with me. Your life has changed, and finishing school here would be unrealistic," Diane Stewart explained to Paige.

"This is bullshit, and I said I am not going anywhere! This is my life!" Paige said loudly, displaying her anger as she stood and leaned with her hands on the table toward them like a young lioness.

Mrs. Stewart stood up herself and leaned on the table facing Paige as if it was a challenge. "Leave us," she said to the two men, without losing eye contact with Paige.

The attorney and liaison quickly stepped outside. The door shut behind them.

Mrs. Stewart leaned in more and said to Paige calmly, "Young lady, I will not tolerate this foul language and rude behavior. Do I make myself clear?" Paige just looked at her like she had two heads.

"Do you understand?" she asked again, just as stern and expecting an answer.

"Yeah," Paige replied

"Yes, ma'am," Diane said, correcting her.

"Yes, ma'am," she said, mocking Mrs. Stewart and rolling her eyes. Paige took a deep breath and put her hands on her hips. Diane crossed her arms and waited for her to sit.

Once Paige was seated, Mrs. Stewart said, "Now, I know this is a shock to you; but, you will do exactly what I say. And yes, you are leaving. This is not your life. Your life hasn't even begun." Mrs. Stewart lectured.

Paige was now upset and shaking. She didn't know what else to do but freak out.

"We are ready to leave," Diane said to the liaison.

"Wait, seriously, I am an adult. I have a choice, don't I?" Paige asked Mr. Daniels in a desperate voice.

Mr. Daniels then explained, "You are only 17 years old. Your birth certificate was falsified to reflect an inaccurate date and year. Therefore, you are not a legal adult and cannot make the decisions of an adult. I am sorry."

Paige put her head in her hands and said, "I can't believe this is happening." Paige looked up at Mrs. Peterson. "So, what happens if I refuse to go? I mean, you can't gag me and drag me away," she said.

Mrs. Stewart turned her head to the side and gave her a look that said, "Don't try me."

Mr. Daniels explained, "If you do not go with Mrs. Stewart, who is your guardian, you will be homeless. You will no longer be a student here. Your formerly known parents have no means to support you. You have no money, no car, no home, and no known identity. Your license is invalid because you are not the person named in the photo. You cannot even enlist in the military because that would require a parent or guardian's signature."

Paige listened to the words, "No home, no money, no car." They brought back painful memories of worrying about if she would have a home the next week when the rent came due.

Paige didn't say anything, so the liaison said, "As you wish, we are finished here. I will have someone escort Mrs. Hutchinson to get her belongings."

Mrs. Stewart replied, "We need to leave immediately."

Paige stood and began to pace with her hands covering her face. The door shut, leaving her and Mrs. Stewart alone again. "Seriously, I have made a functional life here. I do not want to leave. Is there any way I can stay?" Paige asked as she hoped for an alternative.

"There is no way you can stay." Mrs. Stewart said.

"This is not fair," Paige said out loud, expressing herself.

Diane looked at her and said, "I will explain more on the way."

Paige stood with her head resting on the solid white wall in front of her. She had been crying, but it is just now that she noticed her tears flowing down her cheeks. She hid her face. She felt defeated. Her life had all been a lie, and this stability she had finally achieved at the Academy had vanished in a matter of minutes. She wanted to see Natilee and Jude. Maybe they could help. How was she going to leave the only people she loved and who loved her?

Within minutes, a knock at the door revealed Paige's dorm chief, who escorted them to her room.

As Paige unlocked the door, she said, "I need to see my friends before I am forced to leave." Paige went into her room and took a large bag out of the closet.

"You will not need that bag. Only bring personal things. You will not need anything else," Diane said.

Paige looked confused, but she grabbed a jacket, her journal, and the pictures she had of her friends, and her Academy blanket. Natilee walked into her room, unaware of the news.

"Hey, hey, what is going on? Who is this?" she asked, referring to Mrs. Stewart.

Paige looked at Mrs. Stewart and asked, "May I have a minute alone, please?"

Mrs. Stewart nodded and went into the hall without closing the door. Paige collapsed in tears around Natilee.

"What's wrong?" Natilee asked, confused by her friend's obvious distress. Paige tried to explain quickly what was happening. She couldn't stop the tears as she hugged her friend. Jude ran into the room to find them embracing and was immediately upset. Mrs. Stewart, who had been standing outside the door, knocked as Paige cried in the arms of her friends. Paige hugged her friends tightly as the door opened.

"We need to go," Mrs. Stewart said.

"I need a minute," Paige said and closed the door.

"It will be ok. We will help you fix it." Natilee said.

The door opened. "It is time to go." Mrs. Stewart said as she reached in for Paige's arm.

Paige pulled away. "Let's go." Mrs. Stewart took her forearm into her right hand then placed her arm around Paige's, walking her away from her friends. Paige was in full sob cry mode, and she hated to cry. It made her feel out of control. She kept her face down and attempted to wipe her eyes without making a scene. As they left the main hall, Jude appeared outside. He was out of breath with red splotches on his cheeks, like he had been running.

Jude blocked Mrs. Stewart's path, startling her, and asked, "May I see her for just a minute before you leave?"

Mrs. Stewart replied, "You can say goodbye to her outside the car."

A black Suburban was parked in front of the Academy entrance. Mrs. Stewart then, after a few seconds, got in behind the driver, the door was opened for Paige on the opposite side. Paige closed the door to block their moment together from Mrs. Stewart. Paige wiped her face, then looked up at him. Jude smiled at Paige as if they had just breathed a breath of peace that halted time.

Jude said softly, "You didn't think you could get away from me without saying goodbye, did you?" He grasped her hand.

Paige smiled through teary eyes and then reached up to hug him. He embraced her and breathed her in. He nuzzled her neck slightly and then kissed her. This took Paige by surprise, but a welcomed one. She kissed him back and stared up into his eyes.

Not knowing the words to say, he said desperately, "Don't leave me."

The window rolled down, and Mrs. Stewart said, "Anastasia, it is time to go."

Paige didn't respond. She was so engrossed in Jude she couldn't hear anything but his words and feel his body next to hers. She kissed him again, and their embrace tightened.

"I don't want to go, but I don't know how to stay," she said to him.

"Anastasia, get in the vehicle. It is time to go," Mrs. Stewart said impatiently.

"I don't like her," Paige whispered to Jude.

"I am so sorry," he replied.

Diane heard that comment but didn't respond. Jude opened the door, and Paige got in, sinking in her seat. She put her hand out the window grasping his.

The driver looked back and asked, "Are we ready?"

Diane replied sharply, "Yes, Anastasia, remove your hand." As she let go, the car started moving.

Paige exhaled heavily and leaned back, slouching against the seat, and gave Mrs. Stewart a piercing look. She heard Jude beckon for her, and she sat up quickly, peering out as they drove away. She could see him through the window. He was waving and yelling her name in a desperate voice. Paige panicked and turned and hastily attempted to unlock the door.

She screamed, "Let me out of here! I don't wanna go!" She beat her hand on the tinted glass. The car didn't stop. "I said stop the car, now," she screamed at Mrs. Stewart.

"Stop. This is ridiculous," Mrs. Stewart said in a calm tone.

"I don't wanna leave, please, please," Paige asked through her tears, looking at Mrs. Stewart with her hands up in a pleading pose.

"Do you really want me to put you out on the side of the road?" Mrs. Steward asked, her voice rising.

Paige didn't respond but glared at her with hatred in her eyes.

"Exactly, so stop acting like a child." Mrs. Stewart said, clearly agitated at Paige's outburst and behavior.

CHAPTER TWO

Stowaway

Paige cried silently as she wrang her hands, shuffled her feet, and pointed her toes inward. This was an unconscious coping mechanism she had always used when she felt scared or upset. The ride to the airport was short, and soon they were walking to a private jet. Paige would have normally been in awe of such lavish transportation; but she was too upset to even notice. Paige boarded the plane and sat down, placing her bag in her lap. She looked around and could see she was the only person on the plane. She had everything she owned with her in a navy Jansport book bag. She looked at her phone. The phone she had paid for with scholarship money. That was the only valuable item she had. She had her license/identification card, her school meal card, and a debit card. She had a couple of hundred dollars in the bank, and that was supposed to last her until the end of the month. She didn't even have a change of clothes with her. Paige felt like she was being kidnapped. All that was missing were ropes around her hands and feet. She was angry and scared of leaving the home she had made at the academy. Other than Jude and Natalie, she had no one else in the world. Mrs. Stewart sat beside her on the plane, just one seat between them. Paige didn't say a word to her. She didn't know what to say or even ask. How do I even feel about her? On the one hand, she promised a better life, and, on the other, she scolded her for her behavior and locking me in a car.

Once they had ascended, Mrs. Stewart said, "Why don't you lie down and rest?" She pointed to a sofa.

Clearly exhausted, Paige got up and moved to the sofa without arguing. She curled up on her side with her academy blanket hiding her face. She didn't want to cry, but she couldn't help it. She sobbed, wiping tears away with her blanket. She cried herself to sleep, exhausted from the emotional day.

Mrs. Diane Stewart watched her niece. She watched her shoulders shudder under the navy and gold blanket with each gasp. She turned her head away, trying not to become emotional. Diane wanted to hold her, but she closed her eyes and held her breath. Diane knew her niece was a stranger to her and that she wouldn't understand her affection. So, she waited, and when Paige was asleep, she retrieved another blanket, and covered her, then gently patted her head.

When she awoke, Paige felt groggy. Mrs. Stewart saw she was awake and brought her a warm cloth for her face.

"Thanks. Who are you, and where are my parents?" Paige asked calmly and somewhat hoarsely.

Mrs. Stewart responded, "I am your aunt Diane, your father's sister. You may call me Aunt Diane."

"Oh, I didn't know that. I kinda freaked out, didn't I?" Paige asked.

"Yes, you did," Diane said.

"This is so weird, like so crazy," Paige replied.

"Anastasia, you're going to be fine," said her Aunt Diane.

Paige didn't say anything but looked uncertain.

"What?" Diane asked, reading her expressions.

"Can you just call me Paige?" she asked.

"Paige is not your name. I understand you are not accustomed to it; but Anastasia is who you are. So that is what you will be called." Diane said.

Paige didn't feel like arguing. The plane landed in Chicago, and as they drove through the city, Paige asked, "What are we doing here?"

"This is my husband's family's home. We will be here for a few days before we go back home. Your parents are not here, although your father sent me to get you. He has not told your mother or brother of your discovery. He wants to bring you home himself." Diane explained.

"When will I meet him?" Paige asked.

Diane replied, "He will be here tomorrow afternoon, and we have a lot to accomplish before then."

Paige immediately became frustrated and nervous at the same time. "So, I don't mean any disrespect by saying this, but I feel like this isn't lawful," Paige stated, attempting to be respectful in hopes of a positive response.

She wanted to scream at her new aunt, but she knew it wouldn't do any good. She felt like her life had been stolen. The life she had worked so hard for.

"Well, you are a minor, remember that. I do understand. You may feel you have little control right now. But this is not illegal. In fact, it would be unlawful to resist. This is a transition, so it will be difficult. You have only just begun to live your life," Diane tried to explain.

"Well, I should have a choice on whether or not I wanted to leave school," Anastasia spat.

"You had no choice in that matter, Anastasia. You live in a different country. Your home is in England with your family. You have been discovered. Your parents and family, including myself, have been praying for your entire life to find you, and it is a miracle we did. So, you will be going home, and that is that," Diane stated matter-of-factly.

Paige thought about the words her aunt had just said. How could someone have been looking for her all this time? All those times she had wished to leave or for someone to find her, and now, when she gets it all together, she is yanked from her home.

"I am so freaking confused. I know you say my parents have been looking for me, but, I mean, what the hell took so long. Now, I have a life to return to, my friends, my studies, my goals," Anastasia said, frustrated.

"Language, please. And yes, you have friends, but your life was a lie. Your new life will be in England with your family. You are in no position to make a choice. You have not experienced your new life," Diane clarified.

That was a valid point; although Paige didn't want to hear it. She did have friends and a past, but she felt like somehow her life had been erased. Most of her past, she didn't mind being erased, but she felt like part of herself was being erased with it. She took her iPhone out and began to text Natilee. She told her of her arrival in Chicago and that she would be there for a few days. Immediately, Jude snapped at her, and his face was silly and smiling. She responded back, but not with a photo, just a text. She was still angry and knew she would not look very reassuring. She wanted to text him and tell him to come save her. To come and steal her away, but she didn't.

CHAPTER THREE

Introductions

Phillip had already arrived earlier in the afternoon and was sitting at the desk reading the information on Richard Peterson when Diane entered the room. He looked up to see Diane approaching him.

"Philip, I am glad you're finally here," she said as she walked in.

He looked up and smiled, putting down the paperwork in his hands.

"Sister, how is my daughter? I am concerned, especially after reading these records on the Peterson'," he said.

"I don't know how the child wasn't in jail or property of the state," he said as she sat down across from him. "Tell me, how did it all go at the college and bringing her here?" he asked, smiling.

"It went alright. Although, she wasn't and still isn't thrilled about being taken away from her life," Diane said, making quotation signs with her hands at the word life. "She is strong-willed and emotional. She doesn't know who she is and who she isn't. I haven't told her much about her family or her lineage," Diane said.

"Oh my Diane, you worry too much. How can the child understand who she is if you do not tell her?" he said as he sat back in the chair. "Is she like her mother or me?" he asked as he drank a sip of bourbon out of a glass.

"She seems to be a lot like her mother when it comes to her outbursts. I thought I was going to have to use force to get her in the car at the school," Diane said as she raised her eyebrows and smiled.

"Oh my, well, we can't have that. Do you think she is ready to come home?" he asked.

"I think so. I just don't want you to expect her to be a princess. She has lived a very different life," she warned.

"I am aware of her difficult upbringing. I want to give her all she desires. The child has been neglected," he said affectionately.

"She doesn't desire material things. She needs love and structure. She has been on her own for some time, and she needs to be reined in and broken," Diane said.

"We are not talking about horses, Di," he said, laughing.

"You know what I mean," Diane said.

"Well, go get my daughter. I am ready to meet her," he said as he stood and stretched, pulling his shirt down and standing tall.

He looked over at Nellie to his left and said, "How do I look?"

She replied, "Dashing," and smiled up at him.

At that comment, Diane said, "My word," and walked out the door to retrieve Anastasia.

Diane led Ana to the study. It was lit beautifully by multiple lamps, and she could see him across what felt like a huge room. When they entered the room, he stood tall, looking out the window. He turned just in time to see her cross into the room. His smile lit the room even more than the lamps. To Ana, it felt like she floated across the room.

Diane stood in between them and said, "Anastasia, this is your father, Phillip."

"Hi," Ana said softly.

"Phillip, this is…," Diane started.

He interrupted her, "I know who this is. She is the spitting image of her mother."

He walked over to Ana and held out his hands to her. She met his gaze, then put her hands gently into his.

"Anastasia, I am your father. Your mother and I have searched for you your entire life," he said tenderly.

Ana had an overwhelming feeling she couldn't describe.

She didn't know what to say but said, "Hi, this is all such a big surprise."

He pulled her hand toward the sofa and said, "Sit down, dear. I understand this is all surprising. I hope you will be happy in our home and with us, your family."

He spoke slowly and carefully, choosing his words. She wanted to interject and ask a million questions; but she felt it wasn't the right time.

She politely responded with, "Yes, sir."

Out of the corner of her eye, she saw Diane nod her head and smile. She imagined her aunt was astonished by her polite behavior.

Her father continued, "I will have to learn all about my daughter. My hope is for our bond to be as close as if you had always been with us."

Immediately, Ana thought of the envelope with her name on it. She wondered if her aunt had spoken to her father about its contents. Her father went on to say that he wanted her to meet her mother as soon as possible. He kept speaking of how happy they would be and how excited he was that she was finally home. He seemed to be very pleased and sincere when he spoke of how he had missed her and loved her. Ana sat and listened to him. She found it hard to get a word in, not that she really knew what to say anyway. At last, it was time for dinner, and he led her to the dining room.

Before they crossed into the room, Phillip slowed, leaned over, and whispered to her, "I understand this is all new for you, Anastasia. But you must know, you are an important part of this family."

Ana smiled a little, not knowing how to respond. Dinner was served, and Ana focused on trying to use her utensils correctly. During dinner, Diane and Phillip discussed travel back to the United Kingdom. The plan, according to Phillip, was to travel back the following evening. Diane felt that they should wait until Ana had more time to adjust, as well as to finish all the necessary paperwork with the attorney. It seemed to Ana that she might never get the opportunity to have a voice in this decision.

Finally, Diane said, "Well, maybe we should ask Anastasia?"

Ana quickly responded, "Actually, I would like a few more days to adjust, and I was hoping to see my friends before leaving."

Diane looked at Phillip, and he simply said, "Four days enough time?"

"Yes," Ana said quickly.

Diane then said, "I think we can use two days for travel, and a day in Virginia will be enough."

Ana felt like she had been shorted, but at least she could go. She wondered why her time was being limited with her friends.

"I am moving to another country. I would like to spend more time at the Academy with Natilee and Jude. I mean, when will I ever get to see them again," Ana pleaded.

Phillip nodded, "A day doesn't matter to me, Diane."

There was a pause, "Four it is then," Diane said quickly, as she put her napkin on the table.

Ana could tell Diane was not pleased.

"Ana, you may be excused. I know you will want to arrange the visit with your friends," Diane said.

"Yes, ma'am," Ana said as she pulled her chair out.

"Thank you, sir," Ana said before leaving the room.

He nodded, smiled, and said, "You're welcome, dear."

Ana texted both Nat and Jude as soon as she got into her room.

Natilee texted in response.

We have to go out! Jude and I are gonna skip class, so don't worry about keeping us out too late.

Ana agreed and promised to discuss the details soon.

We miss you, Paige. I still don't understand.

Ana simply responded I miss you, friend, so much.

They stayed up late discussing their time together, and she fell asleep with her phone in her hand. She awoke to feel the blanket being pulled up over her arms. She opened her eyes slightly to see her aunt placing her phone on the nightstand. Ana closed her eyes feeling tired, yet safe.

The next morning, Ana slept in until eight. Her phone woke her with a text from Jude.

I can't believe you're really leaving. Another message popped up immediately. I want to spend the whole two days with you.

Ana responded, I know, we will, every minute.

They texted until 8:30ish when Nellie knocked and entered the room, "Hey honey, your daddy is downstairs and wants to tell you goodbye."

"Oh crap," Ana said as she pulled on a sweater over her t-shirt and straightened her sweatpants.

She pulled back her hair, then rushed down the stairs. She slowed as she heard her aunt in the next room.

"Phillip, I wish you wouldn't have allowed her to stay longer than I had planned. She is not a little girl,"

He responded, "Diane, she is my little girl, and it is one day. What is the fuss?"

"She needs to disconnect from her life here, not kindle unrealistic relationships," Diane said to him.

"Let her see her friends now. When she gets home, it will all be new to her, and she will need to talk to her girlfriends," Phillip replied.

"The girlfriend is not who I am worried about, Phillip!" Diane said, exasperated. "What if he tries to get her to elope with him?"

"That is why I sent you. Diane, I am sorry. Please, I just need to ensure she is safe and brought home."

Ana walked into the room.

"Good morning Anastasia, I am leaving to tell your mother of your discovery. I will see you in three days. Try not to worry your aunt. She loves you very much," he said as he walked over and hugged her.

Ana asked, "Three days?" looking at him.

"Yes, dear, you will still get to see your friends. But your aunt is right. We need to get you home," he said simply.

Ana didn't pull away, but she only said goodbye.

"Goodbye, and Ana, you can call me dad if you would like," Phillip said.

"Ok," she replied, then she paused.

Diane made small noises as if she were queuing Ana to acknowledge him. Ana looked at her out of the corner of her eye, then back to her father and said, "Goodbye, Dad."

He walked out, and Ana started toward her room.

"Ana, we will leave for Virginia in the late afternoon," Diane said.

Ana mumbled as she walked away, "Why are we even going for one day? That is stupid."

"Well, we could go straight home if you would like?" Diane called out to her as she walked away.

Ana stopped walking and said, "No, I'm good."

Later that afternoon, the attorney came by, and they finished the paperwork. Soon, they were in the car heading to the airport for the flight back to Virginia.

"Why did you tell him that about Jude? It isn't true. We are not dating," Ana stated as she looked out the window.

"Oh, so you kiss boys you are not dating?" Diane asked.

Ana rolled her eyes and crossed her arms on her lap.

"It isn't like that," Ana replied.

"Then what is it like? Would you like to enlighten me?" her aunt asked.

"You wouldn't get it," Ana said.

Ana felt like she could never win with her. She couldn't decide how many days to visit her own friends, she had to respond with ma'am and sir, and she couldn't even choose her own name. This was weird, and she wasn't sure how great this life was going to be. But what choice do I have, she thought. I have nothing, and I can't run away. They will come and find me.

CHAPTER FOUR

The Academy

She was so excited. She hardly ate her breakfast. Her iPhone was buzzing every few seconds with new messages from Natilee and Jude.

"Ana, we are staying in the hotel downtown a few miles from campus. We will take you over and bring you back tonight," Diane announced as they drove from the airport.

"Well, actually, we wanted to go downtown, to a place we hang out. Then, I was gonna stay with Natalie overnight," Ana replied.

"Ana, that isn't a good idea. I would rather you not stay over," Diane responded.

"We will be out late. So, it just makes sense, don't you think? I could text you when we get back to the dorms," Ana suggested.

Diane thought for a moment. Diane was afraid to let her stay. She had just found her, and she couldn't let her go now without knowing she would be completely safe and secure.

"No, Ana, you can have them pick you up, and you can stay out with them, but you must sleep at the hotel," Diane said.

"Why can't I stay with Natilee?" Ana asked.

"Because you can't," Diane said.

"But, Aunt Diane, I will be ok," Ana argued.

"Anastasia, I am not discussing it. The answer is no. Do you understand?" Diane asked sternly.

"No, I do not," Ana said tersely.

Ana was silent and stared down at the floorboard of the car. They were at the hotel by 1:30, and Ana was more than ready to evacuate the premises. Before she left, Diane handed her a new iPhone and asked for hers.

"What is this?" Ana asked.

"Well, you have a new phone now. You should transfer your contacts, and my number is in there under favorites," Diane clarified.

Ana said, "My friends will be here any minute. I'm gonna go down and wait."

Diane gave her a curious look, "Oh, have them come up. I was hoping to officially meet them. I don't want them to remember me as the stranger who stole you away," Diane said.

Ana smiled, "Ok."

"I expect you in by two a.m. Please text me, and I will have you picked up. Please be safe, and please do not break curfew," Diane asked.

"Ok, I mean, yes, ma'am," Ana said.

Fifteen minutes later, the doorbell rang, and Ana greeted her friends. She introduced them to her aunt.

"Natilee and Jude, this is my Aunt Diane. She will be taking me to England in a few days."

Natilee and Jude both said hello to Diane. She had risen and walked over to meet them.

Diane asked, "What do you three have planned for the evening?"

Jude responded first, "Just gonna hang out and get some dinner."

Natilee finished, "Prolly eat then walk through town, maybe hang out and watch some classmates do some karaoke."

Diane looked at them, inspecting their movements as they stood in front of her. She couldn't help it. She had once been scorned by her daughter's rebellious ways and had learned to be critical of her friends.

Ana caught her staring and said, "Aunt Diane, we are going to leave now. Ok?"

Diane heard her, then smiled at them and said, "Yes, what time do you plan on returning?"

Ana replied, "I'm not sure, but surely not past two, right guys?"

Diane laughed a little laugh and replied, "midnight to one o'clock is more realistic for a teenager. Nothing good ever happens after midnight, Anastasia.".

Ana was not happy about the time nor the comment.

"Ok, sure. See ya later," Ana said.

She did not want to argue about time. Ana walked over to speak to Diane as if she didn't want her friends to hear.

"I will text you when I need a ride home, or if anything changes," Ana said, looking Diane in the eye.

"Thank you, please keep me updated; especially, if your plans change. See you at twelve-thirty. Be safe," Diane said.

"Yes, ma'am," Ana replied, smiling.

Natilee and Jude looked at each other, puzzled by the response Ana had given her aunt. To them, it was like hearing a different person.

As they walked out, Natilee said, "Hey, you ok?"

Ana replied, "Yeah, it just feels so weird. I don't know how to explain it.

"It's like you have someone who cares about you, like you have an actual family, right. You know, like Jude and I have?" Natilee tried to explain.

"Yeah, I guess, except they are all strangers," Ana said, almost embarrassed. "Let's just go."

Jude had driven, and they soon headed back to campus. Naturally, they piled on his bed like always and began to discuss their plans and the events of their night. Their conversation transitioned to their future as friends.

"Maybe we can fly over, or we could come to Chicago?" Natilee said.

"Yeah, maybe I could go to college here? That's what I am hoping for anyway. I mean, this is my home," Ana said.

Jude would graduate the next May, but Natilee and Ana had another year after him.

"So, I guess the military is out?" Jude asked.

"Yeah, pretty sure about that. I don't think my British parents would allow me to join the U.S. military," Ana responded.

They left the dorm and drove to get dinner at a place they visited often. They sat and watched some guy they didn't know sing. He was pretty good, and he sang some popular songs. "Hey, let's take a shot! We need to relax!" Natilee exclaimed.

"How? We're underage." Ana asked.

"I can get some, or I know Jude has friends that can. Come on, guys. This is our last night together for who knows how long," Natilee pleaded.

Jude was not usually a rule breaker; although, he would like to have a fun night with his two best friends, especially Ana.

"Yeah, I know a guy. We could go meet him, then hang out somewhere for a while and drink," he said. "But we can't drink here. There's no way they would serve us."

Ana had only ever sipped beer with her academy friends. However, prior to her admission, she had gotten wasted a few times that ended in puking her guts out. She was older now, though and felt more mature. Besides, it was only five p.m., and they had plenty of time.

"Ok, sure, let's go," she said.

They drove west, off of campus, to meet Jude's friend. This meeting resulted in a large bottle of vodka and a six-pack of beer. From there, they decided to drive to the range outside the campus gate and park. It wasn't used this time of year and had places for campfires. It was around seven-thirty when they finally arrived at the range, and it wasn't too cold for a September night. Jude built and lit the fire. Jude drank beer, and the girls had decided to drink vodka. The drinking began with a shot of vodka as a toast to their future. Jude played some music from his car stereo, and they sat in the back of his Jeep with their legs hanging down. Jude sat next to Ana, his leg touching hers. As they kicked their legs, they laughed about funny things that had happened in the previous semesters. Specifically, about Ana punching Terrance Crump in the face when he ran his mouth to her. The vodka was strong, and the girls were chasing it with juice.

After about an hour, Natilee said, "I gotta pee so bad, Paige goes with me."

"Ok," replied Ana.

As they walked into the nearby bushes to pee, the girls laughed.

"I can never pee straight," Ana said, laughing and almost falling, trying to maneuver her legs away from the stream.

Natilee giggled, "I don't have any toilet paper."

Ana replied, "Drip dry girls," mocking their female drill instructor.

Natilee laughed out loud and asked, "Do you think Harrelson shaves her coot?"

"Are you seriously asking that? Hell if I know," Ana said and laughed. "I bet not, and it poofs out on each side like a bush. Oh my God! That is so gross."

"Oh my God, you're right! The poor man who tries to separate those weeds," Natilee said.

"She could probably braid it on each side, like Willie Nelson," Ana added, and Natilee busted out laughing.

They walked over to the fire, and Jude asked, "What's so funny?"

"We were discussing Harreslon's pubic hair," Ana said with a grin.

Jude spat out the beer in his mouth, "Oh God, I'm gonna puke."

Ana looked out into the dark beyond them and thought, God, how will I ever have this much fun or care for anyone like I do these two? How will I ever have friends who make me feel this good? The girls continued to drink, and Ana was feeling a good buzz. Jude walked off to talk to his dad on the phone.

"Paige, you know he likes you. You know he doesn't want you to leave," blurted out Natilee, clearly buzzed.

"Well, kinda, but all of a sudden in a way," Ana replied.

Jude walked up, finishing a beer. He turned the music up, and they continued to drink and talk. Ana noticed how warm she felt and how her cheeks were starting to feel numb.

"Maybe it's the cold air," Ana thought.

She looked at Jude. She could imagine kissing him, really kissing him, not like the other day when he kissed her before she pulled away. He caught her staring at him, and he smiled.

Oh God, forgive me, she thought as she gulped her juice and vodka quickly. Ana put her cup on the tailgate and looked at her watch, 9:47 p.m. I haven't texted at all, Ana thought. She grabbed her phone out of the front seat. One unread message was displayed on the screen. Ana knew she was a little drunk, but she thought she was still good.

The message read, Ana?

That was it. She started to text back, then erased her message, not wanting to worry her aunt. Although, it seemed like she must have already accomplished that.

So, she texted, Hey, sorry I forgot to text earlier. I am fine just hanging out.

Short and sweet, she thought. She saw bubbles and then a message.

Ok, thanks. See you at 12:30.

Ana thought that wasn't too bad. Her Aunt Diane hadn't asked any questions, and Ana hadn't lied. She felt it was a positive interaction.

Meanwhile, at the hotel, it was 9:45 pm, and Diane had tried to avoid looking at her phone. She thought, No text, no call. Ok, she is fine. She is an adult. She was fine before you ever came along, and she is fine now. But she couldn't help it, she picked up her phone looking for a message and for Ana's location. The map pinged her at Randall point.

"Where is she?" That is not downtown?" Diane said to herself. "Ok, maybe it was a last-minute change of plans," she told herself.

She put down the phone and decided to read for a while. Suddenly, at 9:47, she received a message from Anastasia. She questioned herself, Should I ask where she is? Should I just go and get her? She didn't want to overreact. She truly wanted to call Andrea and ask her for advice; but, this time, she couldn't. She felt a tremendous amount of guilt knowing she was solely responsible for her brother and best friend's daughter and truly not knowing if she was safe. She thought a while longer and decided to give Ana a chance.

At eleven o'clock, Jude asked, "Hey, y'all wanna ride with me? There are some off-road trails back here. It'll be fun. I've driven them before."

Natilee replies, "Yeah, I wanna ride with Ryan."

They turned and could see their friend Ryan's truck coming down the road.

"Did you text him?" Ana asked Jude.

"No, I didn't," He responded.

"I did," said Natilee."

"Why did you do that?" Paige asked her.

Natilee shrugged her shoulders like she didn't know. Jude whispered in Ana's ear that Natilee and Ryan had been talking lately.

"Oh, that's freaking great," she said to Jude, as she rolled her eyes.

Natilee ran to Ryan's vehicle, and he yelled over at Jude, "You ready?"

Jude and Ana got into his Jeep and buckled up. Ana was feeling the alcohol and had picked up Jude's beer to drink as they rode. They had the stereo on low. Ana was enjoying being this close to Jude and hoped he would kiss her again.

"Can I hold your hand?" he asked her.

Ana nodded yes. They stopped at an intersection, and Ryan sped off. Ana leaned over and quickly kissed Jude on the cheek, close to his mouth. Then he turned his head and leaned over to kiss her in return. His kiss started soft, and he stroked her face with affection. She tingled all over when he kissed her. He pulled her into him, as close as possible, securing her body to his. Ana thought it might be the alcohol making it happen, but she was very aroused. Ana ran her hand through his hair and down his chest. Her body was yearning to be touched. He maneuvered the Jeep into a parking lot, slid it into park, and cut the lights.

He began kissing her neck, and he said, "I have been wanting to do this for so long."

She breathed, "Me too."

Her heart was beating out of her chest, and she could feel the heat in her face and body. Her head felt like it was rushing. She wanted to slow him down. So, Ana pushed him away long enough to smile at him. Jude moved from his seat, and she pulled the lever allowing her to lie back in hers. He joined her in her seat. He laid beside her and pulled her close to him. His arm lay so her head could rest on it. He kissed her gently, and then they resumed kissing and touching. He slid his hand up the back of her shirt. Ana unintentionally moaned softly, and he pulled up her shirt and bra, exposing her bare breast. He gently brushed his mouth against her nipple, and chills ran up her spine. He began to suckle her nipple, and she put her hand on the back of his head, pulling him in and arching her back. She wanted him to touch her. She unbuttoned his jeans and put her hand between his skin and boxers. She felt him, hard and large in her hand. She felt herself moistening between her legs. He reached into her panties, and she shook, excited for him to touch her. Suddenly, lights lit up the cab of the jeep, surprising them. Someone was behind them.

"Who is that?" asked Anna.

"I don't know, but we gotta get out of here," he replied. They fumbled, trying to return to their original positions. Ana pulled her jeans up and shirt down. Jude began to pull the Jeep away. The vehicle behind them followed faster.

"Who the hell is that? Ryan's truck doesn't look like that." Worried, Ana began to call Natilee, no answer. Then she texted her, no immediate reply.

"There's a road that leads to the highway. I'm gonna take it, but it may be rough," Jude told her.

"I don't care! We just gotta get out of here. Is this illegal?" Ana asked. She thought kinda late to ask that.

"I guess, maybe, but I don't know anyone who ever got in trouble for riding around out here," Jude said, without revealing his uncertainty. Soon, he turned, and the rutted road began to toss them from side to side in the Jeep. Jude pulled behind a thick grove of trees and cut his lights. The vehicle passed only a few minutes later. Jude and Ana just sat there, holding their breath, hoping the vehicle would not return. After a few more minutes, Jude returned to the road and started toward the highway. The road was wet, and water was standing on it. It was hard to differentiate where the tracks were, but he seemed to be doing well. Then suddenly, it felt as if the axle of the jeep got caught on something under the vehicle. The Jeep came to a sudden stop.

"Oh crap," Jude said. He attempted to move the vehicle by rocking and changing gears, no luck. With one large rocking motion, Jude managed to get the jeep to lurch forward. They made it about 15 feet and luckily out of the mud. They both sighed in relief. The Jeep stopped.

"What's wrong?" Ana asked.

"I can't move it. It feels like I broke something on that stump," Jude clarified.

"Seriously?" Ana asked. She looked down at her watch. It was 12:25 a.m.

"Oh hell, what are we gonna do?" Ana asked.

"I will try Natilee again. Maybe Ryan can take me into town," she thought out loud.

"Good idea," he said as he dug for his flashlight.

"Natilee isn't picking up. I'm worried," Ana said.

"It'll be ok," Jude said, trying to comfort her. He worked on the Jeep, and Ana paced.

"What should I do? Should I call or just let her sleep for a while? Damn, this sucks," she said, frustrated. At twelve-forty, Jude insisted she call her aunt.

"Just chill, Paige. You're not a freaking kid. You should have called before now. Why have you waited?" he asked.

"I don't know! Shut up, Jude," she said back to him as she walked away from him and the Jeep. As Ana was dialing the phone, it rang. "She's calling me. I don't know what to do." She was nervous.

"Answer the phone," he said.

Ana answered, "Hello."

"Anastasia, where are you? Are you ok?" Diane asked her.

"Well, I was riding with Jude, and he got stuck, and that is why..." Ana tried to explain, but it sounded jumbled.

Ana could hear Diane talking to someone. "What? You're coming here?" Ana asked.

"I will be there in five minutes. Do not go anywhere," and Diane hung up.

"She's coming here. How does she even know where I am?" Ana asked.

"She probably had us followed," Jude said, kidding.

"Really, do you think that was the person in that car behind us?" Ana asked.

"No, I'm kidding. She's probably tracking you on your new phone," Jude said.

"Oh, yeah," Ana said, relieved for a moment until she thought about it some more. "That sucks! Who tracks people?" Ana asked Jude, offended.

"I mean, my parents might. I'm not sure if they do," Jude said honestly.

"Really, that pisses me off," Ana said, getting angry.

"Paige, look," Jude said. He pointed, and they could see headlights shining through the trees in front of them. A black Tahoe SUV pulled directly in front of Jude's jeep. The driver got out, opened the back door, and Diane got out. The headlights were bright. Jude and Ana were squinting, standing about ten feet from the vehicle. Diane was fully dressed, complete with a black rain jacket when she stepped out of the SUV. The driver, a tan, white male, exited the vehicle with a flashlight, and he was armed. Diane walked up to Ana and Jude.

"Anastasia, why are you in the middle of the forest? You told me you were going to be in town? "Where is Natilee?" Diane asked, looking around.

"We were riding, and Jude's jeep got stuck," Ana explained. Diane stood in front of them, inspecting Ana. She was standing very close to Ana. So close Ana had backed up against the jeep. She felt like she was being arrested. "Have you been drinking?" Diane asked.

"Kinda," Ana replied, warily.

"You are kinda underage. Did you buy her alcohol?" Diane said, pointing at Jude.

"No, ma'am," he replied.

"Then where did you get it?" Diane asked.

"A guy I know," he replied.

"Where is Natilee?" Diane asked.

"She's with Ryan. We didn't know he was coming," Ana tried to explain.

"Really, Ana? Get your things and get in the vehicle," Diane said, not wanting to hear any more of her explanations. Ana opened the back door of Jude's Jeep. The glass vodka bottle fell out.

"Have you two been doing any drugs tonight?" Diane asked them.

"No way! Why would you ask that?" Ana said defensively.

"Why wouldn't I?" she asked them.

"Jude, have you called your parents?" Diane asked.

"No, I called my brother. He should be here soon to try and get my jeep fixed," Jude said.

Jude heard a vehicle behind him. "That must be Ryan. He can help me," Jude said.

"Great. Anastasia, get in the vehicle, please," Diane demanded.

"No, wait a minute. I gotta make sure Natilee is ok," Ana replied, not moving. Ryan and Natilee pulled up. Natilee got out of the truck and ran to Ana's side.

"What happened?" Natilee asked.

"Nothing, we just got stuck, and then the FBI showed up," Ana said sarcastically, insinuating her Aunt's presence. Diane looked at Ana, growing impatient.

"I have to go," Ana said. Natilee hugged Ana goodbye, then the door closed. They rode down the highway back to the hotel. "I'm sorry I didn't call, but time got away from me," Ana said, breaking the silence.

"I am sure it did when you've been drinking. This is exactly why I didn't want you to come back here. You could have been injured or killed," Diane said.

"It's not like I'm drunk. I'm fine," Ana said.

"You're not fine. This is not fine," Diane said, agitated.

Ana's phone buzzed the entire ride. She was quickly texting responses to the messages, totally engrossed in her phone. They walked to the hotel room. Ana said, "I'm going to bed."

"Go ahead and shower first. I will fix you a snack," her aunt said.

"Of course," Ana said, annoyed.

"Ana, you can leave your phone. I don't think you'll need it in the shower," Diane said. Ana reluctantly put her phone on the coffee table. When the bathroom door shut, Diane heard Ana's phone buzz twice. She glanced down at the phone, reading the message, she picked up the phone. The message, unfortunately, confirmed her speculation that Ana was involved with Jude on an intimate level. Diane poured Ana a glass of juice and laid a few crackers with cheese on the counter. Ana got out of the shower and still felt drunk. She stumbled a little as she put on her pajama pants.

Diane sat across from Ana as she ate. "How are you feeling?" Diane asked.

"Ok, I guess," Ana admitted.

"Do you drink often?" Diane asked her.

"Not usually. Jude is a really good guy. I want you to know that. I know it looked really bad," Ana said.

"Hmm, I want you to be honest. Did you and Jude have sex?" Diane asked.

"Oh my God! Why would you ask that?" Ana said shockingly.

"Because you are drunk, and you were in a dark forest, alone, with an 18-year-old male, who you're attracted to," Diane said.

Ana started, "So..."

"And, because your jeans were unbuttoned when I arrived," Diane said as she drank her tea, not missing a beat.

"No, no, we didn't. Oh my God. Why does it matter anyway? And again, we aren't even really dating," Ana said.

"It matters because there are risks involved if you did. Hopefully, you are aware of that. Is there anything you want to talk about?" Diane asked in a caring tone.

"No, nope, I'm good," she said, finishing eating. After a few minutes, she asked, "So, you're not mad?"

"No, I'm not mad. I am concerned. Although, I am relieved now that you have assured me nothing happened that you may later regret," Diane said.

"Thank you for the snack," Ana said.

"You're welcome," Diane said.

Ana awoke at seven-thirty with a headache. As she sat up in bed, she remembered her phone and reached for it. Natilee had responded again and was apologizing. Jude had sent a message and a snap of a wrecker hauling his Jeep to the shop, with a goofy grin. That made her smile. She texted him, telling him she had survived the ride home and the walk of shame. It wasn't really a walk of shame, but he knew what she was referring to. Ana dressed slowly, not looking forward to the rest of the day. Especially with her head pounding.

"Ana, do you want to eat breakfast soon? You look like you need it this morning," Diane asked as she popped into Ana's room to check the status of her young hungover niece. She could tell she had been crying, and she wondered why. Diane had to keep reminding herself that Ana was not a child. She knew she had a past, and at seventeen, she was surely able to lead a successful life. Although, her actions last night did not reflect those of a mature young adult. But the past was the past, and Anastasia was her only niece. The niece she had wanted to find for all those years. Now, she was here in front of her. A beautiful young girl, who had been laid aside for years by the Americans that took her. She was unique, fierce, and emotionally driven. Diane was determined to give her all the stability she needed to become a mature young lady. No matter how she had to do it.

"Yeah, sure, that would be great," Ana replied. "What time are we taking off today?"

Diane replied, "Around ten-thirty." They left the hotel and ate at a small restaurant. Diane didn't mention the night before, only the fact that Ana needed to eat and rehydrate. Ana was texting her friends. Jude seemed worried about Ana leaving and the status of her emotions after what they had shared the night before. He texted; Maybe I can come by?

Ana's phone kept vibrating until Diane finally said, "Is everything ok with Jude?"

Ana placed the phone on the seat beside her leg. It vibrated again, and she looked at it but chose not to pick it back up. Ana and her aunt waited in the lobby of the private section of the airport. Diane read while Ana texted and laid on the couch, listening to music. Jude texted I am here. Can we talk?

Ana, guilt-stricken from the night before, asked Diane, "Jude is here, and I wanna talk to him. May I go out and talk with him?"

Diane didn't want this to happen. It was gonna be hard enough. To her, Jude meant more heartache for Ana later. "He can come in and talk with you before you leave," Diane said.

"Can we not have any privacy? I am an adult, and we are just friends. I just wanna walk outside, not to another county," Ana said, displaying annoyance.

Diane responded calmly, "Anastasia, we are leaving in less than an hour. No one else is in this lobby. He can come in here or nothing. This is the same friend you were lost in the forest with last night, intoxicated, doing who knows what. You have had enough alone time with him."

Ana was angry at her aunt for restricting her but was angrier because of what she said about the previous night. "God almighty, this freaking sucks! You're so frustrating!" she almost yelled as she turned back toward the window.

"I'm glad you know how to express your feelings. Your actions last night frustrated me, and now you're letting your emotions control your situation," Diane responded, as she looked through her glasses at her book.

"What are you, a shrink?" Ana said sarcastically.

"Not exactly, but I have had a lot of experience with my own teenage girl," Diane responded without looking up. The calm way she responded angered Ana even more.

Jude came in and waved sheepishly to Diane as he walked with Ana to the other side of the room. They sat on the floor, in a corner behind Diane. Diane turned the television on to create noise for her niece. Jude apologized for taking her to the range, and especially for the four-wheeling trip. He regretted that terribly because of Ana's outcome and his busted Jeep. Jude's dad had not been pleased last night when he called him to come out to the range. His dad called his uncle, who towed his Jeep in. Jude's dad lectured him all the way home about drinking and making bad choices. He also said he would be paying for the repair and borrowing his mother's car otherwise. For Jude, his consequences didn't matter right now. His mother had agreed to let him use the car only for the morning, and because she knew Ana was leaving. Jude's father didn't tell his mother he had been drinking last night. Jude was glad, or he would never get to borrow anything with wheels. As they talked, the time flew by, and Ana walked him out to his mom's car. He hugged her, they kissed and embraced. He got in the car and drove home, not knowing if he would ever see Ana again. Ana walked back in before Jude pulled off. She didn't want to be standing in the parking lot, watching him drive away. She walked into the small terminal where her aunt was waiting for her. Ana saw her and held back tears. "Let's go," she said to her aunt.

They boarded the plane, and Ana took her seat. The plane was small, but they still had room to get up and move around. Diane received a text from Phillip and called him, "What do you mean you haven't told her? Philip, I think you need to prepare her. Ana is not a puppy. Where is Drake?" She paused then said, "Of course he is. Well, there might not ever be a time when they are together. You have to tell her, and she has to understand before Anastasia comes home." Diane got up to avoid being heard, "Phillip, you know how your wife is. She is going to expect Ana to be the perfect child she has imagined all these years. Ana is not like that," Diane said. They agreed that Phillip would tell her today, then he would tell Diane when to bring her to her new home.

They made it to altitude, and Ana wanted to sleep. "Are you tired?" Diane asked.

"Yes," she replied.

"Well, you had a very late night last night," Diane stated.

"Yeah, I'm sorry I didn't call when I knew I wouldn't be back," Ana said sincerely.

"Why didn't you?" Diane asked in response.

"Because I knew you would be mad, and I would rather just avoid that," Ana said.

"So, you would rather wait and let me Find you in a forest twenty miles from where you said you were going to be," Diane said in an authoritative tone. Ana just looked out the window.

"So you're just going to stare out the window?" Diane asked, almost challenging Ana.

"No," said Ana. She moved her head sharply with her eyes focused on Diane.

"Alone, with Jude drinking alcohol. You're underage, Ana. What if he had wrecked? He was also drinking, I assume," Diane continued.

"I didn't intentionally lie to you, and I wasn't drunk. It isn't what you think about Jude," Ana tried to clarify. "We just went there to hang out with Natilee. Then she ditched us."

"I am very glad you're safe, but if you were the adult you say you are, you would have called. And you wouldn't ride or drink and drive. Anastasia, you didn't even know where you were!" Diane said.

"I knew kinda where we were. You didn't give me a chance to explain. You just called in the Calvary and had me extracted. And, I have known Jude for a long time, and he isn't going to take advantage of me. We are not stupid," she spat.

"I hope not, and if so, I hope you were responsible," Diane said.

"Oh my God. I do not wanna talk about this with you. Can we just drop it? I screwed up, I lied and drank, but we did not do anything, seriously. Can I just lie down?" Ana said and put her face in her hands. Ana got up and crashed on the sofa for the next two hours. When she awoke, she ate a snack, and Diane had a binder lying beside her. She opened it, and Diane came over to sit beside her.

"I thought it would be good for you to see your family and learn some about them prior to meeting them. The first part is about your birth and your disappearance," Diane said kindly.

"You made this?" Ana asked after she picked it up.

"Yes, for you," Diane said.

"I realize this may be upsetting for you, but it is a part of your life. Do you want some privacy?" Diane asked. Ana shook her head no. She didn't think the pictures of her parents on the day she was born would affect her. She read the clippings from the newspaper about her disappearance and saw pictures of her parents with faces full of sorrow. Diane was in the photos, as well as a small girl with blonde ponytails. These pictures would be sad for anyone to see, but her sadness was greater when she saw her parents and thought of the pain they must have felt. It was difficult to imagine herself as the child of the two people in the pictures. As she turned the page, she read the title of an article, Lord and wife Andrea Hutchinson search for their missing infant, Anastasia.

Ana blurted out, "What is a Lord? My dad is a Lord?"

Diane replied, "Yes, he is a Lord and an entrepreneur. Your father's title, as well as his economic and political success, means a lot to your family. So, that's why I didn't want the whole world to know your true identity until you were ready to know yourself. Even though your birth and disappearance may have been seventeen years ago, the entire country knew about it. You could be getting a lot of attention for a while."

Ana took a while to let that information sink in, then continued flipping through the book. Pages were filled with pictures of her brother Drake. He was sixteen, and she could see the resemblance to their mother. To Ana, it felt weird thinking of having a mother, or father, or siblings. Could this really be her life? All those years, she worried and felt embarrassed because of her parents and the life she led, and it had all been a lie. Ana asked more questions about the book, then just listened to music. The plane landed, and Ana was exhausted. They got in a black Tahoe and drove away. "Where are we going?" she asked her aunt.

"We are going to my home. We will go to yours tomorrow, maybe," Diane informed her with a smile. They pulled through a gate set in some sort of stone wall. It was as though they had left a city street and entered a garden or park. The drive was made with small stones, and the tires against the stone made a sound that reminded Ana of riding her bike down a gravel road to her friend Jerrica's house. They pulled around to the front of the house, and a man stepped out to greet them. Diane and Ana got out of the car as the man came toward them smiling.

"Ana, this is your Uncle Jeffrey, Jeffrey, this is our Anastasia," she said. Ana smiled in return.

Jeffrey turned to Ana, "Anastasia, I am so happy to meet you. Please come in and make yourself at home." He seemed very nice, and despite his facial hair, he didn't seem too gruff. They went in and settled down in the living area. The house was beautiful and larger than any home Ana had ever been in. The house had stone incorporated into the walls and huge wooden beams in the foyer, reminding Ana of a church. They ate dinner, and Ana excused herself from the table. Diane told her where her room and bathroom would be, and she went to lie on the bed to text Jude and Natilee. Jude had texted a few times, asking if she had made it and if she had met her mother. She wondered how it would be to meet her mother. She thought she would feel awkward and hoped she didn't make her mother feel disappointed or like she was too distant. How should she feel? Is there a right way? Ana asked herself. Ana always wanted to know the right way. She had begun life by watching and learning the correct way. Her grandparents, or the Peterson's parents, had always taught Ana to go beyond her parents and strive for greatness. She was always told how not to be like her parents. Ana was taught to be independent, so leaning on a parent would definitely be awkward for her. I have no idea how to be this girl. She thought. This wasn't school. This time she had no direction or instruction book to read. Ana had to let someone else control her life, and she didn't know how to do that. Jude and Ana FaceTimed for a few minutes, but that was interrupted by her aunt tapping on the door. She told Jude goodbye quickly, as the door opened.

"Ana, can we talk for a minute," Diane asked softly.

"Sure, whatever," Ana said casually. There was a sofa in the room, her aunt sat there, and Ana joined her.

"So your father is supposed to talk to your mother tonight and tell her that he has found you. I want you to understand that your mother is going to be very emotional when she meets you. Your mother, Andrea, is my best friend, and she has longed for the day you would be found. Truly, it is miraculous you were found. So, this will be very emotional. Depending on how she is in the morning, we will go over to the house. She will be happy either way, although your mother is the type of woman who likes to be in control of herself. She will not want you to see her as an emotional mess. Do you understand?" Diane asked.

"Yeah, I guess," Ana answered.

"You will love her, Anastasia," Diane said. She smiled and took Ana's hands in her own.

"You are so much like her. I am very excited for her to get to know you. I already feel like I know you so much more, just in the days we have spent together," Diane said. Ana looked at her and smiled. Then, that smile turned into a frown, and Ana cried.

"What is wrong, my darling girl?" Diane asked as she reached up to touch her face.

"I don't know how to feel. I am happy, but I am sad too because I miss Jude. I want to love her, but what if she doesn't like me. I'm not perfect. I am broken," Ana cried. Diane pulled her to her chest and held her like a child.

"Shhh, child, you are wonderfully made. Do you know that verse from Psalms? It is my favorite. Ana, she will love you. It just might take a while for you two to get on the same page. You come from very different worlds," Diane said. Ana began to calm down, and her breathing slowed.

"Do you want me to lay with you until you go to sleep? I used to do that when my daughter was upset," Diane asked. Ana had never had anyone ask that, but she nodded her head yes. Ana had already changed into pajamas, so she laid down in the bed, and Diane laid behind her. Diane placed her hand on her arm and held her. Ana felt a tear fall down her cheek. She was crying again and not for the newfound situation, but for the old one. Her mind floated back, and she remembered times when her former mother would be depressed. She remembered how she would drink too much and end up a crying mess on the bathroom floor. She remembered her dad beating on the door and cursing above her head. Ana would scream at him to leave her alone, and he would. Ana would sit with her mother and hold her, singing to her until she fell asleep. Then, the twelve-year-old would put her mother to bed. Ana was always the mother. She made it all ok again. Ana cried now because she had never experienced this feeling before. If this was love, then she had never been loved. She fell asleep, and Diane kissed her head, leaving her perfectly nestled in the covers.

Diane spoke to Phillip and rode over to check on Andrea. Philip said she was in shock, so Diane knew just what to do. When Diane arrived, Andrea was in her day clothes, draped across a sofa, drinking a glass of wine. "Andy, what is wrong with you?" Diane said in a jovial tone.

"Can you believe this? Andrea asked as she stared at Diane.

"Yes, I can, my friend. She is real, I promise," Diane replied. "Drink this wine, and we will talk," Diane smirked.

"What is it?" Andrea said.

"She is just like you, looks like you, and is stubborn like you. You will love her," Diane said as she took a drink of her wine.

"Oh Diane, I can't believe this is real, that she is here. I'm in shock. Why didn't you tell me?" Andrea asked.

"I couldn't let you know until we knew," Diane said.

"Oh, I hope I am enough for her. She is almost an adult," Andrea said.

"She's your child, and she will love you. You're more than anything she has ever had. I am so glad she is home," said Diane, and they sat there for a long time together.

CHAPTER FIVE

Meeting Mother

The next day, Ana woke to the sound of a knock on the door. She opened her eyes to the morning sun shining brightly in the room. Ana saw her aunt poke her head in the door. "Good morning, do you want to come down for breakfast?" she asked.

Ana nodded yes, still partially asleep. Diane nodded in response and closed the bedroom door. Ana rose and placed a navy robe over her shoulders before leaving the room. She saw her reflection in the mirror and stopped. Should I wear this? Should I dress before I go downstairs? Ana asked herself, feeling insecure. Shrugging to herself in the mirror, she shut the door and walked downstairs.

As they ate breakfast, her aunt asked, "Well, are you ready?" Her aunt sounded nervous herself.

Ana finished chewing, "For what? To meet your mother? Yes, sure, I guess." Ana said.

"Great, we will go over today then," Diane replied.

"What do I wear?" Ana asked.

"Anything should be fine," Diane answered. Ana felt embarrassed to ask for further guidance, so she didn't. Ana took quite a while to get ready. After trying on many things, she decided on khaki chino pants, a navy sweater, and Tom's shoes. Again, she looked into the mirror. She felt like she was wearing a uniform, but at least it looked neat. Ana knew she lacked any sense of fashion. In the past, she had looked at mannequins in department stores for reference. Although, she always felt like the mannequins wore too many layers. She always felt insecure about her appearance, never acknowledging her pretty features. Ana met her aunt downstairs with her bags. She expected some kind of comment, but her aunt didn't make one. Ana was very nervous on the ride over. What am I supposed to be like? What will she be like? All kinds of questions were running through her head.

"You're going to be fine," Diane said calmly, trying to ease her nerves. They arrived and went in. The house was very nice. It was old and elegant looking. It looked like something out of a novel, Ana thought. They were greeted by the housekeeper, Nellie. The same lady from Chicago.

"Hi," Ana said, happy to see a familiar face.

"Oh, am I happy to see you? You're home," she said, smiling at Ana.

"You're here?" Ana asked as Nellie pulled her jacket off her shoulders.

"Yes, this is my home too," Nellie said.

"Oh," Ana said, looking at Diane for clarification.

"I asked Nellie to accompany me to Chicago, but she is usually here," Diane said.

"Where are they?" Diane asked.

"Upstairs, but I will let them know you're here," Nellie said. Ana looked into the room off from the doorway. It looked like what used to be called a den or parlor by the old people she knew. There was a large set of steps to the right that went up way up. They were white and gray. The railing was exposed and revealed the doors to the upper rooms. Ana looked around, and Diane noticed her taking it all in. In the den were shelves of books and pictures of landscapes. It was cozy looking with two large armchairs and ottomans, and a sofa. There wasn't a TV in this room: a book and a pair of reading glasses laid on the small table by the chaise longue. Soft throws were folded and draped on the backs of the chairs and one on the foot of the lounge.

"We will wait here," Diane said to Nellie.

"Great, do you want any water or juice?" Nellie asked Anastasia.

"No, thank you," Ana replied, still looking around. Ana had walked to the French doors and was looking out of the glass. In the distance, she could see a large black horse eating the grass. She stared at her watching the sun reveal her shiny coat, taken back by her build and beauty.

Andrea knew they were there. She was in her room when she saw Diane's car pull in the drive. Andrea had dressed in a navy blouse and mustard chino pants, brown flats. She put on her necklace, the one that Phillip's mother had given her the day Anastasia had been born. Philip walked in from his study. "She is here. Are you ready?" he asked, looking excited. Andrea looked at him and then back at herself in the full-length mirror. Andrea looked in the mirror and exhaled slowly. Phillip put his hands around her. "You look beautiful. Don't be nervous. This is a great day." he said, smiling. He leaned into her and kissed her.

"Let's go," she said to him and smiled. She felt like she was going for the biggest interview of her life. She took Phillip's hand, and he walked her to the steps. She let her right hand glide on the wood railing as she descended the steps. She saw Anastasia standing below her in the den, looking out the glass doorway. The light was illuminating her hair, and her hand was resting on the door frame like she was engrossed in whatever she was viewing. Phillip didn't speak but smiled at Andrea when she looked at him. Diane connected with Andrea's eyes as they slowly descended the steps. Tears welled in Andrea's eyes as she watched and carefully walked down the carpeted steps toward them. She didn't want to interrupt her daydream. No one spoke. Nellie stood off to the side of the steps and took Phillip's arm at the bottom of the steps. Andrea dropped her hand and gracefully walked toward her daughter, facing the door. Time was still in that moment for Andrea and everyone in the room. Anastasia was unaware of the significance her presence brought. Andrea took a deep breath and attempted to control her emotions, her heart was racing, and the urge to embrace the child in front of her was almost too much to bear. Diane smiled and nodded, signaling Andrea it was ok. Andrea looked beyond the glass and saw Anastasia was staring at Shotsley, Philip's black mare.

Anastasia felt the vision of the horse had calmed her. She was in the scene. Ana could even feel the soft slick hair on the horse's neck under her fingertips.

"They are majestic animals, aren't they?" Andrea said, breaking the silence in the room. The voice sounded familiar to Ana. She had heard it before. The voice had broken the spell the horse had put on her. Ana looked down but didn't turn around. She was trying to draw the voice from her memory.

"Yeah, they are." She said, then she dropped her hand from the door and turned around.

She turned around to see a smiling face, a face that she had seen before. She gasped a little when she saw her. She was tall and beautiful, her hair auburn and in large curls around her shoulders. She had inviting blue eyes that seemed unnaturally deep and soft-ivory looking skin. She looked like porcelain, Ana thought.

Andrea had her hands clasped in front of her to keep herself from moving them. She had no idea how to begin introducing herself to her daughter, but she had no doubt she was her daughter. She recognized herself. It was like looking backward in time. Tears kept welling but had not crested the lids of her eyes yet.

Andrea said, "Hello." and smiled a simple smile.

Anastasia was in a silent trance, staring at Andrea like she was trying to memorize her every feature. Diane leaned in and touched her arm, and Ana came back to reality.

"Hello," Ana replied felt like Andrea's presence took up the whole room.

Tears were all over the room yet encapsulated in their owner's eyes.

"Anastasia, I am Andrea Hutchinson, I am your mother," Andrea said.

"Ok," Ana said, still not knowing what to say.

"Welcome home." Andrea said, and her voice cracked. Ana stepped toward her mother. Andrea closed the distance and came to her. She put her hands on Anastasia's upper arms, anchoring herself, and said, "It's ok. I know you don't know me, but I loved you even before you were born." with tears flowing down her cheeks. Ana had tears in her own eyes, and her heart was aching. Ana nodded her head, yes, and her eyes cried, Ana leaned in, and Andrea embraced her, almost catching her in a way. Andrea rocked her back and forth for a few seconds, feeling Anastasia breathe heavily through crying sobs. Andrea pulled her back and moved her hair out of her face.

"Would you like to sit down on the sofa?" Andrea asked.

"Yes," she replied shyly. Ana couldn't help but look at her mother and breathe in her every movement. Ana looked up and saw a family portrait on the table of Andrea, Phillip, and her brother. Ana's mind reflected back to a trip to the beach with her old parents. There were no family portraits that she could remember of the Peterson's. On that trip, her dad had gotten sunburnt after one day, and her mother had left with him, leaving her with her friend's family. It had been the best vacation she had ever had. Swimming in the pool and walking in the waves at night with her friend and her family. Her mom and dad had gone to a beach once before, but they had left just two days in. Her dad had slept the whole time, and for some reason, when he woke up, it was time to go. She never questioned the reason. That was the last vacation they had. She was maybe eight. Ana thought to herself. You should be used to change. Your old life changed so quickly.

"Anastasia, are you ok?" Her mother asked, awakening her from her thoughts.

"Yeah, sorry. I was thinking about something," Ana said as she looked over to her.

"Anastasia, this is your home. It has always been your home, even though you have never lived here. Your aunt tells me you enjoyed the academy very much and had some close friends you were upset to leave," Andrea said. Ana just nodded. "What were you studying? Had you declared a major?"

Ana sat up, "No, I was only in general studies. I won't declare my field until next semester, but I guess I won't be doing that now."

"We will discuss your future later. Unfortunately, no, you will not be going back to that school," Andrea said nicely.

"Why not?" Ana asked quietly.

Diane looked at Andrea, who simply replied, "Because this is your home, we are your family, and the U.S. is just too far away." Andrea was very calm, and she understood Ana's desire to go back to her school with her friends, but it wasn't negotiable.

"But I have a life there, and my friends are there. I was doing well, and I had plans," Ana argued.

"Your life is here now. Your plans have changed. You will make friends here. I really think you will enjoy it here. We have many schools and other opportunities for your future here," Andrea tried to explain.

"So, you're saying I'm stuck here, and I can't go back there until I'm eighteen," Ana said frankly, not concerned about her mother's emotions. Andrea looked at Ana, then at Diane.

"You should take a tour of the house now, and we'll talk about school later," Diane said. Andrea led Ana out of the main room and through the house.

Phillip and Diane stayed behind. "What do you think?" Diane asked Philip.

"I think Drake might be the calmer of the two," Philip said smiling.

"She is certainly not passive," Diane responded.

"What do you think Drake will think of her?" Diane asked.

Philip replied, "He will like her, but he could be a bit jealous."

"My thoughts exactly, but he's so into sports and school he will not be home much anyway, at least until summer," Diane stated.

"Well, maybe he has matured some this semester while he has been away," Phillip said, laughing to himself. Drake was a free spirit and was hard to keep on task. He had always been that way and had once even been expelled for it.

"When is Drake expected to come home again?" Diane asked.

"Andrea said he will be home tomorrow," Phillip answered.

"Wow, that is soon. Well, I guess it is now or never," Diane said, clearly thinking bringing Drake home so quickly was not the best idea.

"Di, you worry too much, she will be fine. She is part of this family, and she is strong," Phillip said, trying to convince her.

"Strong as she may be, she is not used to this lifestyle, and it is all so new to her. She is surrounded by strangers, in a home she doesn't know," Diane tried to clarify.

"Diane, she has had you for almost a week. You are close to her, aren't you?" he questioned.

"Yes, I feel that we have gotten that way," she answered.

"Then she has you to guide her through. You are very protective of her already. It almost sounds like you're talking about Laurel," he said as he smiled.

"No, Philip, protective is right, but for different reasons," Diane said, annoyed at his comment.

"Ana, this is our home. It has been in your father's family for centuries. We moved here just before you were born. As you may know, I was born in America and lived there as I grew up. Your father went to college there for a few years. That is how we met," Andrea explained. They walked through the main floor, which consisted of a large great room, a study, a dining hall, and a kitchen. As they walked upstairs, Ana saw an area tucked away with a ladder and curtain covering most of the ladder. Ana was going to ask about it, but Andrea had started to tell her about the other rooms, so she thought she would ask later. The house was beautiful, with shiny wood floors, tall ceilings, and wall-mounted lights illuminating the halls. Ana felt like she was in a museum or at Hogwarts, but without the spiderwebs and transforming staircases. They passed another living area, but this one had a huge TV and more modern furniture. It seemed to be a very comfortable space where people could relax. Andrea said on most nights, Drake was home. He would end up there with either friends or her and Philip. Andrea kept walking and stopped at a double door entry.

"This is your room. I hope you like it. It was a nursery, of course, when you were born, but when you were taken, your father had it changed. Although, he didn't take down the curtains, and he kept the rocking chair by the window," Andrea said. She opened the door, and Ana walked in. The carpet was an ivory white, and the walls matched. The curtains were a pattern of light blue and mauve flowers mixed with off white. The bed was large, very pretty, and soft. A desk faced the wall, and a chaise lounge sat across from the bed. The closet was also large and connected to the bathroom. It seemed surreal to Ana. There was a baby picture on the side table, next to a rocking chair facing the window.

"Is this me?" Ana asked as she picked it up.

"Yes, Anastasia, that is you and I on the day you were born," Andrea said as she put her hand on Ana's shoulder.

"I went ahead and ordered some clothing for you, just a few things I thought were essential. Your Aunt Diane told me she didn't give you much time to get any of your things. Is there anything you need? Is there anything you want to ask me or talk about?" Andrea asked, sitting down on the bed.

"No," Ana responded, although what she really wanted to say was, what am I doing here? Ana toured the rest of the house and took a walk outside in the garden. The yard ended in a wooded area. Adjacent to the wooded area was a pasture that connected her aunt's home to her new home. The stables were closer to Diane's house, and the distance was not convenient. They had several horses, with a barn and stables. That interested Ana more than any feature on the property, except for the pool. Pools are always fun, thought Ana. As she studied the pasture from a distance, she looked at the horses. She had always loved admiring horses and found them to be a perfect image of strength and beauty. Andrea stared out at the pasture, letting all the new settle around her.

"Do you ride?" Andrea asked.

"I have before, but only a few times. Always wanted to, though," Ana said.

"Diane is a great equestrian. She will teach you," Andrea said. After the tour, Ana ate lunch with Andrea and Diane. For the rest of her first day at home, Ana stayed in her room mostly, except for when she took a walk outside again to talk to Natilee on FaceTime. Even though she called Natilee, she thought of Jude and their last interaction. She yearned to see his big brown eyes and thick perfect lips.

"What are you gonna do, Paige? What is your new mother like?" Natilee asked.

"I have no idea really what my life will be. I am just here; that is all I know," Ana said.

"Is she nice? Does she look like you?" Natilee asked.

"She seems nice. I mean, I don't really know her yet. I do look like her, I think, but she's prettier than I am," Ana answered.

"Have you talked to them about coming back here?" Natilee asked.

"Not really, but it doesn't look like it's going to happen. It looks like I'm stuck," Ana replied.

"Are you going to college? Do you have a hot brother or cousin I could meet?" Natilee said as she laughed."

"Yeah, what the hell was that the other night when you left with Ryan? Were you planning that crap?" Ana asked.

"Are you complaining? It looked like you and Jude were very busy when we got behind you," Natilee said.

"What the hell, that was you? You scared the hell out of us, and we got stuck trying to evade you," Ana cried.

"Hey, calm down. We didn't mean to scare you, but if you wouldn't have been making out with our best friend, you wouldn't have been so ready to leave the scene. Paige, you are so uptight. Are you scared of your new family? I mean, they all but took you hostage," Natilee said.

Ana replied, "No, that's stupid, Nat. I just don't wanna talk about it. I don't even know who I am, much less what I'm gonna do." She said goodbye to Natilee and Snapchatted Jude. She took a photo of herself with a pouty face and sent it to him. He replied with the same, which made her happy. She shoved the phone in her pocket and went in search of the kitchen for a snack. It took her a minute to find the kitchen, but to her surprise, Nellie was there.

"Hello Anastasia, I'm happy to see you. You hungry?" Nellie asked.

"Yeah, I am. Sorry, I'm still not used to my name."

"I bet would you rather me call you something else."

"Ana is good, and yeah, I am kinda hungry. Where's the food around here?" She felt comfortable around Nellie. She reminded her of some of the ladies she grew up around. Ana had worked since she was fourteen. At the place she worked, there were a few older women who she confided in, and who cared for her, gave her advice.

Nellie said, "Come on, Ana," as she walked with her to the pantry and the large refrigerators. Ana's stomach began to growl. "This is where all the food is, and if you want anything special, you just tell me, and I will have George get it. Drake has his favorite snacks I always have for him when he is home. But I don't get alcohol. He tried that once, and it didn't work." Nellie chuckled.

Ana smiled at Nellie and thought that wasn't a very smart move, but he was sixteen. Ana thought about herself at sixteen. It felt so long ago. She had begun her life at the academy when she was sixteen, or she thought she had been seventeen. Her life had been such a lie. Ana ate some cheese, chips, and soda. She sat down to eat at the counter while she watched Nellie prepare dinner. "Do you care if I sit here with you?" Ana asked Nellie.

"No, honey, you're fine. You can sit here as long as you like," Nellie responded with a smile. "Everything going ok. How was it meeting your parents?"

Ana finished chewing and said, "Yes, it was fine. I just wonder how this is all gonna work." Nellie looked at her like she didn't understand what she was talking about. "I just don't know how to do this. No one has ever really been my parent. I just did me."

"Oh Ana, I don't know what to tell you. Besides, it is going to take time for them to feel like your parents, and as far as where you go from here, you live your life as you never have before. You have a family who loves you. Nothing will ever change that. Live out your dreams. Most kids would kill to be in your shoes." Nellie was trying to reassure her.

"Yeah, I know you're right. It's just so different from what I'm used to." Ana finished her snack.

"I know it is, I mean, I can only guess it is. But, if you need to talk, you can talk to me anytime. I will be here for you just like your family is." Nellie stopped what she was doing and looked at Ana.

"Thanks, Nellie, I appreciate it," Ana went over and hugged Nellie. It was a short hug, but Nellie could feel the girl letting the wall down that guarded her heart. Nellie could tell Ana had raised herself, and she also knew that it didn't matter how strong she thought. There was still a little girl inside of her just wanting her momma.

Ana was in her closet looking through her clothes for something to wear to dinner when Jude snapped her. Hey.

She responded with, Hey. That was code for, are you there.

I wanna see you, Jude wrote. She responded with a picture of her face, smiling. He responded with the same picture; except he was shirtless. What a great picture, she thought. She had never, before their trip to the range, flirted with him. Although now, she felt they had gone beyond flirting, and she felt more comfortable expressing herself. She went to the bathroom, peed, then changed her shirt. She stood in the mirror and looked at her body. She saw herself in the mirror but looked more at the background surrounding her. She saw the bathroom with the big tub and glass shower. She could see the white carpet and the lamplight on the chaise lounge. She felt confident, and for a minute, she let herself be Anastasia, the girl who had grown up in this room. Her phone vibrated. It was Jude again, shirtless, flexing and making a silly face. She pulled her hair down and turned her body to pose for a selfie. She looked at the picture and thought, what does it matter and sent the picture to him. She couldn't help but feel a little scared and risky at the same time. She put her hair back up and heard a knock at the door.

"Ana, it's me," Diane said. Ana grabbed her phone, threw it on the chaise, and pulled her shirt over her head. Diana had opened the door. "Oh, I'm sorry. Are you ready for dinner?"

"Yeah, yes I am, I guess."

"How was your time with your mother?"

"It was good, I think. She seems very nice." Ana couldn't help but think about Jude seeing her in her bra in that snap. She was clearly distracted. Ana's phone buzzed, alerting her to a new Snapchat. Jude was typing, followed by another vibration, then another vibration followed by another. Ana didn't pick up the phone, but she couldn't stop looking at it.

"Anastasia, are you ok? You seem flustered?" Diana asked, concerned.

"I'm good, just my friends from home texting me."

"I hope you find your new room pleasant. I am very glad to have you home."

"May I ask you a question?" Ana asked. "What is the plan for me? I feel like I should be doing something, kinda like I'm wasting time." She asked because she had been thinking about it all day, and she didn't feel like she could ask her mother.

"Ana, it's hard for me to answer that, but I think you should try to relax and enjoy getting to know yourself and your family. You have always had to try very hard, and here you have time to find yourself. Your parents will discuss all your options for a wonderful future," Diana said.

"So basically, you said all that to say, you don't know." Ana rolled her eyes.

"No, it's true. And no, I can't tell you the future, sweetheart," Diane clarified. They walked down to the dining room. When they arrived, Phillip and Andrea were already seated. Diane guided her to her seat. She sat across from her mother and next to her father. As she sat down, in the light of the room, Ana's hair shined the exact color of her mother's. She was like a reflection of her from years ago. Andrea smiled, and her eyes held tears.

"Anastasia, I hope you're hungry. Nellie has prepared a wonderful meal for us tonight. Diane, will Jeffrey be joining us?" Andrea said.

"Not tonight. He will be working later than planned. When will Drake be coming in tomorrow?"

"He should be here around noon."

"Does he know about me?" Ana blurted out as she almost choked on a carrot.

"Your father and I are going to tell him once he arrives," Andrea said and smiled, picking up her fork.

"Ah, I think you should tell him before he leaves. Where is he anyway?" Ana said, frankly.

"He is away at school. Why do you think we should tell him before he arrives?" Phillip asked.

After Ana finished chewing her piece of meat, she said, "Because he might not be as happy as you are. I mean, he has been an only child all his life. I would want some warning. I mean, not everyone likes surprises."

Phillip looked at Andrea, and they smiled at each other like they had a secret language. "I think he will be just fine finding out once he gets here," Andrea said.

"Ok, whatever," Ana continued. She was interrupted by Diane clearing her throat. Ana looked over at her and took the hint to shut her mouth quickly.

Diane then changed the subject. Dinner was over, and Andrea asked Ana to join her in the family room. That was the room with the T.V. she learned. They all sat on the couches as the TV played in the background.

"What did you do at the academy for fun?" her father asked her.

"Well, we would chill or watch movies. Sometimes we would play cards or other games."

"What type of cards did you play?"

"We would play rummy, or Phase Ten, or UNO. Just whatever." Ana paused. "You wanna play?"

"Sure, would you two ladies like to join us?" They all agreed, and before she knew it, her father was drinking wine and seemed to be very comfortable. Ana liked to play cards. It allowed people to have a conversation without having their individual attention on the other people. It took away the tension.

"Ana, do you like horses?" her father asked.

"Yes, I do. I have always believed they were strong and majestic." Ana looked at her hand.

Diane looked up and said, "What are you hinting at, brother?"

"She just looks like she would like to ride horses." He grinned.

"Diane, you know how he is," Andrea said.

"Did you know your aunt has excellent equestrian abilities? In fact, her daughter..."

He stopped mid-sentence because Diane interrupted him. "Anastasia, I ride, and I will take you sometime. But horses are a hobby, not a career. You need to know that upfront."

Ana replied sheepishly, "Ok, awkward.". Andrea laughed, then Phillip joined in.

"Di, she is hilarious. Look, you are even smiling," Phillip said. They continued to play as Ana's phone rang. It was a FaceTime with Jude.

She turned to Diane. "It's Jude. I'll call back in a minute."

"No darling, you can call now. We are all about to go to bed anyway," Andrea said.

Ana took her phone and headed towards the stairs. "Oh, Diane, are you leaving?" she asked before she left.

"Yes, but I will come tell you goodbye before I go."

Ana skipped her way to her room and FaceTimed Jude. He was excited to see her, and he was still shirtless. "Do you walk around naked at home often?" she laughed.

"Only if I'm talking to you," he said smiling. He asked about her day, and she told him about Drake coming home. "Have you looked him up on Facebook?"

"No, he's only sixteen, but I probably should, huh."

"Yeah, I hope he isn't an asshole or some sissy boy with manicured nails."

"Nah, I doubt it. I imagine him as a jock or maybe a little nerdy, I bet. I mean, how could you not be living here." They continued to talk for a while then Ana took a shower.

"Who is Jude?" Andrea asked Diane.

"He is a friend of hers. They are close."

"How close?"

"Pretty close. She's never said they were officially dating, although there was an incident before we left that suggested they are involved."

"You know she will have to end it. It's not feasible for her to be dating a boy in another country. Especially now, when she's trying to find herself in this family," Andrea said matter-of-factly.

"I am aware, Andy. But I see no need in taking away her only friend. Besides, he is an ocean away."

"Well, we need to keep that situation under control."

"I know," Diane sighed. She knew Ana would not take it well if they told her she couldn't have a relationship with Jude. She had chosen not to tell Andrea or Phillip about the night at the range, and now she was especially glad. Maybe the relationship would fizzle out. Maybe Ana would be too preoccupied with her new life to worry about him. Diane walked upstairs to tell Ana goodnight. She enjoyed kissing her head and seeing her peacefully lying in her bed. This act was so natural to her. She had done it for years when her own daughter was still at home. She knocked on the door and opened the door slightly. She told Ana goodnight and goodbye.

Ana was sitting in her bed with her blankets around her. "See you tomorrow?"

Diane told her yes and left for her own home. Ana smiled, and Diane cracked the door as she left. Later, Ana went back down to the kitchen for a snack.

When she passed her mother's room, Andrea saw her and said, "Anastasia, do you need something?"

"No, just going down for a snack."

Andrea walked over to her and said, "Ok, dear, goodnight." Andrea leaned in to hug her, and she said, "I love you, Ana."

Ana hugged her back, "I know." That was enough for Andrea. She understood that Ana would not automatically love her, and she knew that when Ana was ready, she would love her in return.

CHAPTER SIX

Home

Andrea believed it would be easier for Anastasia to adjust to her new home if she had a daily routine. Even though Ana had college credit, she was enrolled at the high school Drake had gone to prior to his move to the preparatory school. "So, I have to go to a high school?" Ana asked, as her mother was explaining her plans.

"Yes, for now," Andrea answered. Ana would get her college credits transferred, but she had to pass a comprehensive exam. Once she passed the exam, she could officially begin college classes. Ana didn't care for high school. When she had enrolled, the staff and students treated her weird, fragile, almost like she could be broken. She guessed they thought she had been abused or tortured her whole life, prior to her discovery. On the fourth day of school, reporters showed up at lunch while she was eating outside, asking her to do an interview on how she was finally found. Phillip then called the school and asked for more protection. They didn't come to the school after that. People weren't mean to her but weren't nice either. In the second week of school, she made a friend named Brittani in Chemistry Lab. Brittani's dad was in the U.S. Air Force and was stationed in the area on a permanent assignment at the U.S. Embassy. Brittani was funny, and they got along wonderfully. Ana's comprehensive exam was in two weeks, and she had studied intermittently at the request of her mom. Ana had also gotten permission to drive and was driving to school daily in her BMW. The BMW was brand new and red. She couldn't believe she had a car, much less a BMW, SUV. She enjoyed driving, she felt freedom when she drove, and she could get to the stable easier than walking. She loved going to see the horses and had gotten to know the stable keeper as well. His name was Travis Burns. He was a freshman in college and cared for the horses and stables for her Aunt Diane and Uncle Jeffrey. His parents were close friends of theirs. Travis was shy and awkward but very handsome. It took Travis a week just to say the first word to Ana, but after that, it seemed they were talking a lot. Ana found herself at the barn more than at home. Sometimes her aunt would be there, and they would ride together until dinner. Other days, she would ride alone, and Travis would join her later when he came around to feed. Ana received a text randomly asking if she was coming to the stable that day. She didn't recognize the number but soon found it to be Travis. He had gotten her number from Diane. From that one text, Travis and Ana frequently communicated from then on. Ana felt like it was ok because she wasn't in a relationship with Jude, and she really wasn't in a relationship with Travis either. Ana liked Travis as a friend, but that was it.

Ana was not eager to sit for a three-hour test, so when Brittani suggested they go hang out with some friends instead of going to fourth period, she all but jumped in Brittani's car. Her exam was at 5:30 p.m. She didn't ask permission. She assumed she would be back in time for the exam. She imagined she could rush through the exam, pass it, and be home before nine. Brittani had older friends. Her sister was older and in college. So that day, Brittani and Ana went downtown to a local pub to socialize with her friends. Ana didn't tell her mom because she thought she would be back in time for the test. "I'm gonna get a drink. You want one?" Brittani asked Ana.

"Sure, one shouldn't hurt, but I'm underage,"

"Watch," Brittani ordered a drink, without any question from the waiter.

When Ana ordered, the waiter asked for her identification, and Ana knew she had been caught. Although the waiter, a male in his forties, said, "Oh, hello Ms. Hutchinson, here you are," as he handed her back her I.D.

Ana smiled in response and, after he left, said to Brittani, "He knew my name."

Brittani said, "Yeah, I could tell." Within a few minutes, the waiter returned with both girls' drinks and an appetizer that they hadn't ordered. "It's good to be you," Brittani said to Ana.

Ana smiled and said, "Yeah, maybe." Ana and Brittani drank while they laughed and enjoyed the company. She was having fun, fun like before, with her friends Natilee and Jude. The mixed liquor drinks were good, and she liked the way she felt, so relaxed, silly, and happy. So, she kept drinking without a thought of her exam or how anyone else may feel about it. When she looked down at her phone, it was five 5:22. She had to squint hard to see the numbers. "Oh crap, Brittani, look, it's five twenty-two!" Ana said.

"Oh well, did you really think you would be taking that exam today?" Brittani said as she laughed.

"I'm not about to go take it now. I am kinda drunk." Ana replied. "I will just take the next one," and drank her fourth drink. It seemed like the more she drank, the warmer she became. Ana and Travis had been texting, and the conversation had gotten a little loose. She was saying things to him she would never say in person.

"We gotta go," Brittani said. Ana looked, and it was 7:00 p.m.

"Yeah, will you take me to the stables? I wanna stop and see Travis."

"Oh, why do you wanna stop and see him?" Brittani smiled. "I just want to kiss him," Ana said. Brittani had drunk as well but wasn't near as intoxicated. Brittani dropped her off at the stables and promised she would text when she got home safely. Travis was in a stall with one of the horses when she came up. Ana came up behind him and hugged him. This surprised him, and he smiled.

"What has gotten into you?" Travis asked, smiling at her.

"I don't know," Ana said shyly.

"You've been drinking." He laughed. "You better hope your mom or aunt don't catch you." He teased her, knowing it would be trouble if she did get caught. He reached down and pulled her close to him from the waist and kissed her. She kissed him back. This was their first kiss, and from there, it seemed to move really fast. She wanted to kiss, but she didn't want to have sex with him. She knew that much. She wasn't ready. She started breathing rapidly as he put his hands under her shirt, and when he unbuttoned her pants, she backed away.

"I can't do this," Ana said quietly. "I want you to take me home." He didn't argue. Travis dropped her off at the edge of her driveway, hiding his truck from anyone who may be watching. Travis had worked at the stable for a while and knew it wouldn't be a great idea for them to get caught up together. He feared Diane and Jeff would fire him if they knew.

Meanwhile, while Ana was out with Brittani, the school called. Andrea answered, and the school principal informed her that Ana had not shown to take her exam. Andrea tried calling Ana as she drove to the school but couldn't get her. When she arrived at the school, Ana's Jeep was parked there, but Ana was not there. Andrea called Diane crying and terrified. "Diane, Ana is gone. She didn't show up for her exam, and her Jeep is here at the school."

Diane called Anastasia multiple times. With no answer. The phone went straight to voicemail. Diane attempted to locate her, although it looked like she was either out of range or had turned off her phone. Andrea left the school and headed back home. Andrea called Phillip in a panic. Diane was trying to keep her calm but was having a hard time. Phillip was worried and asked Diane to help her. Diane said, "I will find her, Phillip."

Andrea just stared at her phone on the counter and cried. Diane hugged her. "Hey, she will come home," Diane said.

"What if someone has taken her away from me?"

"No, I think Ana has some explaining to do. I think this is Ana, out with friends and losing track of time." Diane was trying to reassure her. At 9:00 p.m. Diane's phone pinged Ana, and Diane could see Ana's blue dot cross the front yard. "She's home."

Ana softly walked into the dark foyer and through the hall to the stairs, attempting to sneak to her room. "Stop right there, young lady," Diane said loudly from the shadows of the kitchen. Ana turned around and flopped down on the steps, sitting, waiting, anticipating a lecture from her aunt. Andrea watched her from behind Diane and went from crying to anger in a matter of seconds.

"Anastasia, where have you been?" Andrea demanded as she turned the bright light on over Ana's head. "Why didn't you take your exam today?" she asked before Ana could answer. Ana was caught off guard by her mother's tone and volume. The light made her squint, and she felt really drunk all at once. Ana looked up, not knowing if her mother was done yelling at her or not.

"Speak," Diane commanded.

"I went with my friend Brittani after third period. I was planning on coming back to school, but I lost track of time, then it was too late. Sorry mom," Ana explained and looked at the floor.

"Look at me when I am speaking to you." her mother said. Ana looked up at her mother.

"Why is your car at school?" Diane asked as if it was her turn to interrogate her.

"I wanted to get home, so I just had her drop me off," Ana said, lying.

Diane could smell the alcohol on Ana's breath, and her intoxicating look was all too revealing. "And have you been drinking?" Diane asked. Hearing this, Andrea turned around and paced and was shaking her head. Both of them were glaring at Ana, waiting for a response. Ana was silent. "There is no reason to lie, young lady," Diane replied to her.

"Kinda," Ana responded as she put her hands on her face and looked down.

"You are drunk. There is not a 'kind of' to it." She turned to walk away then came back, infuriated.

"Anastasia, blatantly, you chose to miss the exam. You went out, without permission, with people we don't know and got drunk." Andrea pointed in Ana's face.

Diane stood back and watched, then she asked, "Brittani brought you home? Are you sure? Then why did she drop you off at the end of the drive?" Diane didn't know the answer, but by looking at the patch of muck on her shoe, and the piece of hay stuck to the back of her shirt, she knew Ana hadn't come straight home.

"Yes, Brittani brought me home," Ana lied. Andrea and Diane looked at each other. Ana's face was like a window to her soul. She couldn't lie very well. Something was up.

"So, you didn't go by the stables?" Diane asked.

"Brittani dropped me there, and I walked up from there. What's the big deal?" Ana knew she was getting caught in a lie and was getting frustrated and tired of the conversation.

"Why did you turn your phone off?" Diane wanted to know.

"I don't know," Ana replied.

"So, you did turn it off, so you must not have wanted to be disturbed."

"What were you doing, young lady, that you didn't want to be interrupted?" her mother asked, glaring at her through her navy round-shaped glasses.

“Nothing, I just turned it off.” Ana lied again.

“That is a lie.” her mother said accusingly. Ana and felt like she was going to cry.

Andrea paced and placed her hands on her face and tried to breathe. Unable to control her frustration, she leaned over and pulled Ana’s chin up, forcing her to make eye contact with her.

“You blatantly missed your exam by choosing to go out without permission, drinking with people we do not know, and you turned off your location on your phone, and now you're lying to me. Anastasia, I thought someone had taken you, Ana. You wouldn’t answer the phone, your car is at school, and you’re not. That doesn’t paint a very pretty picture. I just found you a little more than a month ago. I thought I had lost you forever,” Andrea explained.

This made Ana feel sad and guilty. “I am sorry, Mom,” Ana said, now crying.

Andrea was getting emotional herself, so she turned and walked away. “Go shower, then come down for your dinner.” Andrea pointed up to Ana’s room.

“Mom, I got carried away, and I...”

“Go, Ana,” her mother said. Ana felt like a failure with a capital F. She wanted to crawl under a rock and hide. She got in the shower and sat under the water. She felt terrible and somewhat sick. Her head hit the back of the wall, and she began to spin. She closed her eyes and passed out. Andrea and Diane knew she was taking way too long. Andrea went into her bedroom and knocked on the bathroom door. Ana grunted something. Andrea opened the door, and the bathroom was full of steam. She opened the glass shower door, and Ana was holding her knees to her chest with her wet head laid on her knees. Ana looked drunk and sick. “Anastasia, are you ok?” her mother said.

“I am so sorry,” Ana mumbled.

“Let's get her out,” Diane said, remembering doing this same thing with her daughter. They turned the water off, and Diane handed Andrea a towel.

“Ana, get up.” her mother said.

"I don't want you to see me," Ana said through sobs. She was embarrassed but still so drunk.

"Ana, here I am covering you, now get up," Diane said as she covered her with the large towel and pulled her arm. Ana stood up and held the towel tight around her.

"I will get her pajamas," Andrea said, and she left Ana in with Diane.

Ana was looking somewhat better, and she looked at Diane and asked, "I am in trouble, aren't I?"

"Yes, you are," Diane answered truthfully. Andrea came in and exchanged a look with Diane.

"I can do it," Ana said.

"Don't be silly. You could fall. Here, there is no reason to be embarrassed." Andrea said as she slid her shirt over her head and gently pulled the towel down. Diane was holding on to Ana's other arm. Ana put her arms through the shirt and was humiliated. She started to snub like she was going to cry again.

"Stop crying. You're already dehydrated." Andrea told her, tired of the tears. "Come on. You need water and maybe a snack." Diane said, holding her arm. Andrea sat her down on the chaise lounge. She used the towel to dry her hair as she sat. Ana felt like a child or invalid.

"Mom, I am sorry for this," Ana said. Andrea came from around the chaise and looked into her eyes.

"I am sorry you did this as well," Andrea said.

Ana held up her arms for her mother. Andrea wanted to resist her, but she embraced her. Her anger was still there but had cooled. Diane walked in with the water and crackers.

Ana started to talk again about the night, but Andrea said "We will talk about this in the morning, now. Let's get you feeling better." Diane smiled at Andrea as Ana's head was rested back on the chair, with her eyes closed. Ana ate a small amount and drank a large glass of water, and took two ibuprofens, then went to sleep.

The next morning Ana slept till nine, which was late. She came to breakfast, and the smell of the eggs made her feel faint. "May I be excused?" she asked as soon as she sat down.

"No, drink this at least. You don't have to eat anything yet." Nelly said, handing her what looked like tomato juice.

"Is that a raw egg?" Ana asked, looking at the glass with the yellow yolk at the bottom.

"Yes, and drink it," Nellie said in a not kidding way.

"You should listen. She knows what she is doing." her mother said from across the table.

Ana chugged the drink and said "ugh." as she finished.

"I am going back to bed," Ana said.

"Fine, but you will be up by eleven and ready to work outside with your aunt and me," her mother said. "Doing what?" Ana asked.

"That doesn't matter. It is part of your punishment." her mother said.

"What is my punishment? I was supposed to ride with Brittani today." Ana asked with a teenage look of disgust on her face.

"We will discuss the details later, but I assure you will not be riding today." her mother said with a smirk of her own.

"Whatever," Ana said and went back up to her room. At ten minutes till eleven, Nellie came into her room. "Up and at it. Your mother is waiting on you." Nellie said.

"I feel like crap," Ana admitted.

"You should now get up," Nellie said.

And dressed and walked downstairs and out of the garage. Ana saw her aunt's car, and she followed the sidewalk around to a patio. "Have a seat, let's talk." her mother said as Ana walked up. The sun was beaming on her, already making her squint.

"You look like you're on trial," Diane said, smiling.

"I feel like I'm at the Judgement."

"Sit down," her mother said. Ana sat down on the iron chair and looked at them. "How are you feeling?" Diane asked.

"Like hell," Ana said.

"Well, what do you expect after behavior like that?" her mother said.

"Mom, I didn't mean to get drunk. It kinda happened," Ana said, trying to be passive. Diane nodded and looked at Andrea.

"Anastasia, that type of behavior is not tolerated. You were impulsive and irresponsible. You not only missed your exam, but you put yourself in danger and then turned off your location. Ana, I thought you were gone, stolen, or worse. Do you understand how that made me feel?" her mother said.

"Yes, I do, and I am sorry to both of you. Especially you mom, I wasn't thinking." Ana said sincerely.

"So, I have called Professor Finn, and you will be in class with him after school for the next month. That way, you can be fully prepared to take your exam." Andrea said frankly.

"Ok," Ana said, expecting that.

"And you're on restriction for a month, school and home only. I will take you to and from school." her mother said.

"Seriously?" Ana said, truly shocked. She had never been grounded before.

"Yes, ma'am." her mother said. Ana didn't argue. She knew what she had done.

Diane watched their interaction. She was proud of Andrea for controlling her emotions and Ana for keeping her mouth shut and accepting her punishment. "Now, let's get to work. These shrubs don't get pruned themselves." Diane said, standing up. Ana followed and carried load upon load of trimmings for her aunt. Her mother did some, although mostly weeded around the flowers.

"I mean, shouldn't we have a gardener?" Ana asked her mother.

"We do." her mother said from a seated position.

"And why are we doing it?" Ana asked.

"Because we wanted to," Andrea answered. Ana nodded and kept carrying.

The next week, on Monday, Andrea drove Ana to and from school. They would get home around 5:30 p.m. Ana didn't mind staying home, but it had only been three days. "I'm gonna go down to the stables, Mom," she said as she passed by the kitchen.

"Are you finished with all your assignments?"

"Yes, all but Professor Finn's assignments."

"Ana finished means finished, with all of it. You're not going anywhere unless it's all done."

"Yes, mother," Ana said, in a sarcastic tone, as she walked back to the study. The assignments grew in number every day. It seemed like as she finished one, another was added. She was spending all her time looking at textbooks. Ana felt like she would never get to go back to the stables. After she asked the first time, she hadn't asked again. She had managed to ride with her Aunt Diane on Saturday afternoons when she would come by and ask for her company. On Thursday evening, of the third week of her sentence, Ana decided to ask her mother again for permission to go to the stables. "Mom, may I go to the stables. Diane is down there today," Ana said, trying to persuade her mom.

"Ana, Diane will be here soon. Your dad is coming home this evening. Tomorrow is Friday, so you can go to the stables this weekend." Andrea said, hoping this would please her daughter.

"Oh really, like he will be here for dinner?" Ana asked, worried about what her father would say about her drunken night. She still felt terrible about it. She was especially sorry for lying and worrying her mom, but she missed the horses and hanging out with Travis and Brittani.

When Ana saw her father, he was calm, cool, and collected as he sipped a glass of beer in the study. The T.V. was on, but he was reading the papers in front of him. Drake was home as well. He was sitting on the couch, watching T.V., and playing on his iPhone as Ana passed.

"Anastasia, come here. I haven't seen you in a while," Phillip said as she stood outside the door.

Ana went into the room and greeted him with a hug.

"Hi, dad," she said meekly. He kissed her head, and she moved to stand beside his desk, pretending to look at the books on the shelf against the wall.

"Doing well, I assume?" Phillip asked as he looked at his paper.

"Yes, sir." Ana was nervous and didn't feel like she knew her father very well. He was often away on business.

"School going well? Have you thought about your major?"

"School is school, but I don't hate it," Ana said. Drake looked up at her. She felt stupid.

"Ana, just get through high school. College has a lot less drama and is a lot more fun."

They went to the dining room for dinner, and Ana was puzzled. Did he know about the exam? She wondered what her mother or aunt had told him. He didn't seem to be upset with her at all. Dinner was ready, and everyone seemed pleasantly happy. Jeffrey and Diane were there, and Diane and Andrea each held a glass of wine. Before the food was served, her father asked Nellie to bring the wine to the table. Nellie began to pour, but Phillip interrupted her, "Let me," he said as he got up from his seat.

Andrea smiled at him as he went around the table. The table was set with wine glasses at every seat. That was how Ana had always seen it at dinner, so she wasn't alarmed. Ana sat across from her mother and beside her father. Drake was diagonal from her, seated between his mother and uncle. Diane was seated beside Ana. As her father came around the table, he poured wine into the glasses and spoke jovially to them. He stopped at Ana and held the wine over her glass. This confused her. "Anastasia, would you like wine? I have heard you enjoy drinking with your friends?"

Ana's face turned red, and she looked down. She knew he knew she had been caught drinking. "Anastasia?" he asked again, demanding a reply.

"No, thank you, sir," she said, keeping her eyes down. Andrea and Diane looked at each other, then at Ana with empathy.

"Wait, did you ask her if she wanted alcohol, Dad?" Drake sputtered out, getting everyone's attention. "She's only a year older than me. Why didn't you ask me?" Drake had no knowledge of what was really going on.

"Anastasia, please educate your brother. Do we believe that underage drinking is acceptable behavior." her father asked.

"No, sir." Ana looked down at her plate; hot tears welled in her eyes.

"Oh God, you got caught drinking? Oh, that sucks," Drake blurted out loud. Diane gave him a look and changed the subject. For the rest of the dinner, Ana didn't speak unless she was directly asked a question. She refused to make eye contact with either of her parents. She was embarrassed, angry, and ready to leave the table. Ana had her cell phone in her pocket, and it vibrated, then twice more. She didn't attempt to take the phone out of her pocket.

Her mother heard the vibration and gave Ana a look.

"Mom, may I be excused, please?" Ana asked.

"Yes."

Ana stood up and took her plate and water glass to the kitchen. She put them in the sink and burst into tears. She ran up the steps to her room. She went to her room, shut the door, and locked it. She answered her texts and snaps from Natilee, Jude, and Brittani, then laid down on the chaise lounge. She had almost fallen asleep when her mother knocked on the door and tried to turn the handle. "Ana, open the door."

Ana jumped across the floor and unlocked the door. Startled by her mother's tone. "I'm sorry, Mom, I fell asleep studying," she tried to explain.

"Ana, I'm sorry for scaring you, but we do not lock doors."

"Ok, I'm sorry." Ana apologized.

"Tomorrow, I have a meeting at eight a.m. sharp. Your dad will take you to school, and I will pick you up."

"Can I not drive, just for one day?" Ana was hoping for a light at the end of the tunnel.

"No, I'm sorry. Your restriction is one month, and it has only been three weeks." Andrea put her hands on Ana's shoulders and pulled her in. "I love you, Ana. Just because I'm not giving in to you doesn't mean I don't love you."

Ana pulled back to see her mother's face. "Mom, that embarrassed me so bad when dad did that." Ana began to sob big tears. Andrea sat her down and held her.

"I know, I don't think he meant it to be that much of a display. You're going to be fine. You're smart and beautiful. We all make mistakes. We all mess up. We have to learn from those mistakes, not repeat them, and move on," Andrea said, then put Ana's phone on the nightstand, covered her daughter, and kissed her head. She had dreamt about doing this so many nights before.

Ana looked at her mother with sleepy, slightly swollen eyes. "I love you, mom."

Andrea felt her heart swell with warmth. "I love you too, sweet daughter of mine."

Phillip was downstairs, sitting by the fireplace. It was still spring, so the cold night air created enough of an excuse to light the logs. Drake was lying on the couch texting when Andrea entered the room. "Well, what are you two doing? Nothing it looks like."

Phillip turned around. "How is Anastasia?"

"She's ok, but she's humiliated. That was harsh, Phillip. She doesn't know you well enough for that, and then Drake's comments made it worse." She looked at Drake.

"What, nobody tells me anything. How was I supposed to know to keep my mouth shut? I was surprised that the princess had done something wrong. What did she do?" Drake said.

"She skipped her placement exam and was missing for four hours, while your mom and aunt were frantically looking for her," Phillip said.

"I thought she got caught drinking?" Drake asked, looking confused.

"When she came home, she had been drinking," Phillip clarified.

"I can handle the alcohol better than the lying Phillip," Andrea said.

"Yes, she lied to your mom about where she had been," Phillip said Drake. "She had been at the stables. Why would she lie about that anyway? Diane couldn't find her phone location. It was very scary. Drake, don't even try turning yours off. It's obvious you don't lose signal where you live," Andrea said.

"Wow, now I don't feel like such a rebellious child. Don't be so hard on her though Mom, she is new. She probably did whatever she wanted in her old life. She really didn't have much in the way of parents, right?"

"No, not according to the files," Andrea said. "Well, she is grounded for one more week and has to stay after school for an extra class with Professor Finn until then. She's hating it, mostly because she doesn't have time to go to the stables in the evening. I should have just restricted her from there." Andrea sipped a cup of coffee.

Drake remembered that Travis worked for his aunt at the stables and couldn't help but wonder if maybe there was something going on between him and Ana. He went to bed, leaving his parents alone, but planned on talking to his sister the next morning.

Andrea sat on the sofa next to Phillip. "I miss you when you're away," she said.

"Can you believe we're raising two teenagers?" Phillip said and smiled. "Do you think we should have told Drake about what Ana had done?" Phillip was second-guessing his decision.

"Well, there are no secrets in this family, Phillip, no use in hiding it. We forgive easily, learn from it, and move on."

"Yeah, I guess you're right. I'll talk to her tomorrow. I didn't realize that what I said would humiliate her so much, and I didn't anticipate our big-mouth son saying what he did. I'll go down to the stables tomorrow. Maybe we can ride."

They sat there in silence, watching the fire and feeling full. With their two children asleep above them, they finally felt content and happy after all these years. Andrea kissed Phillip softly on the cheek. Phillip had missed his wife, especially seeing her happy. He stood and tugged her hand to pull her to him. His chest against hers, he could see something youthful and playful in her eyes, something he hadn't seen in a long time. Taking the opportunity, he passionately kissed her, and she didn't pull away but instead pushed closer to him. He kissed her neck. She closed her eyes. He was so handsome standing with her, and he felt so strong against her, something they had both forgotten. They stood there kissing, like two young lovers, when they heard a sound but disregarded it as Nellie. Ana walked by the door. Seeing them, she turned her head quickly toward the other direction. Andrea and Phillip smiled, "That was inappropriate for our daughter to see," Andrea said, still standing in his arms.

"Awkward maybe, but not inappropriate. They need to know their parents love each other." He turned off the light and headed to bed.

Andrea went toward the kitchen. "Ana, you ok?"

"Yeah, my phone was buzzing and woke me up. I wanted some milk."

"Who was calling you at this hour?"

"Oh, just Jude. He was out with some of our friends at a place we used to hang out." Ana finished her milk and put the glass in the sink. Andrea had taken Drake's phone at night when he lived at home. Maybe she should consider taking Ana's, but she didn't want to restrict her communication with her friends at home, she thought.

"Ok, goodnight, love." Andrea left the kitchen, heading to her bedroom.

Ana followed, going to her own room. She saw her mother enter their bedroom and close the door. Ana blocked the thought of her parents having sex from her mind. "Yuck," she said aloud as she entered her room and got in the bed. She had never seen the Peterson's show affection toward each other. It was kind of comforting knowing her parents loved each other, although it was necessary to exclude the thought of them as lovers. That was just weird.

The next morning, Drake knocked on Ana's door. He entered and said, "Get up lazy, let's go do something fun. I'm only home for the next few days." Ana didn't move out. Drake threw a pillow from the floor at her head. It hit her, but not very hard.

"Hey! Stop you twerp," Ana said, smiling back at him. She threw a bigger pillow at him while getting out of bed.

"Well, it worked, come on, I'm hungry." Drake headed down to the kitchen. "You want an omelet?" he asked her and Nellie.

"You cook omelets?" Ana asked.

"Yeah, Nellie lets me cook all the time, right Nellie?"

"Yeah, he can cook, but he makes a big ol' mess every time," Nellie said, laughing. He made two omelets for Nellie and Ana.

They were eating when Phillip came into the kitchen. "Oh, look who's cooking. Chef Drake," he said when he saw his son.

"Hey Dad, you want an omelet? Is mom still asleep? Do you think she will want one?"

"Sure, I'll dine with these fine ladies, and your mother should be down shortly."

Drake was finishing two more omelets when his mother walked into the room, her wet hair in a towel. Ana thought she looked flushed, which brought out the color of her eyes. They all ate together. "Drake, what are you doing today?" Andrea asked.

"We are going riding, just around the service roads near the barns. We need to check some fence that Ana was worried about. Right, Ana?" Drake said. He looked at Ana for support. Drake knew Ana didn't have the keys to her car, but he wanted to see what they could get away with.

"That's interesting because Ana isn't driving right now," Andrea said as she sipped her coffee.

"I'm going to drive," he said.

Andrea squinted at him. "She can drive. You're way too dangerous. Don't do anything stupid." She smiled as she looked at both of them.

Ana was amused watching this interaction and was impressed that Drake had come up with that story so quickly. Soon, they were in the ATV headed down the road. "Hey, how did you get mom to let us go?" Ana asked.

"I don't know. I just figured it was harder for her to tell us both no. What happened anyway?"

"I messed up. I really don't wanna talk about it."

"Hey, I'm just glad I'm not the only one who gets in trouble." Drake was trying to make her feel better. "You wanna know what I did?"

"Sure, maybe it will help me not feel so much like a loser."

"Once, I had a party at our house. It was supposed to be small, but my friends invited a bunch of people I didn't even know, and one of the punks crashed into the fence. As if that wasn't enough, I was supposed to be staying with Aunt Diane, so when I didn't show up, she came over to find a bunch of other people passed out on the carpet in the living room and me. I woke up to her yelling in my face and Uncle Jeff pulling guys up by their collars. It wasn't good. I puked all over the white carpet. But the worst is what got me into prep school. I was with a few friends who vandalized the gym at the high school one night. I was drunk and almost got arrested. I was friends with a lot of older boys. Mom called them thugs. Anyway, those thugs left me there that night while they ran. Dad and mom came and got me. I was afraid for my life. I thought dad was going to pulverize me."

"Oh my god, you're nuts. I would never do that stuff."

"I wouldn't either now. I have matured. I mean, that was last year." He gave her a cheeky smile.

"And now, mom and dad trust you?" Ana asked unbelievably.

"Trust me, they do more than they did, but I'm not sure I could get away with too much."

They rode for a while, and Drake showed her where he liked to hike. They stopped by a creek, a place he used to go swimming when he was a kid. The place was quiet and tucked into the side of a mountain. "They say there's a cave, but I've never found it," Drake told her as they walked along the creek.

"Is there a trail that comes here? We could ride the horses," she asked him.

"Yes, it takes a little while, but it's an easy ride," Drake answered. They went down to the stables on their way back to the house. Travis was there. His truck was parked out front. "Dad's here, wonder why?" Drake said.

That made Ana nervous. They walked into the stable and saw Travis saddling Shotsley, a black mare, and their father adjusting the stirrups on another mare. "Hello, thought we would go for a ride. Drake, saddle your horse, and we will show Ana some of the places we like to go." Drake went off to get his horse.

Ana walked up to Shotsley, and Travis smiled at her secretly. "Thanks, Travis."

"Oh good, you know each other, Travis. You want to join us?" Phillip asked.

"Nah, Mr. H, I better not. I'll be here to help when you all get back."

They mounted their horses and rode through the field down by the creek. Phillip would point and talk about each place they went. They visited the same spot Drake had taken them and got off to rest. The three of them sat down on the ground and watched the water. Phillip nudged Drake and signaled him to give him and Ana some privacy. Once he had walked away, Phillip said, "Anastasia, I'm sorry if I embarrassed you last night. I didn't mean for it to turn out the way it did."

Ana looked up at him. "Dad, I understand. I'm just not used to being told what to do, and when, or being punished." Ana looked back at the water.

"Ana, you are our child, and we love you. You're just in high school, you're not out on your own, and we want the best for you. All of us need boundaries, and you're being punished because you lied, drank alcohol, and skipped your exam. That is part of our job as parents. Do you understand that?" Phillip tried to explain.

"I know that. It just feels weird to have someone --." Ana paused.

"To care about you?" Phillip asked.

"Yeah." A tear ran down her cheek.

"We will always love you. It's true. Nothing can change that," her father said.

They returned to the stables around two o'clock. Travis was still there, just like he said he would be. He took Phillip's horse as soon as he dismounted. Andrea had come to visit and was standing there waiting to greet them. Phillip walked to her, they embraced and kissed hello. Ana looked at Drake, he shook his head at the display of affection, and Ana smiled in agreeance. Drake dismounted and walked his horse into the barn. Andrea held the bridle while Ana dismounted. "Thanks, Mom." Ana led Shotsley to her stall.

Andrea hadn't been to the stables in a number of years, and it felt unfamiliar. Drake returned to get his tack. "I can carry something for you," Andrea said. As she looked in the tack room, she saw Travis handing Ana the riding equipment and gear. They moved in sync without speaking, like they had done this very thing thousands of times.

Andrea approached the door and a startled Ana. "Oh, Mom, thank you!" She took the piece of equipment out of Andrea's hands.

They were soon finished with the horses and were headed back to the house for dinner. Andrea had walked down to the stables, so she rode with Phillip back to the house. "Who is that guy at the barn?" she asked Phillip.

"That's Travis. He's worked for Jeffrey and Diane for a couple of years. He keeps the stables for them. I think he goes to the University."

"Does he work there often?"

"I don't know, Love." He could tell she was pondering something. "What is it, Andrea?"

"Nothing, dear," Andrea recalled how much Ana had been at the stables, almost every day, before restriction. She decided she would ask Diane more about Travis and how much he worked there. She had a feeling that made her uneasy. She would call Diane before dinner.

On the ride back to the house, Drake broke the silence with a question. "Ana, what is up with Travis?"

"What do you mean?"

"Come on. I'm not gonna rat you out."

"What do you think you know? We're friends, we text."

"No, it's not obvious, but I heard you've been spending a lot of time at the stables. I can tell you two have spent a lot of time together."

"What is it, Drake? Spit it out."

"Ana, Mom will not approve of you dating, especially him. Don't let them find out. Better yet, just don't date him," Drake advised her.

"Drake, what's the big deal? I'm 17, and we're not dating anyway. I've had a boyfriend and even made out with one or two," she said and laughed.

"That was before. Now you're Anastasia Hutchinson. Mom and Dad are not gonna let you date someone like him, trust me."

They got back and had dinner as a family. After dinner, they laid around in the living room and watched T.V. Ana laid across the couch with her feet tucked into her mom. Every now and then, Andrea would rub her foot or squeeze her toes. Ana would smile at her mom in response, although the smile was a poor display of how happy she felt deep inside. They all went to their separate bedrooms. Andrea had a missed call. It was Diane. She was returning Andrea's call she had missed earlier, so Andrea called her back. "Tell me about Travis," she said to Diane.

"Why?"

"How much does he usually work?" she asked before explaining her reasoning.

"He works about five days a week, but I don't know exactly. That's Jeff's deal."

"How old is he?"

"Why are you asking about Travis?"

"Because I'm wondering how much time he and Anastasia have been spending together."

"Oh, what's up?" Andrea told her about the scene she witnessed in the tack room.

She tried her best to describe it to Diane. "It was like they were very comfortable around each other."

"That doesn't mean anything, Andrea, and he is twenty-two."

"I don't know. I have a feeling about him."

"How is the restriction going, and the class after school?" Diane tried to take her mind off of Travis and Ana.

"It's fine, as good as you would expect. She is completing her assignments. She hasn't gotten to go to the stables until today but has asked twice and was upset when I said no."

"Oh, she is hating that," Diane said sarcastically. Soon, they hung up the phone and went to bed.

Drake left on Sunday evening to go back to school. He had learned to like the prep school and had made a lot of friends there, although not the kind friends he had prior to leaving home. Ana received a text about an hour after he left.

Be Good.

Ana laughed to herself and thought, I am good.

The next week went much like the previous three, with long days of homework sitting in the study. She tried to work ahead but would get distracted by texting and end up wasting time. It was the last week of her sentence, as she called it, and she had so much to do, but she was over it and just didn't care if the assignments got completed. She desperately wanted out of the house. Wednesday evening, her mother had a late meeting at work, so she dropped Ana off at home before going back to work. "Mom, is there any way I can go to the stables? I need to get out of the house." Ana was trying hard to earn her mother's sympathy.

"Are your assignments complete?" Andrea knew they weren't.

"I just have one to do, and I can do it before bed. Mom, just this once, I won't stay long." Ana was pleading.

"Absolutely not, you know the rules," Andrea said quickly, digging through her briefcase.

"Mom, please. You're going to be gone anyway." Her mother looked at her but didn't respond and kept gathering her things. "I should just go. You wouldn't even know." Ana said under her breath.

Andrea heard this, and it upset her. "No, ma'am. You are not going, and do not leave this house." She slapped her hand on the counter in the kitchen, startling and infuriating Ana.

She didn't want to sit in the house for three more days over sheets of math problems and analogies. Ana was angry, and didn't care, as she rolled her eyes and said, "Whatever, this is so ridiculous." Ana spatted at her.

"Excuse me?" her mother asked.

"I have sat in this house for almost a month, God you are being such a bitch to me. It is so fucking stupid!" Ana yelled, revealing her anger.

Andrea was appalled that her daughter would speak to her like that. Ana had never raised her voice before, much less cursed at her. Andrea stepped over in front of Ana and slapped her across the face, hard. She just could not believe Ana would speak to her that way or that she had just slapped her. Ana bent over and was holding her face. "Young lady, you will not speak to me that way." Andrea was shouting and pointing her finger in Ana's face, shaking with anger.

Ana was in shock. She couldn't believe her mother would hit her. Ana's emotions went from anger to fear and regret in a matter of seconds. Her mother walked out of the room. Ana dropped to her knees with her face in her hands, sobbing uncontrollably. Andrea walked back in from the garage. "Anastasia, get up and sit down at this table. You will do these assignments correctly and will not leave this house." Ana was crying and shaking but was following her mother's orders. Andrea was still fuming as she began to rant. "How dare you speak to me that way! Those words should not even be in your vocabulary, young lady. I am not going to change my mind about your punishment. You should know that by now. You skipped your exam. That was stupid. You have to do well on it. You could have already taken it if you wouldn't have chosen to get drunk with your friends and do who knows what. Then, you lied and shut off your phone. Remember that? Now that was stupid. You did this, not me." Andrea was yelling as she leaned over the table at Ana. Ana didn't dare look up at her mother. She had never seen her like this, and it scared her. Andrea walked into the office, got her bag, stopped in front of Ana, and said, "Do not leave this house, young lady. Do you understand?"

"Yes, ma'am," Ana replied meekly. She had stopped sobbing but was still clearly upset, and she didn't look up.

"So, you're not going to look at me when you speak to me?"

Ana stuttered slightly, not knowing whether to say yes or no. "Yes, ma'am, I understand." Ana looked up sheepishly at her mother. Andrea turned and left the house, slamming the door.

As soon as she was gone, Ana broke down sobbing, laying her head on the table. Her face hurt, but not as bad as her heart. Nellie walked into the kitchen a while later. Ana was working but still snubbing. "Child, you're gonna be ok. Your momma told me what happened. You hungry, honey?"

Nellie felt sorry for Ana. Nellie always thought a little snack made everything better.

"No, ma'am," Ana said, wiping away her tears. She tried to finish the work in front of her, but her mind wouldn't stay focused. Finally, she just put something on the paper and put it away. She went to her bathroom and looked at her face. Her left cheek was still read. She couldn't stop the tears from running down her face, even though she wanted them to stop. She wanted to apologize, to fix it. She heard a knock at her bedroom door.

"Hello Ana," she heard Diane calling as she stepped into the room. Ana quickly ran from the bathroom to her aunt. "Anastasia?" Diane asked as she embraced her. "What happened, Anastasia? Where is your mother?" Diane was serious.

"She left to go to a meeting. I asked her if I could skip my homework and go to the stables. She said no, and when I asked again, she hit the counter with her hand and told me not to ask again. She slapped me --"

Diane interrupted, "Is that the whole story?" Diane already knew there was more to the story. Andrea had called her and told her she'd slapped Anna because of something Ana had said to her. Andrea was upset and had asked Diane to check on Ana. "What did you say to her, Ana?"

Ana started to cry and mumbled the words she had spoken to her mother. Diane was surprised at what she had said. Knowing Andrea's temper, it was not surprising she had slapped Ana, although now Andrea felt bad. Ana added, "Now she's gone, and she forbade me to leave the house."

"What did you expect, Ana? You knew that was wrong."

"I really screwed up. I don't know what is gonna happen."

"So, you're worried that you will be punished for this?"

"Yeah, I'm already grounded. What happens now? But, I mean, I don't know how I can fix it."

"Yes, you do. She's your mother, and you have disrespected her. How you fix it is you obey her, and you apologize."

"I'm never going to be able to go to the stables again."

"Considering what you said, I'm surprised she didn't do worse. If you act like a disrespectful child, she will treat you like one." Diane walked around to Ana's window.

"I feel so bad. Did she call you?" Ana sat on her bed, looking defeated.

"Yes, she asked me to check on you and make sure you didn't leave."

"Great, well, I'm not going anywhere, so you can leave."

"I'll be downstairs. Darling, you will survive," Diane said as she left the room.

Ana stayed in her room and texted Travis all the events of the evening. He wanted to see her and talk, but she told him no. She couldn't think of disobeying her mother now, and besides, Drake said she would be furious, and she'd already had enough of that. Ana called Drake. "Hey, what's up? I just cursed at mom, and she slapped the hell out of me, and she scares me. She left and isn't back yet." Ana was trying to sum up the story.

"Oh crap! She slapped you? What did you say?"

"I kinda said she was being a bitch and was fucking stupid."

"I bet she is livid. Be glad you're not locked up in the cellar. I'm glad I wasn't there. Are you ok? Is she ok?" Drake asked sincerely.

"I'm fine. I just feel terrible, Drake. I'm really sorry."

"I know you are. Did you tell her?"

"No, she left for a meeting and sent Aunt Diane over here to guard me. It's like they're a tag team."

"Yeah, they are like that, sometimes I don't know who is worse," he said laughing, trying to lighten the conversation.

"What do you think she will do?" Ana asked her brother.

"I don't know. You're already grounded. Have you been hanging out with Travis?"

"No, she won't let me go down there."

"Ana, be careful with him, he's a lot older than you, and he isn't a guy you're compatible with."

"What do you mean?" Ana asked, feeling dumb.

"He's not like us. He's different."

"What the hell does that mean?" Ana heard her mom pull up. "I gotta go. Mom just pulled up."

"Bye, sister, it will be ok," Drake said, trying to comfort her. She had such a sick feeling in her stomach. She felt like she could vomit. She heard her mom downstairs talking to Diane. It was nearly eight p.m. Her mom came up the steps, went straight to her bedroom, and closed the door. She didn't even look in Ana's direction. This made Ana feel even worse. Ana didn't come out of her room that night, and she cried herself to sleep. So did Andrea. She regretted striking her child, especially in the face. She knew how that felt, but Ana was also wrong.

Nellie woke Ana up a little early on Wednesday morning. "Ana, wake up. Your mom wants you downstairs to eat breakfast with her." Ana heard that and wanted to fall back in bed.

"I don't wanna go. Oh, Nellie," Ana said as she hugged her.

"Baby, I heard the whole thing. Now, you've got to face her sometime, might as well be now."

Ana dressed for school and took her book bag to the kitchen, sitting it beside the chair as she sat down. Andrea looked up from the paper she was reading. Ana looked at her, then down in shame. "I'm sorry, Mom," Ana said, looking down.

"Eyes up, young lady. What are you sorry for?"

"I'm sorry for speaking to you that way. Andrea's expression softened, and Ana began to cry. "I'm so sorry, Mom, please forgive me." She fell into her mother's lap.

Andrea held her, pulling her up to sit on her lap like a little girl. "Anastasia, I love you, and I forgive you." She kissed Ana's head. Andrea felt like she should apologize for striking her, but she didn't want Ana to forget this encounter. Andrea was just as stubborn as Ana.

CHAPTER SEVEN

Found Out

Phillip came home that day, and he picked Ana up from Professor Finn's class. Ana said hello but didn't want to invoke much conversation. "Ana, you're grounded for another week, and you are not going to the stables at all until we say so," her father said.

"Yes, sir." She had expected that much of a punishment. The rest of the week was uneventful. She went to school, came home, and then went back again. Her mom didn't hold any grudges, it seemed, and Ana tried to let it go. She took her exam that Friday and had to wait on the results for another week. She had scored very high in math and English, which is what she needed to get into St. Catherine's. Her mother worked there as an English professor, and this would make her parents happy. She was given the keys to her car on Saturday and was finally ungrounded. Ana didn't jump up and down when she was given the keys, but she really wanted to. She spent some of her time riding and the other she spent with Brittani. The next Saturday, one week after she was released, Ana met Brittani for coffee at ten a.m.

"Do you want to come ride with me this evening? You can help me not get too close to Travis," Ana said as she smiled.

"Sure, I'll go, but you have to go with me to the drama club meeting, it's today at one."

"Ok, sure." They drank their coffee and laughed about things that had happened at school. Ana went to the meeting with Brittani and sat in the back listening. They were discussing the upcoming production and casting. Ana thought she might have been in a drama club if she had been raised as a normal kid. But it was never an option for her. The play had three main actors, a lot of minor parts, and was set in the United States. Unfortunately for Ana, most of the faculty and staff knew her story. Rarely someone would mention the kidnapping, but when they did, it was always awkward. The director was a young lady. She seemed to be very young and more like a peer than an instructor.

"Ana, will you audition? We would be honored to have a true American in the show," the director asked as they were leaving.

"I don't know if I'm any good."

"An actor is better when they have a diverse life background. I bet you have been through more life experiences than most middle-aged adults. Just try it, here, I'll give you a script." Ana took it and smiled.

"Ana, that is freaking awesome. You should audition," Brittan said as they walked out.

"I'll think about it." Ana drove down the road and thought about what the director had said. She thought she would at least read the script. They stopped at Ana's so she could get clothes. Ana introduced Brittani to her mom and Nellie. Brittani was very polite and simply said hello.

"Where have you two been this morning?" Andrea asked out of curiosity.

"We went to a drama club meeting at school," Ana replied.

"Really?" said Andrea. She was clearly not expecting that answer.

"Yeah, Mrs. Hutchinson. The director asked Ana to audition, I think she would be great," Brittani said with enthusiasm.

"Yes, I do too Brittani, I think that is an excellent idea. I was involved with theatre as a teen, and I really enjoyed it," Andrea said.

"I'll think about it," Ana said. "Come on, Brittani. Mom, we're going down to the stables to ride for a few hours."

"Be careful, dear," Andrea said as they walked out the door.

"Thanks, Britt, now she's going to be on me to be in the play. She's all the time telling me I would enjoy school more if I would get involved," Ana said.

"Sorry, but she is right."

Ana snarled at her, "Shut the hell up." Ana slapped Brittani's arm and smiled. When they got to the stables, Travis wasn't there. So, the girls had to saddle their own horses. They rode off, but Brittani could tell Ana was bummed.

"I can't help he isn't here, so cheer up," Brittani said.

"I know, it just sucks. I wanted to see him."

"Did you tell him you were coming?"

"No. Remember? I'm not supposed to see him, and it's not a big deal anyway."

They rode the trail to the creek; Brittani was impressed with the scenery. "We could have a great time here," Brittani said. "Do you think your mom would let us camp out here? Aren't you a boy scout or something?"

"I'm not a boy scout, I'm a girl, and I just spent some time on trips at the Academy where we learned how to survive on our own out in the wilderness," Ana clarified.

"See, you are a boy scout," Brittani said, ignoring Ana's obscene sign language.

"I doubt she would let us anyway, with just us. She's scared to death someone will take me again."

"What if Drake came, and he had some friends come?" Brittani suggested.

"Are you nuts? Do you think she's going to let me camp with guys? Dream the hell on." Ana laughed at the idea.

"Maybe we could pitch it a different way, not like a party, but like a game, and we just stay the night after."

"Ok, Alice, you're in wonderland. There will have to be supervision. You're crazy, but it would be fun." Ana admitted. They rode back to the stables, and Travis was there.

"Well, look at that. Nice, very nice," Brittani said, teasing Ana. "

Shut it up." Ana rode up to him and said, "What's up?" teasing him. He smiled and helped her off her horse. They got the horses settled and sat down facing the pasture and the house.

"Ana, I'll be right back, just running to the car," Brittani said.

"Ok." Ana looked puzzled.

Brittani came back with a bottle of brown liquor. "Y'all, got cups, or are we going to drink right out of the bottle?" Brittani asked, holding the bottle up with a mischievous grin on her face.

"Oh my God, are you stupid? I just got out on parole," Ana said, laughing.

"Oh, chill out. There isn't enough for us to get drunk," Brittani said. "Well, I'm going to drink some of this while we sit here, and I'm going to imagine we are out on the prairie. I just rode in on my black stallion, and I'm waiting on my hot-ass cowboy lover to ride up. He got held up because he had to shoot some robbers in town." Brittani took a drink.

"Well, if you're that, then I'm a cowgirl. I just got in from the range where I had to shoot a wolf because he was trying to eat your lover's face off," Ana said, laughing.

"Was that before or after the shooting of the robber?" Travis asked.

"Hand me that," Ana said. She took a drink and passed it to Travis. They took turns drinking the whiskey until it was gone.

"I gotta pee, come on," Brittani said. Ana got up and walked her to the bathroom. When they walked into the bathroom, Brittani asked, "Are you buzzing?"

"Yeah, are you?"

"Yeah, don't get crazy. Here's some gum. I can't have my best friend getting put back in prison."

"Yeah, that would suck so bad." Brittani and Ana went back outside.

"I gotta get going, Ana," Travis said.

"Ok, I'll walk you out," Ana said, jumping up to follow him.

Brittani pointed at her as she walked away and mouthed, "Two minutes, and I'm coming after you."

Travis was parked at the back of the barn. He usually let the owner's park up front so they could get into the barn easier. He walked to his truck, and she followed him. "I'm sorry I couldn't come here for the past month," she said.

"It's ok. You're here now." He leaned into her and kissed her softly. She was surprised but didn't resist. The alcohol was stronger than she thought.

He kissed her hard, and she was kissing him back. He picked her up and set her in the driver's seat of his truck. He leaned into her and kissed her neck, then pulled her shirt down and nuzzled near her breast. She pulled him closer as he stood between her legs, in a position that, if they were unclothed, would be dangerous. His hands quickly grabbed at her pants button, and then his hands were in them, pulling at her panties. Ana thought this was fast, but she didn't say anything. She reached to touch him, and he unbuttoned his pants quickly to give her access. As his fingers advanced further, she gasped. It was painful, and she backed away. He pulled her back down toward him, and he pulled at himself like he was going to put it inside her. Ana thought this couldn't be happening. It was too weird. She moved back then suddenly. They heard a car door slam and a beep as the doors locked.

"Oh God, who is that?" Ana was frantically scrambling out of the truck and ran inside the basement of the barn. She had to get upstairs to Brittani, but she had to maneuver around equipment in the dark. She tripped and fell over something, "Son-of-a-bitch," she said. The object was metal, and her shin was hurting. When she tripped, she knocked over a gas can that made a loud echoing bang on the concrete floor. The alcohol didn't help her move in the darkness, and her nervousness only made her clumsier. When she reached the top of the steps, her heart was racing, and she was out of breath. She didn't know if it was because of what had just happened with Travis or what she feared would happen upstairs. She listened at the door and could hear Brittani talking to Diane.

"What is that sound? Where is Ana?" Diane asked, looking back and forth.

"Oh, hello. You must be Diane. I'm Brittani; Ana has told me so much about you. We went riding today. You know it's beautiful over there near that rock bluff," Brittani said as she tried to think of where Ana could be.

"Is Travis here?" Diane asked as she walked toward the back of the barn. Ana met her at the top of the steps. "Ana, what are you doing down here?" Diane asked.

"I was just looking for a different water bucket for the mare. Her's is broken." Ana said.

Diane walked by her and looked through the basement, then went outside. She knew Travis had been there because his boot prints were all over the ground in the red dirt, and so were Ana's. Diane went back upstairs to find

Brittani and Ana sitting on the porch looking at their phones. "Ana, when did he leave?" Diane asked.

"Who?" Ana responded, playing dumb.

"Travis, when did he leave?" Diane asked.

"Not too long ago, he said he had to do something for his dad." Ana was making it up as she went. Diane walked back in the barn, leaving them on the porch. Brittani looked at Ana and busted out laughing. Ana smiled, trying to whisper, "Shut up, you idiot."

Diane walked back on the porch and said, "Are you going home for dinner?"

"Yeah, I guess," Ana replied.

"You guess?" Diane stared at the both of them.

"Come on, Brittani, we gotta get going," Ana said.

"Bye see you later," Brittani said to Diane.

The girls got into the jeep and drove down the drive. Diane looked around the barn and shut off the lights. She threw her an old broken horse bridle she had found lying on the step into the garbage, and she heard glass break and thought that was odd. She leaned over and found an empty whiskey bottle. She must have hit it just right to break it. She thought surely Ana had enough sense not to drink this close to getting off restriction. Maybe it was Travis'. He was older and maybe drank here on evenings when he was alone. Diane decided to go to dinner at the Hutchinson house.

"Oh my God, that was so close, I almost had a heart attack, and I almost broke my damn shin," Ana said, then asked, "Brittani, you staying for dinner?"

"Better not, I need to get home." Ana dropped Brittani off at her car, and she left.

Travis called, and she answered. "Hey, you ok?" he asked.

"Yeah, but I'm still shaking. That was too close," Ana said.

“Don’t worry about it. We can go somewhere more quiet next time,” he said.

“I’ve got to go,” Ana said, ignoring that comment.

“No, I want to talk to you,” he begged.

“What is it, Travis? I’m probably already screwed with my parents. We are not a thing. My mom will freak the hell out if she finds out I messed around with you,” Ana said impatiently.

“I don’t know, but I don’t want to lose you,” he replied.

She pulled over. She was at the beginning of the driveway, and she didn’t want to be on the phone when she pulled in. “I’ve got to go, Travis. I am sorry, but this can't happen. I like spending time with you, and messing around with you is ok too, but it’s going to suck if my parents find out. I am watched like a hawk, and this isn’t worth it. We could never date, you know that. I’ve got to go.” She hung up without a goodbye. She was irritated at the whole situation, but especially at herself for making out with him the first time. It was like she had opened a door that couldn’t be closed. Even though she knew better, she couldn’t help being physically attracted to him, but she didn’t like how he moved so fast. She was secretly glad they had been interrupted. When she got home, she saw Diane’s car in front of the house. “This is freaking great,” she said to herself.

When Diane arrived at the Hutchinson's, she found Andrea in the kitchen looking at her phone. “Why is Ana sitting on the side of the road at the end of our driveway?” she asked Diane.

“What? Let me see. How long has she been there?” Diane wanted to know as the dot started to move.

Andrea responded, “Maybe five minutes or so.”

“Well, I found an empty liquor bottle in the trash at the barn. I don’t know if it was Travis’ or Ana’s.”

“Are you kidding me?” Andrea said, raising her voice.

“No, but don’t say anything. I’m looking into something, just trust me. I think it will reveal itself soon enough.”

“Was he there today with them?”

"Yes, but he was gone when I looked for his truck. I don't know how long he was there."

"So, what is the deal with them? God, I hope nothing," Andrea said. They heard Ana coming in the side door from her car. Andrea nodded to Diane as Ana came through the door.

"Hey, mom. Hey Aunt Diane, I didn't know you were coming over here," Ana said.

"Yes, a last-minute decision," Diane said.

Ana thought to herself, yeah, I bet it was. "Well, I'm going upstairs to shower and change clothes before dinner."

"Ana, wait, stay for a minute. Tell Diane about the theatre club," Andrea said.

"Oh yeah, the director asked me to audition—no big deal. Whew, I got hot riding, I'm sweaty," Ana said, pulling the hair off her neck and into a ponytail. As she pulled her hair back, a red mark was revealed on the left side of her neck. It wasn't very noticeable but was definitely there. "Be back down in a minute." Ana left the kitchen for her room. She was relieved to get away from her mom and aunt. She felt like Diane was there to rat her out to her mom.

"Did you see that?" Andrea said.

"See what?" Diane asked.

"On her neck, I swear it looks just like somebody has been sucking on her neck." Andrea was clearly convinced it was what she thought it was.

"No, I didn't see it, but I wasn't on that side of her either. You don't know that for sure, don't go crazy, Andrea. Wait until we can talk to her, don't jump to conclusions."

Ana took off her clothes, showered quickly, dried off, and brushed her hair. As she pulled her hair back, she saw the same thing her mother had seen. She was shocked. "Oh my God, that asshole." She looked closer in the mirror. "I'm dead. Just call the funeral home now because if I'm not dead, I will want to be. What am I going to do?" she said to herself. She called Brittani and told her the entire situation in a minute flat.

"Oh God, Ana, you're screwed. Mom and Aunt Hawaii 5-0 are on the case," Brittani exclaimed.

"What am I going to tell her?" Ana asked in desperation.

"What is your plan? How are you going to explain that?" Brittani started laughing.

"Don't laugh. That was an asshole thing to do."

"Sorry, you're right. Looks like he was trying to mark his territory."

Ana huffed, "I've got to go. I just heard my mom yelling up the stairs." Andrea had called Ana, but by no means did she yell. Ana didn't wear foundation or concealer makeup, so that option was out. So, she wore her hair down and a bulky sweatshirt to dinner. "Dear Lord, let her vision fail or give her explosive diarrhea so she won't be glaring at my neck," Ana whispered, going down the steps. Then she apologized for that prayer, "Sorry, I know that isn't nice, Amen."

When she went into the dining room, the table wasn't set, which was odd. She walked into the kitchen, where her mom and Diane were setting the small kitchen table in the breakfast nook. "We're going to eat in here, it's just us three, and it's less work," Andrea said. Ana sat down almost across from the two women. "I would like to pray before we eat. We really should do this more often, to give thanks."

Ana and Diane bowed their heads. "Dear Heavenly Father, we are so very thankful for our food, our home, and our family. Lord, please forgive us for our wrongdoings and help us to search ourselves and be honest with you in confession. God, help us to fight the flesh of the body from all temptations. Don't let us fall into sin and temptation. Thank you for this meal and my wonderful daughter, whom you have blessed me with. Amen." Andrea looked at Diane, who couldn't believe Andrea had just prayed that. Diane almost laughed and couldn't help but laugh.

That prayer would make a nun confess to fornication, Diane thought.

Ana wanted to bang her head against the table. She thought that was probably a better option than finishing the meal. They ate and shared casual conversation. "Ana, I was worried when you were late, and when I looked, you were up at the end of our drive for a while. Was something wrong with your car?" Andrea said casually.

"Why are you tracking my every move? Ugh." Ana couldn't help it. She hated that they had her on GPS.

"Why do you have a problem with me tracking you? You are my daughter, and it is my vehicle you're driving. Do you have something to hide, young lady?"

"I'm not arguing any of that. It's just -- nothing," Ana gave it up. "I was on the phone, so I just pulled over."

"Who were you talking to?" Diane asked.

"A friend of mine who was freaking out and wanted to talk. Why do you ask?"

"Just wondering who would be so important for you to stop?" Andrea said.

"Just a friend Mom, I don't like to be on the phone while driving." They had begun to eat, and a few moments passed.

"Anastasia, can I see your phone?" Diane asked as she smiled at her.

"Sure, I just did the new update." Ana handed it to her. Diane scrolled through the phone, then laid it down in front of Ana. Diane then picked up her own phone, pulled up Travis's contact information, and laid it beside Ana's phone.

"Were you talking to Travis?" Diane asked. Ana nodded, screen to screen each phone displayed the same cell number, but Diane's had his name identified on the contact. "Just wondering why, you would need to talk to Travis on the side of the road?" Diane said as she looked at Andrea and crossed her arms.

"May I be excused for a minute? I don't feel well," Ana said, trying to get away.

"No," they both said in unison. Ana didn't say anything. She just looked at the phones.

"Anastasia, I thought you were hot. Why are you wearing that sweatshirt and your hair down? You never wear it down after you shower." her mother said.

"I was trying to hurry down so you wouldn't have to wait on me," Ana said. "Anastasia Danielle, pull your hair back for me," her mother requested.

Ana thought she looked like a prosecutor revealing her secret piece of evidence to win the case.

Ana felt like slapping the table and refusing. Instead, she asked, "Why?" She was tired of playing their games. Ana laughed sarcastically, put her hands on her face, and leaned forward in her chair, getting agitated. Ana looked down at her wrist, "I don't have a hair tie, I'll go get one," she said. She turned in her seat, trying to act cool and calm.

"I have one. I'll put it up for you." Her mother smiled and batted her dark blue eyes through her navy glasses as she stood up and walked behind Ana. Ana had backed herself into a corner, and she had no choice but to sit there. "Sit up, Ana. What is wrong with you?" Ana moved her chair back from the table and sat up in the chair like she was at the salon. Andrea began to run her fingers through her hair, and Ana felt like she could vomit as her mother pulled her hair into a ponytail. "There," Andrea said, revealing the red circle on Ana's neck under her ear. Ana just closed her eyes tight, hoping to make herself invisible. Ana could hear Drake telling her to be honest, but stubborn was a word that would define Ana for years to come. "Why don't we go upstairs and have a little chat in your room?" her mother suggested as Nellie began to clean off the table. Ana followed them up the stairs, and Diane closed the door. "Ana, come here," Andrea said. She put her in front of the mirror and stood behind her. "What is that?" Andrea asked as she pointed to the spot on Ana's neck.

Ana closed her eyes, "Oh, I got hit by a branch when I was riding." She instantly realized how stupid that sounded. Andrea couldn't believe what just came out of her daughter's mouth.

"Young lady, that is a lie!" Andrea said and couldn't help but grin. "Explain that!" Andrea demanded, pointing at Ana's neck again.

Ana started to stammer. "Mom, I had no idea that was there, and --."

Andrea said, "I am warning you. Do not lie to me, little girl." She walked away from Ana before she slapped her. Ana turned around and went to sit on her bed, holding a pillow against her stomach.

"So it seems you're not going, to tell the truth, so let me give you my version. This is just my hypothesis, mind you. This afternoon, you and your friend, and probably Travis, were drinking at the stables, right?" Diane asked. Ana just looked up. She was not amused.

"Answer her, Anastasia," Andrea said sternly.

"Yes, but it was very little," Andrea hung her head and rubbed her forehead.

"So when I arrived, you were around back with Travis doing something that caused that hideous thing on your neck?" Diane said.

"I don't want to talk about this," Ana said to Diane with squinted eyes. She was getting very angry with them, and she wanted to choke Diane for making a display out of her. Diane sat down and started flipping through Ana's phone. There were no text messages from Travis, but she could see where she had called Drake, probably on her way from the barn.

"Well, if you really want to know, you can call Drake, Andrea," Diane said. She opened Ana's Snapchat and opened a Snap from Travis. It was a chat message that read, I still want you. She showed the message to Ana, and Diane read it out loud, "I still want you."

"Anastasia, you better start talking," Andrea said aggressively.

"Mom, that is misleading. I am not dating him," Ana said to her.

"I want you. What does that mean? Have you had sex with Travis?" Andrea asked her.

"No, we have not. I promise you we haven't." Ana said, desperately wanting to be believed.

"Anastasia, were you with him the night you missed the exam? Is that why you lied about going to the stables?" Andrea demanded.

Ana sighed heavily and answered, "Yeah, but we didn't have sex. That was the first time. Mom, please, believe me, I'm telling the truth."

Andrea was pacing the room. She picked up the phone and Facetimed Drake. He answered, "Hello, Mom?" looking very shocked to see her on Ana's phone.

"Drake, have you known about this guy your sister has been messing around with?"

"Ah, ah, kind of, but not really."

"Ok, good enough, I will talk to you later."

"Mom, don't hang up. It isn't as bad as it looks."

"Drake, shut up," Andrea said, and she hung up the phone. She sat down in the rocking chair at the window.

"Aunt Diane, please, believe me, he has never sent me a message like that. Really, we have only messed around twice, and the last time was for like five minutes. Really, you have to believe me." Diane just looked at Ana.

Andrea said, "Start talking and be honest from the beginning."

"About Travis?" Ana asked.

"Yes, about Travis. What else is there?" Diane said.

"I was just going down there to ride. He was really shy, and we seemed to get along well. I didn't even really consider him a friend, though, because of his age. But the more we were around each other, the more I kind of noticed him. Anyway, the night of the exam, I was kind of drunk, and I had Brittani drop me there because I wanted to see him. I just wanted to kiss him," Ana explained. She put her hands in her lap and looked at her feet.

Her mother shook her head. "Ana, keep talking, and there is no such thing as kind of drunk."

"We just messed around, then I came home, and all hell broke loose."

"What does 'messed around' mean?" Diane asked.

"I mean, I don't know how to explain it. We just made out and stuff, but I don't remember all of it." Ana was trying to make it sound as benign as possible.

"If you don't remember some stuff, then you don't know," Andrea said.

"No, I remember Mom. God, I don't want to talk about this," Ana said, clearly agitated.

"I don't care if this is embarrassing you. You need to own it. What happened today?" her mother asked.

"Brittani and I were there, and Travis had to leave. I walked him out. We messed around like before but more involved. Then you arrived, and I just about broke my damn leg trying to get upstairs, and now you're overreacting," Ana proclaimed as she stood. Andrea looked at Diane. She could feel the heat rising to her face.

"Do not speak to her that way. You and I have been down that road before, and it doesn't go very far," Diane said as she stood in front of Andrea, blocking her from Ana's view. Ana didn't say anything but looked up at Diane and her mother with big eyes. Ana couldn't lie. Her facial expressions betrayed her every time. "So you're saying that if I pull the video, it will show you kissing Travis, and that is all?" Diane asked.

"I'm not sure what you'll see. I'm not even positive there is a camera," Ana responded with an arrogant tone.

"Answer and stop showing your ass," her mother ordered. Andrea was now standing beside Diane in front of Ana.

"I don't know, and why do you care?" Ana said as she sat down on the bed, avoiding her mother's gaze.

"Why do I care? Are you kidding me?" her mother asked.

"Explain Ana, we need to know," demanded Diane.

"I don't know what it will show. He was laying on top of me, we were kissing and stuff," Ana said. She was so embarrassed; she closed her eyes and pressed her forehead against her knees. "I regret it. It was too fast and weird. Mom, I swear!"

Andrea was emotionally confused and upset. She paced with her hands on her hips. "Ana why were you even messing around with him if you know you can't date him?" she asked.

"Because, I don't know, it felt good."

Diane was watching her like she was playing defense. She said, "So, nothing."

Ana didn't understand what she was asking. "What?" Ana asked with her hands up in the air.

Diane was having difficulty finding the correct words so as not to throw her best friend over the edge. Andrea stood at the opposite side of the bed with her arms crossed. "He didn't insert his -- there -- right?" Diane finally scrambled together.

"No, no, oh god, no! He had his hand down my pants, but no, he didn't put it inside me, we didn't do that," Ana said.

Andrea threw her hands up in the air after hearing that. "Oh no, it's not a big deal," Andrea said, mocking her. Ana saw the disappointment on her mother's face.

"Mom, I am sorry. Please, I promise we didn't, please believe me," Ana pleaded.

"Give me the phone, I'll call him, and you can hear it for yourself that we didn't," Ana said as she picked up the phone. She dialed Travis and said, "Shhhh, don't say anything.' Ana looked at them. Travis answered, and Ana put him on speakerphone.

"Hey," Ana said.

"What's up?" he asked.

"Mom is pissed at me because she thinks we were having sex at the barn," Ana said, then put her hand up, signaling her mother to be quiet.

"She is such a bitch," he said, sounding drunk. Andrea gave Ana a mean look.

"I mean, we weren't even close, right?" Ana asked, kind of laughing. "I mean, you didn't put it in me, so we didn't," Ana asked, worried.

"Ana, you're such a virgin. You would know if I put my dick in you, I only had my fingers inside. I was getting ready to put in you, though, and fuck you hard, just like you wanted. I'm going to make you scream," he said. His voice was creepy on the phone. Ana walked to the other side of the room, trying to turn the speakerphone off quickly. Her mother and aunt followed her.

"Oh my God," Ana said.

Andrea jerked the phone out of her hand and said, "No, that isn't going to happen. You are never going to touch, or see, or speak to her ever again, you low-life." She hung up the phone. Ana shook her head and covered her eyes with her hands, thinking maybe that hadn't been a good idea. She sat on her bed and waited. Andrea's face was red. She was clearly angry. Ana looked at her but didn't know what to do. "That was a nice conversation. So you didn't, and I am so glad. But he was going to, 'Fuck you hard, like you wanted?' Anastasia, really?" her mother asked, totally irate.

Ana had tears coming down her face. "Mom, I don't know why he said that. He sounded drunk. I have never said anything like that to him," Ana said.

"Ana, he was planning to take your virginity and make you scream. Do you know what that means?" Andrea asked.

Ana had tears in her eyes as she said, "No."

Andrea exhaled, feeling exhausted. "When you have sex for the first time, it's usually painful. He was saying he was going to go hard, causing you pain, and you would scream," she explained.

"Momma, I'm going to be sick," Ana said, and went to the bathroom and vomited.

"That guy is dangerous. Who talks to a seventeen-year-old like that?" Andrea asked Diane.

"My thoughts exactly. I don't think Ana knew that would happen." Diane said.

Diane looked at Andrea, who was looking down at Ana, who was crying on the bed, hiding her face from her mother. "You say you didn't, but the truth is, if your aunt hadn't pulled up, you would have had sex?" her mother said.

"No, Mom, it hurt. I was going to stop him," Ana said.

"Are you bleeding?" her mother asked.

"I don't know."

Ana then received a text from Drake. Diane was still holding Ana's phone. She picked it up to read it, "Ana, please call me now, it's important." it read out loud.

"Will you handle that, please?" Andrea asked Diane. Diane didn't want to leave Andrea, but she did need to take care of this, so she left the room.

"Anastasia, look up at me. You are seventeen years old, which means two years ago you were fifteen. Two years ago, he was twenty. That's a huge difference." Ana heard her mother but was getting frustrated that she didn't believe her. Ana laid down on the bed, her head buried beneath a pillow.

"Andrea, you need to hear this," Diane said as she walked in holding Ana's phone. Andrea stood up to look at the phone. It was Drake.

"Hi, Mom. Where is Ana?" Drake asked. Andrea turned her head so he could see Ana lying on the bed, holding a pillow over her face. "Oh god, is she ok?" he asked, sounding concerned.

"Yes, she's being dramatic," Andrea said. "What is it? This is not exactly the perfect time."

"I bet, but Mom, I got a message a minute ago from my friend Matt. He heard Travis, at some bar near the University, telling a bunch of guys about him and Ana."

Andrea looked at Ana, who had taken the pillow off her face after her mother's dramatic comment. "What about him and Ana?" Andrea asked unenthusiastically.

Drake felt uncomfortable saying it, but he did. "That he was in a sexual relationship with Ana."

"Imagine that, Ana!" Andrea said.

"Thank you, Drake. I will need your friend's information. I will call you back shortly after I talk to your sister, and we figure out what to do."

"Wait, Mom, there's a picture," he said.

"What? A picture of what?" she asked.

"I don't know," Drake said.

She hung up the phone and said, "Ana, why are you crying and upset? You should have known this would happen. He's a guy. They talk, and show, and boast. So, now we have to deal with this and soon."

"But Mom, I didn't have sex with him, and it was Snapchat. I didn't know he screenshot it," Ana pleaded.

"Ana, even if you say you didn't, I will say it was close. I am so glad your aunt interrupted you, or you would have lost your virginity on video, behind a barn." Andrea went from disappointment to frustration in a hurry. "You are a virgin, correct?" Andrea asked as she leaned over closer to Ana. Diane was hoping this would not turn into a confrontation that Ana had learned from previous experiences with her mother.

"Yes, but you don't believe me, so whatever," Ana said, getting frustrated herself. Ana sat up on the side of the bed. "Mom, he's lying, and who knows what was even said." Ana was in denial that Travis would do this to her.

"Well, he left that disgusting mark on your neck, that looks terrible. Wake up. He's a twenty-two-year-old college guy. You don't think he would brag to his friends about having sex with you, Ana? You have status."

"He's not my boyfriend, god Mom!" Ana stood up, throwing her arm up at her mom, but Diane was faster.

"Anastasia, sit down," Diane said with a warning. Ana sat down, taking her aunt's warning seriously.

"Oh, so if he's not your boyfriend, what is he?" Andrea fired back at her.

"We were just messing around. I know we can't date. He's too old for me. You're making this a bigger deal than what it actually is," Ana said.

"My seventeen-year-old daughter, laying in the seat of a truck with her legs spread for a twenty-two-year-old college guy, is a huge deal. Even if you say you would have stopped him, you probably couldn't have. He was that close. You are not to see him again, at all," Andrea said.

"You can't control who I'm friends with," Ana said to her mother.

"You are my daughter, and I want what is best for you. That doesn't include people or things that are harmful to you. So yes, I will control who you spend your time with."

"Yeah, Mom, I know," Ana answered sarcastically.

"Go brush your teeth. It's time for bed," her mother told her.

Ana looked at her like she was stupid for telling her to brush her teeth and rolled her eyes. "Your goal is to make my life suck," Ana said, heading to the bathroom.

"No, you're doing that on your own," her mother said.

"That is enough," Diane said.

Ana was angry and frustrated. She came out of the bathroom with a toothbrush in her hand and toothpaste in her mouth. "You know, I bet you wouldn't even be upset if you had caught me with my pants down with some ivy league prick you approved of. Right, mom?" Ana asked, being vindictive.

Andrea and Diane were both shocked at what Ana had said. "Anastasia, I am warning you," Andrea warned.

Ana turned around to rinse her mouth. Diane looked at Andrea. She looked hurt, not just angry. Diane went to the bathroom and closed the door behind her. Ana was not expecting Diane in her space, and she backed away. "You know that's not true. You are going to walk out there and apologize to your mother right now," Diane said.

"Well, what if it is true?"

"It isn't, and I do not appreciate how disrespectful you're being. What is wrong with you?"

"She doesn't believe me, and it makes me so mad," Ana said, being truthful.

"And how you are behaving is really convincing her you're not lying?" Ana shook her head and crossed her arms. "You're lucky. If you had said that to me, you would have a handprint across your cheek and toothpaste splattered on the wall, young lady," Diane warned her.

"She already slapped me once," Ana said, looking scorned.

"And yet you're asking for it again? Now Go," Diane said, and Ana walked past her into the bedroom. It was empty.

"She isn't here," Ana said.

"Then go to bed. Goodnight." Diane shut the door and went downstairs. Diane found Andrea making coffee. "Are you ok?" Diane asked.

"What do you think? I need him far away from her, Diane. I don't know what to do with her right now, but she can't be around him."

"We will handle Travis, don't worry."

"Does she really think it would be different if it were a boy of higher social standing?"

"No, she's just being a teenage girl. They like to say things to make their mothers upset and angry. Ana knows better than that." Diane was trying to ease her worry.

"I love her, and this is killing me. Do you think she will try to sneak out of the house?"

"I don't think so," Diane replied.

Andrea went back to Ana's room a few hours later. The lamp was on, and Ana was sitting on the bed with a book in her hand. "Ana, it's getting late. You should sleep," Andrea said, trying to change the tone of the night.

"Mom, I'm sorry for saying that. I shouldn't have said it."

"Do you really believe that?"

"No."

Andrea looked at Ana, seeing her own seventeen-year-old self in her daughter's image. Ana laid down, turned on her side facing the door, and Andrea curled up behind her putting her arm around Ana's body. "Anastasia, I know you're embarrassed, but I have to ask you a question. When was your last period?" her mother asked.

"Mom, please, I didn't have sex with him."

"Ana, when was it?" her mother asked again.

"I think like three weeks ago." Ana turned toward her mother and tucked into her. "Mom, I didn't do it. You have to believe me."

"Ok, I believe you. But my point is, what if he wouldn't have stopped? What if you wouldn't have been caught? You put yourself at risk, even if you say you weren't going to let him. He could have taken advantage of the situation. You're a teenager. He is a man. Ana, he could have hurt you."

"He did. I'm sorry for disappointing you. It got out of control real fast." There was a long pause.

"I know, I was there once myself." They laid in the bed silent and listened to each other breathe. "I love you, Anastasia, no matter what." There was a long silence.

"Mom, do you still want me?" Ana whispered. Andrea felt so sad for this beautiful teenage girl lying in front of her. She wished she could have been there to love her all her life. She loved Ana as her daughter, and that would never change. She knew it would be challenging, and tonight had broken her heart, but she was willing to go through the fire for Ana, and she needed to know that.

Andrea whispered back, "You are mine, I will always want you, and I forgive you."

Ana began to cry, and Andrea held her as she sobbed. "Please, believe me, Momma," Ana pleaded.

"Shhhhhh, now go to sleep." A few minutes later, she said, "I'm going downstairs. Please don't leave the house. I don't know if I can mentally make it through anymore tonight."

"I won't go anywhere," Ana said.

Andrea got up and covered her with the blanket and said goodnight, then went downstairs to talk with Diane. Diane was sitting in the kitchen with Nellie. Nellie walked out when Andrea walked in. "Well, has she calmed down?" Diane asked.

"Yes, finally, I am emotionally exhausted."

Diane agreed. "I talked to Jeffrey. He's going down to the stables tomorrow when Travis arrives to tell him he no longer works for us. Also, I do feel he needs to talk with him about what he's telling people."

Andrea was relieved. "Thank you, Diane. Do you believe her?"

Diane waited for the right words then said, "I think so, and I know it was difficult for her to tell us how far they had gotten. I can't imagine telling my mother something like that. I would have been mortified."

Andrea poured a cup of coffee and sat down. She looked like she wanted to crawl in a hole and hide for a few days. "Well, I asked when she had her last period. That made her very upset. I just wish I could trust her. I want to believe her, and I agree it was difficult for her to tell us about their level of intimacy, but that could be due to her embarrassment. I was embarrassed enough hearing it. No, I can't imagine saying that to my mother either. We never spoke about sex. Diane, truthfully, I don't know if she's ever been in a situation like this before. She said she was a virgin. But who knows what Ana has been through? I know she had a boyfriend at the Academy or a friend that was a guy. Jude, right?" Diane nodded, and Andrea continued, "I didn't think she was involved with him physically, but now I don't know. Diane, I should have talked to her about sex. I was going to. I just haven't yet. I feel like I should have picked up on this." Andrea was exhausted just hearing herself.

"Andrea, you didn't know this was going on, neither did I. You can't stop it if you don't know, don't be so hard on yourself." Diane was trying to comfort her best friend. "As far as her past and Jude, I know that Jude and Ana had some kind of a relationship, although it was fairly new. That last night we were there, she didn't show for curfew. I found out later she had been stuck in the woods alone with him. She said nothing happened, and I believed her, I should have told you that sooner. I was really embarrassed that I let it happen. Andrea, I'm sorry, maybe that would have prompted you to talk to her sooner. I know she really likes Jude. I've seen where she Snapchats him a lot at all hours of the night, or at least she did when she stayed with me. I could hear her phone buzz every time. I do believe she's a virgin, but what she did in her past life we have no say over. I believe her about Travis too, I did look at the video from the barn camera, and she described it correctly. I couldn't see very close, but it didn't look like there was any movement that would indicate penetration," Diane told Andrea, hoping to reassure her.

"I am so glad they were interrupted. That relieves me some. I don't know what to do about punishing her for this. I mean, I just grounded her for a month, and this happened. What do I do?"

"Oh friend, I know this feeling well from Lauren. I don't think you should be permissive though, to me, that would be like you were giving up, and she would feel like it's ok and her actions don't matter. I wouldn't compare last month to this incident. They are totally unrelated with the exception of the dishonesty." Andrea looked at her then stared across the room. "But nobody has the answers, this is, unfortunately, one of those things we all have to deal with, and I'm sorry it has happened this soon. But I do think she's a good kid. She's just stubborn, and truthfully, I don't think she's ever had any boundaries in her life."

"I am not giving up on her, Diane. She asked me if I still wanted her. Yes, of course, I do."

"Friend, she reminds me a lot of you," Diane said as she smiled. "Do you want me to stay tonight?"

"No, go home. I don't think she's going anywhere."

"Ok, I'll come over in the morning, after we go to the stables, to do a well check on Ana," Diane said and laughed.

"I have to find a way to tell Phillip, but I'll do that tomorrow."

Diane and Jeffrey were at the stables when Travis showed up the next morning. They had known Travis for a couple of years, and he was always very respectful and hardworking.

"Good morning, Travis," Jeffrey Said.

"Morning," Travis replied. He looked nervous. They moved onto the porch to meet Diane.

"Travis, we have a problem. Do you know what it is?" Diane asked, holding the empty bottle of liquor. She knew he knew exactly what the problem was/

He answered, "No."

"Andrea and I found out yesterday, after a long discussion with Ana, that you were involved in some kind of relationship with each other. Can you tell me about that, Travis?" Diane asked. Travis didn't answer.

"Well, can you answer a few questions for me then?" Jeffrey asked. "Travis, I strongly encourage you to answer and be honest."

"Yes, sir," he responded.

"When did you start seeing Ana? How long ago?" Jeffrey asked.

"About a month ago or maybe more," he answered.

"Did you ever take Ana anywhere, like on a date?" Diane asked.

"No."

Then Diane asked the most important question. "Did you and Ana have sex?"

"No."

"Are you being honest about that?" Diane wanted to confirm his answer.

"Yes, ma'am," Travis answered.

"Who did you tell that you and Ana were in a relationship? And why did you tell people that you had sex with her?" Jeff asked Travis in an accusing tone.

"I didn't tell anyone," Travis replied defensively.

Jeff walked with Travis to his truck. Jeff's objective was to make Travis understand his time with Ana was over and that he should keep quiet. Travis indicated to Jeff he understood with a nod. After the conversation, Jeff confided in Diane that he thought Travis was more attached to Ana than Ana had been to him. Travis had been shy and clumsy in high school and college, having only a few friends. He was handsome but couldn't seem to commit to any relationship. Although he had plenty of one night stands after drinking at the pub. Travis was obsessive. He wouldn't let go that easily.

CHAPTER EIGHT

Mistakes Have Consequences

Ana came downstairs at 8:30 a.m. to find Andrea cooking breakfast. She had only seen her mom cook a few times, mostly when the whole family would be eating or on a special day. It had been almost three months since she was discovered and had become Anastasia Hutchinson. Ana actually felt like she had been here for years, and sometimes she had to remind herself she hadn't. Her mother looked up, saw her, and smiled. "Ana, come help me make breakfast. I'm making French toast." Ana had worried it would be hard or different interacting with her mom because of her discovering Ana's all too recent sin, but her mom acted the same as always. Ana walked to the bathroom near the kitchen, washed her hands, then joined her mother at the counter. Ana asked what she could do, and her mother asked if she wanted to flip or dip the bread. Ana chose to dip.

"Who's coming to eat?" Ana asked, looking at the pile of toast prepared.

"Your aunt and uncle, we have to talk over a few things," Andrea explained.

Ana didn't ask any questions, but she couldn't help but feel this meeting was due to the recent discovery of the interaction between her and Travis. They were almost done with the French toast when Diane and Jeffrey walked in. Jeffrey sat at the table, and Diane went to pour their coffee. Diane asked, "Can I do anything?"

Andrea responded, "No, we're all done." She smiled and handed Ana a plate of fruit.

Once they started eating, Jeffrey asked Andrea, "Do you want me to discuss it now or wait?" Ana knew what he was really asking if he should speak in her presence.

"Go ahead, Jeffrey. She needs to hear this." Andrea replied. Ana didn't say anything, because she really didn't understand what they were talking about.

"So, I called Drake last night. I have found the boy who messaged him about Ana and Travis. It seems Travis was intoxicated and was boasting about his recent score. I'm trying to term this nicely," Jeffrey said.

"It's ok. You can say whatever you need to. There's no need to sugar coat anything," Andrea said as she sighed.

"I'm sorry, Ana, I know this will not be pleasant to hear," Jeffrey said. This surprised Ana and made her even more uncomfortable.

"May I be excused?" Ana asked, wanting to vacate the area in a hurry.

"No, ma'am, you helped create this mess. There's no need to run away from the reality of the situation," Andrea responded. Her mom was right, but it still would have been a lot easier if Ana could skip this whole conversation.

"I've spoken to Matt Howard, the boy from the pub, who says Travis was boasting about having sex with Ana and was showing a picture on his phone of her. Matt did give me the names of the boys Travis was speaking to, and the one of significance is Scott Trammel," Jeffrey stated. He pulled out his phone to read a text.

"What kind of picture was he showing? Did Matt see it?" Andrea asked as she looked at Ana.

"Matt said he was farther away and couldn't tell exactly."

"What picture did you send him, Ana?" Andrea asked, tired of surprises.

"I don't know," she responded.

"You don't know? I swear, I think you have opportunistic amnesia." Andrea shook her head and tried to focus back on Jeffrey. "Ok, we will revisit the picture later. Go ahead, Jeffrey."

"My concern is with Scott's father, Steven Trammel. Steven has had recent interactions with Phillip on a project," Jeffrey clarified.

"Ugh, I have to tell Phillip, but I was hoping to keep him out of the details," Andrea said.

"Unfortunately, I do feel you should tell him about this possible exposure to Trammel. As far as how much detail, that is up to you and what he inquiries about," Jeffrey replied.

"What about Travis?" Andrea asked. Ana was suddenly interested.

"He is no longer employed by us, and he has been advised to keep his mouth shut. Although, I didn't know about the photos until after I met with him this morning," Jeffrey stated.

"You fired him? Why?" Ana asked.

"Yes, it was absolutely necessary," Jeffrey replied.

"Why? That's crazy," Ana said.

"Because we don't want this relationship to continue," Diane answered.

"It's not a relationship, and it never was. I told you we were not dating, and I just told him that when he called me. Why did he say we were dating? What did he say?" Ana said as she stared at Diane, awaiting a response.

"He didn't say much of anything," Diane responded. Ana was relieved that he didn't go into detail about their time together.

Jeff asked Andrea, "Would you like me to speak to Philip about this before you speak to him?"

Andrea replied, "Yes, that would be great. It will be easier that way, so I don't confuse him." Diane asked when he was due home, but Andrea wasn't sure. Jeffrey rose from the table and left the room. He went to Phillip's office and closed the door. Andrea began to clean off the table from breakfast, and Ana got up to help her. Jeffrey was able to reach Philip on his cell phone and began to explain the incident to him. Jeffrey told him all the main points and how he had let Travis go, and unfortunately, who Travis had told. He skipped the details as much as possible. Immediately after Jeffrey finished, Phillip demanded to speak to Andrea. Jeffrey put him on hold and summoned Andrea from the kitchen. Jeffrey dreaded this because he knew how upset Philip was by his tone. Jeffrey informed Andrea that Philip wanted to speak to her. She sighed, dried her hands with the dishcloth, walked into the office, and closed the door. Ana decided she should go up to her room. She wanted to run away and hide, which she knew wasn't practical, so hiding in her room would have to do. Andrea explained to Phillip all she could while trying to keep the conversation away from the intimate details. Andrea couldn't explain it, but she felt responsible for Ana's behavior. Phillip was upset, to say the least.

"I am coming home as soon as I can board a plane," he told Andrea, almost as a threat. "Where is she? I want to speak to her."

"Phillip, she's upstairs in her room. I think you should wait until you get here after you've had time to think."

"Don't cover up her mistakes Andrea, she's not an infant," Phillip scolded her.

"I'm not defending her. I'm just saying to wait. Give yourself time to think."

"Don't let her leave that house until I get there."

"Dear, please calm down. I need your help. I don't know what to do next. I mean, I just grounded her for a month and took her car. I can't beat her. I just don't know what to do." Andrea was trying to get him to understand.

"Ok, well -- tell her I wanted to speak to her and that I will handle this when I get home."

"Yes, dear, I will." Andrea hung up the phone. She was relieved he had agreed to wait.

Ana was dressed and sitting on her bed, looking at her phone, when Andrea came in. "Well?" Ana asked her mother.

"He is very upset, he wanted to speak to you, but I felt it wouldn't have been beneficial in his state of anger," Andrea said gently.

"Oh, great, that is so good to hear," Ana said sarcastically.

Andrea slapped Ana on the leg lightly and said, "Come on, we'll go ride around for a while. I feel like the walls are closing in on me." Ana got up quickly, and soon they were in her mom's car riding down the driveway. Ana was so relieved her mother wasn't holding a grudge. It hurt her heart to know she had disappointed her mother. Even though she knew she didn't have sex with Travis, it was still wrong what she had done. Since she was a small child, Ana had had a very guilty conscience. Ana thought that maybe it was because she didn't really have any guidance as a child, but the guilt followed her past her childhood and past the Peterson's. Ana had made mistakes in the past that made her feel guilty and remorseful but disappointing her mother, Andrea Hutchinson, had been the worst. She couldn't explain it, and it really felt stupid if she thought about other girls her age and what they had done. But Ana wasn't like other girls. Ana was different and always had been. Ana was the kid who appreciated kindness and had had to let the material things go. She had seen and been through so many trials, that by default, she was calm when everything around her was chaotic. Ana had been to the bottom, had seen the devil, and had survived. She wasn't proud and had always appeared humble, telling herself it could always have been worse. This was worse. This feeling of regret and shame was worse than anything she had ever endured. Not because of Travis, but because she was expected to be better than her behavior, and she had failed in her parents' eyes. She was secretly scared that she would lose her mother, and that made her desperate, seeking repentance from the one who had always fixed it all, God.

Andrea drove down a country road that passed their property and went around a small village of mill style houses until she passed the river. Everything had always been so simple and natural on this route, Ana thought. Andrea stopped at a small white church. The church was so old the siding was cracked, and it had a bell that hung inside a square steeple. The wood rafters were visible from the windows and were a shiny oak, and in many places, shingles had fallen to the ground. The church had been built in the 1800s and had been used for many different things since being built but had had no inhabitants in over a century. Ana asked, "What are we doing, Mom?" Ana looked at the church with great curiosity.

"I want to show you something, come," Andrea said as she got out of the car. Andrea had been coming here for years. The church had no pastor or congregation, but she had visited here because the place gave her peace. As Ana followed her mother, she walked softly on the grass, and her feet slightly sunk with each step. Moss covered the huge trees in the front of the church, and squirrels scattered as they walked, trespassing on their territory. They walked around to the back of the church, where an ancient-looking rock fence bordered the cemetery. A large, wooded gate hung in the center of the front wall, hinged with an iron latch, not locked. Andrea walked slowly through the churchyard to the gate of the cemetery, her shoes wet from the grass. Andrea opened the heavy gate and walked in. The grass inside the walls was extremely soft and green. The grass had been mowed, and around the stones, no weeds were present. The stones were all different; in the middle of the cemetery stood a very tall etched stone that pointed sharply to the sky. It appeared its occupant was a decorated colonel in the Royal Military. There were multiple gravestones of lesser height, each intricately etched in beautiful white stone. Various families were harbored in small groups throughout the cemetery. In the back of the cemetery were five small stones for children's graves, it was difficult to make out the names, but they were all under seven years old. A statue of a lamb lay near a bench facing these stones.

"What is this place?" Ana asked as they slowly walked along the edge of the cemetery.

"I've come here for years. I visited here once as a child with my grandmother when it was occupied by a congregation. Then, as a teenager, I came here with some friends because it was said to be haunted, but I never believed that. After I was married, I would come here to think and to pray when I felt like I needed peace in my life. This place has always brought me comfort." Ana didn't say anything; she just walked beside her mother. Near the left corner of the cemetery, Andrea pointed over the wall. "Look."

Ana leaned over, and right up against the wall on the other side were two small graves. "What are these?" Ana asked, looking hard. She jumped over the wall and dusted off the graves. Wet leaves laid heavy on them. Not being able to see much and getting chill bumps coming up her arms, Ana looked up at Andrea and grinned. She jumped back across the fence, feeling safer on the other side.

"They say the graves outside are those who are unconsecrated," her mother said.

"Oh, but mom, one was a child's grave."

"I know," her mother said. They walked around the cemetery and up to the front of the church. The door was unlocked. They walked into the church, Ana walking slowly behind her mother. The church was walled with off-white paneling and had deep oak pews. The floors were shiny and cracked easily. The rafters gleamed overhead, and the air smelled old like they had walked into a dust-covered book. In the front of the church was a hexagon-shaped area with wood-framed stained-glass windows displaying a lamb, a cross, and a bible. The pulpit was simply a wooden stand. Andrea sat on the back pew with ease, like she had sat there many times before. Ana stood for a few seconds watching her, then entered the pew and sat on the other side of Andrea, not wanting to interrupt her. Silence fell on them, followed by a breeze that came in as the door slowly opened a few inches. Andrea smiled, then looked at Ana, who had an expression of fear on her face, like she had heard a ghost. "Come on. We'll go," Andrea said.

"Ok," Ana replied as she walked quickly out of the church in front of Andrea. It was around 2 p.m., Andrea knew Phillip was due home around three, and she didn't want to be home when he arrived. Phillip had been more than upset when she spoke to him earlier on the phone, and he didn't even know the details, but he was informed about Scott Trammel hearing the rumor about Anastasia and Travis. Scott Trammel was the son of a business associate that Phillip, unfortunately, had the pleasure of dealing with on his current project. Andrea had tried to calm Phillip down, but he wouldn't listen to her. She was anxious just thinking about speaking to Phillip later. He didn't understand how it was to be a teenage girl, and he had forgotten how he felt when he was a hormone-driven teenager. Andrea remembered how it felt to be a young teenage girl, although she had not sympathized with Ana. Phillip was not at all sympathetic and had accused Andrea of taking Ana's side when they had spoken earlier. "Mom, do we have to go home now?" Ana asked. Her tone really said, Mom, keep me safe a little bit longer.

Andrea looked at her and understood what she was really asking. "No, we'll go into town." They rode into town and stopped and ate at a little pizza place. It was a small place owned by a family Andrea knew. Andrea and Ana talked of school and tried to stay away from the subject of Travis or the events that had just occurred at home. Ana seemed semi-interested in auditioning for the drama production, and Andrea felt she would greatly benefit from it. Andrea received a call from Nellie and answered quickly. Ana knew her mother was getting a phone call from home informing her that her father was there. It was all too apparent in her mother's expressions and voice. It was a short conversation between the two, but a lot more was said than was actually spoken.

Nellie knew Phillip and knew he was upset by his abrupt tone with her. He was never rude to her, but she could always tell when he was angry. He came in, threw his bag down, and went into his study. Only there for a few minutes, he went upstairs looking for Andrea and Ana. When he didn't find them, he yelled down at Nellie from over the banister, "Where are they?" His tone wasn't angry, but he was agitated not to find them there.

"They went into town. They'll be home soon," she responded. Nellie was glad they weren't home, but she did call Andrea because she knew it would only get worse the longer, he had to wait. Nellie went into the living room, and Phillip was there looking at his phone. He still had his jacket on and looked up at her when she entered. "What's wrong with you? I know you need to at least take off your coat. Maybe you need to take a shower and relax before they get home?" she said, mothering him.

"You know what's wrong, Nellie. And, you know as well as I do that Anastasia should not have been involved with a twenty-two-year-old man. Why did her mother not know what was going on?" Phillip said, throwing the blame on Andrea.

"Now, I think you're over-exaggerating the situation, and if you're mad at Andrea, you should be mad at me as well. I see Ana just as much as she does, and I had no idea," Nellie said, trying to diffuse him.

"I want to talk to both of them soon. Ana should know better than to behave that way. She is only seventeen," Phillip vented to Nellie.

"Now Phillip, she might have known better or maybe not, we don't know, and it doesn't matter if she did. She's seventeen. Don't you remember how you were at that age?" Nellie was trying to make him think. They both got up to leave the room.

"I'll go shower," Phillip said in passing.

Nellie shook with frustration as she texted Andrea that he was showering. Andrea and Ana finished eating, got in the car, and headed back home. "Are you mad at me?" Ana asked Andrea as they drove.

"I'm not mad. I am disappointed," Andrea replied.

"Dad is mad, isn't he?" Ana asked, looking down at her hands.

"Dad is upset, Ana, but it will be ok," Andrea said, trying to comfort her. Andrea pulled into their drive, and she could see Ana crying silently in the passenger seat. She put the car in park. She dreaded going in. Ana looked at her with big tear-filled eyes for guidance. "Ana, come on, you have to go in." Andrea patted her thigh. She really wanted to pull her close and hold her, but she knew she couldn't caudle her now. It would just create a division of authority. Andrea went in first, and Nellie met her in the hall.

"He's upstairs in the shower, I assume," Nellie said. Ana walked in and went straight to her room. Nellie saw her eyes and looked at Andrea.

"I didn't do it. She started crying on the way home," Andrea responded.

"Oh Lord, I hope he's calmed down. He was in a mood when he got home," Nellie said.

"I'll go talk to him, might as well get it over with." Andrea headed up the stairs.

"Here we go," Nellie said to herself.

When Andrea walked into their room, Phillip was standing at the window, his tie loosened and his jacket off. He looked like he was thinking and undressing at the same time. He turned to face Andrea. "Hello, love," Phillip said and tried to smile. "Where have you two been?"

"We just went out for a drive, and then we got an early dinner," she replied. Phillip didn't seem interested and turned back to face the window. "Phillip, what is it? I mean -- I know you are upset with Ana."

"Upset is not the word I would use, but yes, I am. Scott told his dad. He called me on the way home to inform me of my daughter's new sexual relationship with the stable boy. I'm sorry, did I say boy? I meant a 22-year-old man." He took a drink from his glass of liquor sitting on the dresser.

"I am sorry, dear, I'm disappointed as well." There was a pause, and then Andrea said, "Ana swears she didn't sleep with him." She was trying to calm him and put her arms around his back and over his arms.

He didn't move, but he said, "And you believe her? She is 17 years old. Of course, she's going to tell you that you're her mother." Andrea pulled away, and Phillip turned around, looking for an answer.

"I believe her, I really do. Yes, I know she's a teenager, and they lie. She has lied. I know you think I'm stupid, but I do believe her," Andrea confessed.

"Andrea, what if she's pregnant or has contracted an STD from this guy? I mean, he is twenty-two."

"I've thought of that, Phillip. Do you think I've not thought of that?"

"So what are we going to do? Just hope she doesn't have an STD or isn't pregnant?" Phillip was clearly irritated.

"I will talk to her. What else can I do?" Andrea responded.

"Take her to a doctor, get her checked out. Maybe she'll be more inclined, to be honest with a medical professional. Yes, talk to her. I want to talk to her myself. Where is she?"

"I think she's in her room, but don't you want to wait a while? You seem very angry." Andrea was trying her best to persuade him to wait.

"Stop protecting her, Andrea. I'm her father, I want to speak with her, and I will," he demanded.

"She's just a seventeen-year-old, Phillip. She isn't an adult, don't be so hard on her," Andrea pleaded. Philip walked out of their room, leaving her behind and choosing not to acknowledge her comment.

Ana was in her room playing on her phone when he knocked on the wall before coming through the open door. She immediately sat up, somewhat startled, when he came through the door. Ana stared at him with big eyes, not knowing what to expect. Phillip walked into the room and stared at Ana, seemingly absent for the right words. "You, follow me," he said to her as he walked out of the room. Holding her phone in her hand, she followed him into the master bedroom where Andrea was sitting by the window in a rocking chair. Andrea was surprised to see them enter the room and didn't quite know how to react. "Sit down," he said as he pointed to a stool next to the vanity, across from her mother. "I am very disappointed in you, Anastasia, and I don't know why you would put yourself and your family at such risk. I was informed by an opposing colleague today that you were having sex with our 22-year-old college guy, who also works for us. I found this very disturbing and realizing I had been left uninformed about the whole situation by your mother made me angry." He motioned to Andrea.

Andrea interrupted, "I didn't not tell you --" Phillip cut her off, pointing at her.

"I don't want to hear excuses. I should not have heard this from Trammell Andrea, let me finish," Phillip said, his tone conveying his anger and annoyance. Andrea shut her mouth but was obviously getting frustrated by his comments. Ana looked to her mother, who turned her head away from her view. "Do you have anything to say for yourself?" Phillip asked as he looked down on Ana with his hands on his hips.

Ana just looked at the floor and said, "No, I mean, no, Sir." Andrea gave Phillip and I told you so look.

"Ana, you have nothing to say?" Phillip asked, clearly waiting for some sort of response.

Ana looked up at him, then to Andrea, who sat with her arms crossed, watching her struggle for words. "No, I mean, I am sorry. But Dad, I didn't do what he supposedly told that guy. I told Mom that already," Ana said, pleading for assistance. Andrea didn't offer any words of support.

"You did not have sex with him. For sure, nothing happened, that is what you're telling me? So, he is lying?" Phillip asked her.

"I mean, we messed around, but we didn't have sex, I promise you that. I already told Mom, I'm a virgin," Ana stated, becoming more embarrassed by the topic.

"I don't know what the definition of messing around is, Ana, and I'm not sure you're being honest. And I want you to see a doctor, soon, for a full examination. Your mother will take you," Phillip said matter of factly.

Ana's face turned red. She couldn't believe the words he was saying. "Dad, are you serious? I told you, I didn't have sex with him." Ana was full of frustration. She turned to her mother, "Mom, really? You're gonna take me to a doctor just because you think I'm lying?"

"It isn't a terrible idea for you to be evaluated by a female physician. You need to establish a relationship with a physician anyway. You've never been seen here, and you may be more comfortable discussing certain things with a doctor," Andrea explained.

Ana stood up, stepped toward her mother, looking at her with disdain. "Why are you doing this to me? Because you don't believe me? So now you're going to have some doctors examine me to see if I'm lying." Tears welled up in Ana's eyes. Andrea stood to respond, but Ana cut her off. "Mom, this is so wrong, and you fucking know it."

Immediately Andrea stepped forward, raising her hand. She saw Ana wince and brace herself, closing her eyes while tears streamed down her face. Andrea took a breath and did not strike her but waited. She moved closer, facing Ana. Andrea waited on Ana to open her eyes and said, "Are you finished, young lady?" Ana was immediately embarrassed, she knew she shouldn't have said what she did, and she was humiliated being responded to like a child. Ana just looked at her mother, silence being her only weapon. "Anastasia, you will respect us. You are acting childish and defensive. Do you have something to hide?" Andrea asked. Ana again chose not to answer. "So, since you do not have anything to divulge, we will make the appointment, and you will go. Do you understand?"

Ana felt defeated and inferior, and she answered, "Yes, ma'am," her voice sarcastic. Andrea moved away and walked behind Phillip to their bathroom. Phillip watched as Andrea walked past him. Ana had struck a chord with Andrea, and Phillip hadn't seen Andrea and Ana interact this way. He was surprised when Andrea didn't strike Ana, it was warranted, and he was aware of Andrea striking her for a similar act a few weeks before. Ana stood there; her face flushed with anger. She crossed her arms and then sat down on the stool, fuming. Her father came out of the bathroom.

"Anastasia, I will not allow you to speak to your mother that way. That was very disrespectful, and I am surprised she didn't slap your face. Apologize to her," her father demanded. Andrea was out of the bathroom and standing behind Phillip.

"I'm sorry, Mom," Ana said at his request.

"The exam was my idea. It is not an examination of your virtue. It's so you can be seen by a physician who can be a resource for you," Phillip said. Ana exhaled, waiting for more words to be said as she tried to ignore her emotions.

"Ana, you're on restriction until further notice, and you will be cleaning out the stables daily until your uncle hires someone else to do the job."

"Whatever makes you happy, Sir," Ana said in response, just trying to get out of the room. Ana turned to leave the room.

Andrea was glad that Phillip was there to see this side of Ana, but she also understood Ana's frustration, although Ana was taking all her anger out on her. "Go downstairs and help Nellie and hand me your phone. It is mine until further notice. You're not going to lock yourself in your room on your phone all night," Andrea ordered as she pointed toward the steps. Ana handed her phone to her mother and walked out. She was pissed off at both of them but especially upset at her mother. She walked heavily down the steps to meet Nellie in the kitchen. Nellie took one glance and knew Ana was angry. She handed Ana a knife, and they peeled potatoes for a while in silence.

Andrea waited for her to get out of hearing distance. "Really, she thinks we are going to have her violated to prove a point," Andrea said to Phillip.

"I am not having her violated. I don't know what you're talking about," Phillip said.

"I mean internally examined. Gosh, Phillip, you don't know anything about women's health."

"She needs a physician anyway. This is not going to hurt her. It's just a physical."

"Well, she's going now for sure after that episode of defiance," Andrea said to herself, but Phillip heard. "Phillip, we can't lock her in this house forever."

"We can until we know she isn't going to run away. I am not losing her over some stupid boy."

Andrea agreed and didn't know what else to say. She was afraid to lose Ana again. She was afraid she would run away and afraid she would ruin their relationship by being too hard on her. As Andrea looked out the window, she began to cry. "I'm sorry, I was worried and was trying to find the right way to tell you." He nodded in response that he understood, and she walked into the bathroom, closing the door.

Nellie hadn't heard the words, but she knew Ana and her parents had been in a heated argument. She let Ana simmer down, then asked, "Do you want to tell me what you're upset about?"

Ana looked up and said, "Not really, I'm embarrassed."

"Ok." They kept chopping.

Ana cleaned up the kitchen counter, then Nellie excused her to get ready for bed. Ana didn't mind doing chores, she had done them all her life, but she hated to be treated like a child. Ana walked up the stairs and saw her mother's door was cracked. She walked to the door and looked in. She saw her mother lying with her head in her father's lap on the sofa, they were speaking to each other, but Ana didn't stay to hear the conversation. Her mother's face was still blotchy red, and her eyes looked swollen like she had been crying. They didn't notice her presence, and Ana slipped back into the darkness and went to her room. She felt guilty and wanted to talk to her mother, but she couldn't do it in front of her dad. She messaged Diane on her iPad and said, "Hey."

Diane responded after a few seconds with, "Hi?"

Ana messaged back with a frowning face emoji.

"What's wrong? Why are you sad? Why are you on your iPad?" Diane asked.

Ana typed but then deleted her text. Diane, seeing her bubbles disappear, called Ana.

"What is it, my dear?" Diane asked. Ana FaceTime called Diane. Ana began to cry and speak at the same time. She explained how she felt like her parents were having her examined because they didn't trust her and that she had cursed at her mother and now felt terrible. Diane breathed deeply before answering. "Ana, there isn't an examination that authenticates virginity, and I assume they simply want you to be evaluated by a medical provider. You haven't been seen by anyone here. You know this is not as big of a deal as you're making it."

Ana replied without sobbing, "I don't want to be evaluated. I'm fine. I have no medical conditions. I do not need a doctor to try to scare me into the truth. I told you the truth."

"Ana, you know better than to speak to your mother that way. Using that language provokes her, and you know it. She's an easy target for you, and that isn't fair to her."

"I know, I shouldn't have said that, but I'm still so pissed off," Ana confessed. "Why doesn't she believe me?"

"Do you think I would have made all that up? It was embarrassing as crap to tell you and Mom about what Travis and I had done."

Diane responded, "I agree that had to be embarrassing, but you know we are both women. We were both seventeen at one time. You can tell us anything Ana, I hope you know that."

"I guess, and now Mom is crying, and Dad fussed at her because he thinks she takes up for me. I feel so bad." Diane knew Anastasia was tender-hearted and was very thankful she was empathetic toward her mother, even though she took her frustration out on her.

"Where is she? Have you told her you were sorry?" Diane asked.

"Not really, she's in her room with Dad. She sent me to the kitchen to work with Nellie and took my phone. Nellie sent me to bed after I finished in the kitchen."

"She did, huh," Diane responded. She laughed to herself at her friend's creative method of parenting. "Well, Ana, if you feel this bad, you should apologize, she's your mother. Go to her." Diane was trying to ease Ana's burden of deciding what to do.

Ana agreed and said, "Goodbye, and I am sorry."

"Sorry for?" Diane said.

"For all this," Ana said.

"Thank you, Ana. You don't have to apologize to me, but I do appreciate it."

"Well, I guess I will go."

"Goodnight, I love you, Ana."

Ana replied, "I love you," then hung up. She did feel better about the exam, although she had a feeling deep in her gut that made her want to vomit. She was sorry, and she knew this feeling wouldn't go away until she apologized to her mom. It was like a gnawing feeling that made her feel like nothing would be right in the world again if she didn't apologize to her. Ana got ready for bed and watched Netflix on her iPad for a while. Her dad came by her room to ask if she needed anything from downstairs. He said he was going down to eat a snack. She said no but asked where her mother was. He said she was already in bed and they would talk in the morning. Ana wanted to speak to her alone, so she went to her bedroom. The lights were off, so Ana crawled in the dark to her mother's side of the bed. Andrea wasn't asleep but had closed her eyes, laying with her face toward the outside of the bed. Ana watched her breathe and wished she could take back everything she had done, especially how much she had hurt her mother. It killed Ana to know her mother was disappointed in her. Ana saw how her hair laid against her cheek and how she held her hands near her face. She was beautiful lying there. Ana realized then that she wanted her mother; she wanted to be wanted by her. She needed her and loved her, no matter how upset or angry she became. Ana touched Andrea's arm and said, "Mom."

Andrea opened her eyes and said, "Yes." Ana sat on her knees on the floor beside her mother's bed. "What is it, Ana?" Andrea asked, worried that something was wrong.

"Mom, I am sorry, I'm so sorry. I am such a brat."

Andrea was alarmed by her submissive display and asked, "What are you sorry for?" thinking that maybe it was something other than her recent behavior.

"I'm sorry for it all. I'm sorry for lying and for how I have treated you. Mom, I messed up, and I really didn't mean to."

"Didn't mean to do what?"

"I didn't mean for this thing with Travis to come to this."

"I know you didn't mean to get caught," her mother said as she turned the lamp on and sat up in bed. She patted the bed in front of her and motioned for Ana to sit. Ana sat with her legs bent underneath her, slouching forward. "Explain the pictures?" her mother asked.

"Have you seen it?" Ana asked.

"No, have you?"

"I'm not sure what picture it is. But I have an idea it's a picture of a Snapchat."

"Oh, I see."

"I'm hoping you were clothed in the picture."

"Yes, mostly. I did send him one of me in my bra once. That's the worst, though."

Andrea couldn't hide her feelings well but was trying to stay positive. "That's it?"

"Yes, Mom, please forgive me. My heart hurts because I hurt you," Ana said, sobbing in her mother's arms.

"Child of mine, I forgive you," her mother said as she scooted back and over, making a place for Ana beside her. Ana laid beside her mom as she put her arms around her and said, "Shhh," and kissed her head. Ana stopped crying, and her breathing slowed. Ana felt so safe, so content in her mother's arms, she thought this must be love. Andrea held her daughter, and her heart grew warm as she cradled her. She felt so full holding her, so near, Ana completely safe in her arms.

"I love you, Momma."

"And I love you." her mother said. Then they both drifted off to sleep.

Phillip later came in to find them both asleep, Andrea cradling Ana. Both of them looking so peaceful. Ana's head tucked under her mother's chin. Andrea's arm around her and Ana fingers intertwined in a piece of her mother's hair. He turned off the lamp, cracked the door, and went to sleep in the guest room down the hall. He couldn't bear to interrupt their slumber. Although, before he left the room though he couldn't help but stand and look at them, embracing this moment of his daughter finally wrapped in the arms of her mother, safe and warm. He knew this was what they always wanted. He snapped a picture of the two on his phone, and he couldn't resist sending it to Diane before he went to sleep. Diane's phone alerted as she received the picture. She just stared at it, smiling, with tears streaming down her face. Tears that expressed joy and sorrow at the same time. She felt a peace for Andrea and Ana, and that gave her great satisfaction. This is what love was all about, forgiveness, grace, and the willingness to give of yourself for another without the promise of receiving anything in return.

CHAPTER NINE

Dr. Julie

Andrea made an appointment with a female doctor Diane had suggested. She was young, and Andrea felt like maybe Ana would connect with her. Diane spoke highly of her and thought it was a good idea to get her established. She did not tell Andrea that Ana had called her. She didn't feel like it was something Andrea needed to know. She like that they shared a connection they shared. She had always been close with Phillip and had been very involved in Drake's life. Andrea and Diane had been instant friends as soon as they had met in college, and it was Diane who encouraged Philip to date, Andrea. Although she was a good sister, she was also a loyal friend and was tied equally to them both. She had known other friends who couldn't get along with their sisters-in-law, and she was so grateful for Andrea and her unselfish ways. It had been Andrea that had brought her own daughter home many times, when she'd called her from somewhere, she shouldn't have been. Those times seemed so distant, although, in truth, it had only been a few years ago. At that time, Diane had felt like she was on the brink of insanity. She shook her head as she thought of those nights, the arguments, and some of the things she had seen. It was like a bad dream she had tried to block out of her memory. Andrea and Laurel were close, so were Diane and Laurel, but their bond was different. Diane knew it was because Andrea was younger, and Laurel didn't feel as threatened by Andrea. Andrea had tried to cushion Laurel's fall on many occasions, although Laurel would still end up in trouble. Andrea, like herself, in the current situation, would keep most of the details to herself unless she felt Diane needed to know. Laurel had taken a while to mature, Diane thought, as she tried to rationalize her daughter's past. In fact, the physician Diane had recommended had seen Laurel while she was home, and Diane trusted her judgment.

The morning of the appointment, Ana was not in a cheerful mood when she appeared downstairs for breakfast. Andrea chose not to engage in conversation. "Ready to go?" she asked as she picked up her coffee and headed for the garage. Andrea had taken the day off work; although she had told Ana, she would return her to school around noon, another thing Ana wasn't pleased with. Ana appeared in the car a minute or two after her, carrying her own coffee and eating a breakfast bar. She didn't have her book bag but had her cell phone in her pocket. She only knew that because it vibrated as she sat down. Andrea had given Ana her phone back a day after her last outburst. "Bookbag?" Andrea asked.

"Oh yeah," Ana said, got out of the car, and returned with her bookbag. Once on their way, Andrea turned on the radio, and the tension seemed to decrease.

"So, this doctor is young, and your Aunt Diane recommended her. She said she was very good with Laurel, so hopefully, you will like her," Andrea said as she drove.

"Ok, so what do I do?" Ana asked.

"It's a physical Ana. You don't do anything. They just check you out, take your history, do blood work, you know," Andrea explained. Ana looked confused. "Did you not have a pediatrician when you lived in America?" Andrea asked, confused herself as to why Ana wouldn't know what an annual physical was.

"I went to the doctor when I was sick and stuff, but it was never scheduled. And, I went to the health department to get a bunch of shots before I went to the academy because you know who had lost my records and nobody could find them," Ana said.

"Oh, well, usually a child has a pediatrician that sees them at least once a year. Have you ever been to a doctor as a teenager?" Andrea asked, curious if her another mother had taken her.

"No," Ana answered, she had, but she didn't want to talk about it. Andrea looked at her and thought this could be traumatizing.

"Ok, well, this won't be bad," Andrea said. They got to the office, and customarily they were checked in and placed in a room. Ana was asked to undress, put on a gown, and wait for the physician. "Do you want me to leave?" Andrea asked as she turned around while Ana undressed.

"I don't think so," Ana said. Ana had left on her socks and panties. Andrea saw the socks and wondered if she still had on underwear but didn't ask. The doctor entered the room wearing seal blue scrubs with her hair pulled back in a low ponytail. She looked to be about 35 or 40 years old. She introduced herself and sat down on a stool in front of Ana and Andrea.

"So, we're here for a new patient physical?" she asked, looking at Andrea. Andrea confirmed, and the physician asked who had seen her previously, and Andrea explained the situation, that Ana had just moved from the states. Ana just looked at her like she was waiting on her to perform some kind of magic trick. "Ok, so Ana, I will ask you some questions, and then I will examine you and draw some blood. I'll step out with your mother for a moment, and then I will return." The physician guided Andrea into the hall. "Diane called me yesterday," the doctor said. "She informed me of Ana's arrival here and that she had not had much medical care in the past."

"Yes, that is true," Andrea said.

"Is there anything you're concerned about, Mrs. Hutchinson?"

"Not really, Doctor."

"Call me Julie."

"If you want to wait here in this chair until we get done, I'll come and get you." Andrea nodded and sat down in the chair outside of the room.

Julie entered the room. Ana was seated on the table with her blue gown on and a blanket over her legs. Julie sat down on the stool in front of her. "So Ana, tell me about yourself," Julie said. Ana looked overwhelmed immediately. "Ok, let me start. My name is Julie, and I'm your cousin's doctor. I am thirty-nine years old, and I have one child, her name is Kylie." Julie slouched her shoulders and smiled. Her hair was brown, and her eyes a pretty green. When Julie smiled, her dimples lead to her bright white teeth. She looked normal and real, like a girl who grew up to be a woman, a successful, intelligent woman. Ana saw her slouch, she noticed that her feet turned in slightly, and she noticed she wore a dog tag around her neck.

"My name is Anastasia Hutchinson. I lived in America until about four months ago when I found out that my so-called parents had kidnapped me. I found out my whole life was a lie. I formerly was Paige Peterson, and I was in school and doing well for once. I finally felt like I was free from my dysfunctional life, then I found out the truth. Now I'm home. I have a mother, a father, and a brother that I never knew. I have things I never thought I would have. I have a life that I've always envied others for, and now I feel more like a child than I ever have. I have no control over my life, and I made a mistake," Ana said quickly, then she breathed in. "I'm sure you didn't want to hear all that," Ana said, shrugging her shoulders.

"Yeah, sure I did. How am I supposed to care for you if I don't know you?" Julie asked, not expecting an answer. Julie went on to ask about her medical history, and Ana revealed nearly nothing because she hadn't had much of a medical past. "When did you start your first period?" Julie asked.

"I was fourteen, but it doesn't come every month," Ana said.

"Ok, are you sexually active, or were you before you came to England?" Julie asked.

Ana didn't say anything. "Ana, anything you say is confidential."

"I've messed around, but I haven't ever had actual sex," Ana said.

"That means penetration, I'm guessing, and does messing around mean oral or anal sex?" Julie asked without stalling. Ana became embarrassed, and her face flushed. "I'm just asking, I do not judge, to each their own," Julie said, holding up her arms to show she didn't care.

"Ugh, oral kinda --once, and never anal," Ana said. "Ok, well, as long as you're not sexually active, I won't have to do an internal exam unless you have concerns," Julie said. "Do you have any issues?"

"Well, kinda. I think I've been scratched or something by a guy," Ana said. She explained that she had bled and had some pain. Julie did a head-to-toe exam and talked to Ana while she examined her. When she put her in stirrups, Ana became very nervous and closed her legs tight with her feet still in the stirrups.

"Ana, you're going to have to relax your legs. I'm not going to hurt you," Julie said. Julie could tell Ana was extremely uncomfortable, and she wasn't sure how she was going to get her to relax enough to begin the exam.

Ana put the pillow over her face and grunted, "Ugh, do you have to do this?"

"Yes, Ana, this isn't bad. I just need to look." Ana breathed out slowly and released her legs, but as soon as Julie switched the light on, she was right back shut. "Ana, do you want your mom in here with you while we do the exam?"

"Yes, get her, please. I'm sorry, I'm just freaking out. I don't know what you're going to do."

"She wants you, Mrs. Hutchinson," Julie said to Andrea with her head out of the door.

Her mother came and stood by Ana's head and took the pillow off her face. "Ana, you have to relax. She's just going to look," her mother said. Andrea helped Julie put Ana's feet back in the stirrups.

"Now, take a deep breath and let your legs fall open," Julie said. The sheet covered her thighs so Andrea couldn't see her bottom. "Ana more, I have to be able to see down here. Don't be embarrassed. We are all women here." Andrea gently pushed Ana's leg out, and Ana didn't close them. Julie could see all the normal anatomy, although she noticed a redness near her vagina that looked like an abrasion. "I'm going to touch." Ana closed her eyes. "Ana, are you having any pain?" Julie asked.

"Yea, a little," Ana said. Julie gently pressed near the opening, and Ana nearly came off the exam table. "Ouch, what is that."

"Ana, I need to look further inside. It seems you have an abrasion," Julie said as she worried the abrasion was actually a small laceration. Ana saw her mother shut her eyes and shake her head. Ana knew what she was thinking. Ana braced herself, and Julie attempted to enter her vagina with just a finger. Ana slid back. "Please slide back down here. I'm not going to hurt you. It looks like someone else may have, and I have to see how bad it is ok, so please cooperate," Julie said sternly. Ana slid back down and tried to stay still. "Take a deep breath." her mother said, holding her hands. Ana breathed out and squinted her eyes. "Ana, it's an abrasion, almost a laceration. I have to ask, were you entered forcefully?" Julie asked.

"It was just his finger or fingers, I'm not sure, but it hurt, it happened so fast," Ana tried to explain.

"But you're sure it wasn't a finger then a penis? Did you see it?" she asked Ana.

Ana looked at her mom. "No, I didn't, but it was his finger because my pants weren't down that far," Ana said.

"Are you a relationship with him?" Julie asked.

Ana and her mother answered in unison, "No.

"Well, it should heal with time, although it will cause pain until it heals. You need to stay clean and away from that area for a while." Julie explained.

Julie helped her to a sitting position. "Ana, if you're having this type of sexual activity, then I would suggest you be on some type of birth control."

"No, I'm good. I don't think I'll be doing anything like that anytime soon," Ana said.

"Ok, but if you do or think you're going to have sex, please come back and get birth control," Julie said.

"Ok," Ana responded as her eyes met Andrea's. Julie finished, and Ana felt better about the visit. She was relieved she could see Julie in confidence if she needed to. As she dressed, Andrea and Julie stepped out of the room.

"She reminds me of Laurel a little," Julie said to Andrea.

"Yes, she does," Andrea agreed, smiling and raising her eyebrows. Julie smiled in return.

"How is she, Laurel?" Julie asked.

"She's good, thank you so much," Andrea replied.

"By the way, I am going to have a blood pregnancy test ordered, just in case," Julie said.

"Yes, thank you," Andrea said and sighed.

They left the doctor's office, grabbed a fast lunch, then Andrea pulled into the high school. "Have a good day. I'll see you in a few hours," Andrea said as Ana unbuckled her seat belt.

"Ok, bye, Mom, I love you." Ana leaned over toward her mother, and Andrea kissed her cheek.

"Bye, I love you." That was the first time Ana had done that, and it felt good to Andrea. She waited for Ana to enter the building and smiled as she changed the gears of Ana's SUV, heading toward town. She wasn't going to work today. She had made an appointment with her massage therapist and was meeting a friend for a drink in the time she waited on Ana to get out of school.

CHAPTER TEN

Charleigh

Charleigh walked into the spa to find her friend, in a robe, drinking a glass of cranberry juice, most likely mixed with vodka. "Hey honey, how are you? You look so relaxed," Charleigh said to Andrea.

"Oh, I'm about to go into a coma from all these oils they have rubbed into my skin," Andrea said and laughed.

"Yeah, you smell like baby Jesus," Charleigh said, making Andrea laugh.

"Oh my Girl, you would not believe the week I've had." Andrea smiled, putting her drink to her lips.

"I figured when I got your text saying you needed a rub down and a hard drink."

Charleigh was twelve years younger than Andrea. They had met while she was working on a project at St. Catherine's. Charleigh always made Andrea laugh. She was carefree and witty. She worked as a nurse in the emergency department at the local hospital. Her husband worked out of town mostly, and they had recently been trying to conceive a baby.

"Char, do you want a drink?" Andrea asked as the waitress passed.

"I do, honey, but I need to refrain. I think I could be ovulating."

"Oh god, then you definitely need one."

"Well, I've been reading that alcohol decreases fertility. My app says it's time and my mucosa are just right." She smiled.

"Have you been checking your own cervix again? You are obsessed with your vaginal mucosa. I think it's hilarious."

"No freaking kidding, can you see me with my long ass legs trying to hold my leg up and reach up in there to my cervix. I have long fingers, but still, just not a hobby I want. It's hard as hell. I almost fell this morning and cracked my head. Wouldn't that be great, an ambulance coming to find me with my hand up my vagina, half-dressed, and unconscious?" Charleigh said, making faces as she tried to reenact her experience. Andrea almost spit, laughing.

"You're crazy, girl. You make me laugh," Andrea said. "I needed to laugh today, thank you." She finished her drink. The waitress passed again, asking if they needed anything. Andrea ordered another drink, and the lady walked away.

"Hey, wait, I need a drink also," Charleigh said, then ordered a double vodka and cranberry. Andrea laughed again. "Well, hell, it isn't every day you get to drink with your best friend, the Duke's wife." Andrea rolled her eyes. "Tell me, how is my favorite friend's new daughter?" Andrea told her about the recent incident with Travis and how they had just left the doctor's office this morning. "Oh my, Andy, I am sorry. But you know that's normal teenage behavior, right? Don't you remember how it was to be her age? Oh my god, I was like a horny goat," Charleigh said, laughing.

"Travis is twenty-two. That is not normal."

"Oh yeah, that part isn't so good," Charleigh admitted. "Well, at least it's over, right? At least he's gone. She can't have sex with him if he isn't around."

"He is not employed there anymore, and Ana swears they didn't have sex." Andrea expected a sarcastic response.

"What did she tell you happened, they made out?"

"Yeah, I guess it would be like third base.".

"She told you she did oral?" Charleigh said, almost spitting out her drink laughing.

"No, she said he had his hand down her pants. Is that not third base?"

"No, that's second base. Oh my god, I was gonna say, if she told you she gave him oral sex, she's brave. I would have rather said I was gang banged to my mom." Charleigh laughed.

"Do you think she's lying? I mean, it was difficult to get her to tell us anything. She's so stubborn."

"Us, who is us?" Charleigh asked.

"Diane and I," Andrea answered.

"Oh my god, what are you all, some kind of tag team detectives? Poor kid probably feels like she's getting interrogated by the supreme court," Charleigh laughingly said. "You are hardcore friends, but if she told you that and then didn't lie about it later when the doctor found the abrasion, probably not." She shook her head and smiled. "You need a blog called the Bad-Ass Momma Club, or something, giving parents tips on how to interrogate and give interesting methods of punishment for their teenagers," Charleigh said, making fun of Andrea.

"Funny. You know I'm not that bad," Andrea said.

"No, you're hard, but you love her, and she knows that. Seriously, I'm glad you're that way, my mom would have beat me with a table leg for something like that." Charleigh laughed.

Andrea looked at her in disbelief. "No, seriously, my momma chased me with a table leg one time. She got me too but just a little. But she was bat-shit crazy. We later found out she was bipolar."

"Oh my god, you're not right," Andrea said, and they continued to laugh.

"Exactly what deserves being chased with a table leg?" Charleigh said and laughed. "What did Phillip say? I know he expected more from her." Charleigh sat up stiffly, mocking his proper behavior.

"Well, you know Phillip, he always did the right thing. He doesn't get it. He blames me for not knowing it was going on. He says that I make excuses for her. I don't, though. He just doesn't realize what it's like to be female in these situations."

"Yeah, he doesn't get it; he has a wiener."

"He grounded her, took her car, and is making her work at the stables until a new person is hired. What he doesn't know is that she will enjoy that, but I let it go because she can't just sit in the house on her phone. It would drive me nuts."

"Yeah, and you have to tote her around. Where is he anyway?"

"He's home today, I think he has a meeting, but he'll be home this evening for dinner. Want to come over?"

"It might be a good distraction for Ana, so she doesn't have to think about her injured vagina at the dinner table," Andrea said, laughing.

"Oh my god, yes, for her, I will. How freaking awkward would that be to discuss that all evening with your parents? You all have got to chill." They finished their drinks and enjoyed the sun on their legs. They laughed some more and then drove back to the house in their separate cars.

"You want to pick up Ana? I'm going to help Nellie. I want to have fajitas for dinner," Andrea said.

"Sure, what time do we need to be here?"

"Be here by six. That gives you time to get some clothes in case you want to stay over later." Charleigh stayed over some, especially when her husband was out of town. She loved Andrea like a sister. They enjoyed each other's honesty.

Charleigh pulled up in Ana's car at the school at four p.m. Ana had gotten a text saying she would be picking her up. She had never met Charleigh, but her mom spoke about her a lot. Ana saw her SUV and got in, flinging her bag in the back. "Hey Anastasia, I'm Charleigh, and I'm your taxi today," Char said, introducing herself. Ana smiled. "So, your mom said you're in a drama class."

"Yeah, my friend Brittani is in it, and she likes it, so I figured it would be better than band or something."

"I did theatre in school, and I loved it." Charleigh pulled onto a road that Ana knew wasn't in the direction of her house.

"Where are we going?" Ana asked.

"Well, I figured you needed a little field trip since you're on lockdown?" Charleigh grinned.

"Yes, please, I hope my dad isn't home this evening."

"Well, he is, but I'll distract him." Charleigh winked at her; and. Ana smiled. They sped down a country road and ended up on the farthest side of town near Charleigh's house. "Hey, I am going to grab some stuff from my house. Can you drive? I mean, do you have a license?"

"Yes, this is my car," Ana said, smirking.

"Ok, smarty-pants, you can chill with that," Charleigh said, antagonizing Ana. Ana followed Charleigh in her house. Her big dog almost knocked Ana down when she went through the door. "Brutus, get down." Charleigh pushed the dog down. "He's just excited, sorry." Brutus followed Ana, sniffing her hands and butt.

"You're married?" Ana asked.

"Yeah, Dylan works out of town some. He won't be home till tomorrow," Charleigh explained. Ana looked around at the pictures throughout the house. There were a few pictures of her mother and Charleigh laughing and drinking wine, then one of them close up, standing near a big rock cliff.

"This is my mom?" Ana asked.

"Yeah, it is. Glad you can recognize her." Charleigh had a bag hanging off her shoulder. "Come on. You're driving."

"Where were you? That doesn't even look like her. She's all happy and young."

"We were in North Carolina, and your mom is young. You just don't know it. You know why she's cool? Because she has a cool young friend, me,"

Charleigh laughed. She opened a beer and went outside on the porch. "You want one? Charleigh asked jokingly. Ana looked surprised. "I'm kidding, your mom would be pissed, and she's not grounding me."

"I've drunk before. I'm not a baby," Ana said.

"Oh, I know you have. Now come on." Charleigh finished her beer and got on the passenger side.

She put a beer in a cup, and they left. Ana looked down at the beer and then at Charleigh. "Don't tell your mom, I don't want to hear it, and don't ever drink and drive. I'm riding, but don't do that either. And if you do, don't get caught, and if you do, don't blame me." Charleigh said. Ana laughed and pulled out of the drive. Charleigh had Ana drive around town. She showed her where she worked and where she and her mother hung out sometimes. They also circled around the back road that ended near the stables. Ana saw Travis's truck on the side of the road.

As she looked in her rearview mirror, she said, "What's he doing here?"

Charleigh turned around, "What? Who was that?" Ana slowed down like she was going to turn around. "Is that the guy? Oh hell no, you are not turning around; keep going."

Ana sped back up. "What? I was just going to ask him what he was doing? He doesn't live near here."

"That's the boy that you were caught with. No way. Are you talking to him? You have to let him go, he's too old, and your mom will kill you. I'm surprised she hasn't already."

"I didn't have sex with him. We just messed around," Ana said as if it was news to Charleigh.

"Ok, say what you want to. You're the one with the abraded hoo-ha," Charleigh said, one-upping her.

"Oh my god, I can't believe she told you that." Ana was shocked her mother would disclose her personal information.

"What? I'm a nurse. I don't care. I see that stuff all the time," Char said. "And let's be honest, between you and I, I bet there was probably a little more that went down than that. Maybe not that time, but I'm sure there were other occasions?" She pulled her sunglasses down and looked at Ana. Ana pulled into the top of her drive.

"We didn't have sex. It was close, I guess, but we didn't," Ana said.

"No penetration, right?"

"Right."

"Hey, oral counts as sex, just saying. You can get some bad diseases from that," Charleigh reminded Ana.

"I didn't do that either."

"Good girl, but you know, even if you had had any kind of sex, you could tell them, it is normal," Charleigh said.

"I know. Do you think she'll be chill one day with me?"

"I didn't make your mom cool. She was already awesome when we met. She makes me a better person. Your mom is chill, but she's your mom. It's different; she can't be all crazy with you because she has to be a good influence on you." Charleigh explained. She reached over and slapped Ana's thigh. "Come on. We're ten minutes late. Let me handle it." Charleigh bounced into the house.

CHAPTER ELEVEN

High Road

Andrea looked at her phone. It was 6:10 p.m., the locator said Ana was coming down the driveway. She felt relieved. She was finishing the vegetables and getting ready to put the chicken on. Charleigh came in the door. Andrea looked at her watch and then at Charleigh. "I know, I'm sorry," Charleigh said. Ana sat her bag down near the steps.

"Why don't you put Charleigh's bag upstairs and yours as well," Andrea said. Ana picked up the two bags and headed upstairs as she texted on her phone.

"How was the trip home?" Andrea asked.

"Good, but we saw --." Charleigh stopped, moved closer to Andrea, and whispered, "We saw Travis on the side of the road that goes to the stables. It was weird."

"Yeah, that is interesting. Did you stop?"

"No, I didn't think that was a good idea."

"Yeah, it isn't. They are not supposed to be communicating."

"Well, Ana was surprised as I was to see him." Andrea seemed happy with that statement.

Ana came downstairs with her phone glued to her hand. Andrea and Charleigh chatted, and Charleigh poured Andrea a glass of wine. Andrea gave her a disapproving look, and Charleigh whispered, "Chill, Momma." Andrea shook her head and smiled.

Phillip came into the kitchen. "Look who's here, hey Charleigh," Phillip said. "You want a beer?"

"Yeah, sure," she replied. Charleigh got her and Phillip a beer. Then she assisted Andrea in the kitchen. Ana stood against the counter, texting on her phone. They decided to eat outside since it was such a nice night. Phillip seemed to be relaxed for the first time since he'd been home. They were talking, and Charleigh was letting them in on her and Dylan's plans of having a baby.

"Life changes when you have a child Charleigh, you just wait," Phillip said.

"I know, I know," she said.

"Ana, how was your day with mom?" he asked.

"Fine," she replied as she looked at her phone. She had been texting off and on throughout the meal and seemed distracted.

"How did you like Dr. Julie?" he asked.

"She was very nice."

"Ana, phone," her mother said. Ana put the phone under her leg.

"Sorry, Mom, I'll need to stay after school until five on Thursday and Friday for theatre class. They're having auditions."

"Ok, and don't you have a paper due Friday morning?" Andrea asked.

"Yeah, I'll work on it as soon as I get home." Andrea nodded as she swallowed a bite.

Phillip cleared his throat, and Andrea looked at him. "What is it, dear?" she asked.

"Ana, you have chores to do right after school. I want you in this house before dinner so you can finish your homework, especially if you have a paper," he said.

"But if I can't stay after, I can't audition. Can't I finish the stables then eat dinner later, Dad?" Ana asked.

"Ana, we eat as a family, you know that," he said.

"Dad, why does it matter to you? You won't even be here," Ana said, staring at him. She was right, but that statement didn't please Phillip.

Charleigh stood up. "Anyone want a drink?" she asked.

"Yeah, sure," Phillip and Andrea both said. Charleigh walked into the house.

Ana asked, "May I be excused to go to the stables.

Phillip excused her and said, "I will drive you down." "

No, thank you, I'll walk," Ana said in a low, depressed tone.

Charleigh came back to sit down. "Wow, I thought it was going to get heated," she said.

Andrea shook her head. "She was right. Why should she be in the class if she can't audition.?" she said.

"She's grounded. This is her punishment. We have to follow through," Phillip said stubbornly.

"Dear, you grounded her indefinitely."

"Oh yeah, I did. Well, it hasn't been a week yet. I'll talk to her later."

"Where is she anyway? Charleigh asked.

"She's gone to the barn to clean out the stalls," Phillip said.

Charleigh immediately thought of Travis. "Hey Andy, let me help you with the dishes," she said, motioning to the kitchen. Andrea followed her, carrying dishes. Once they were in the kitchen, Charleigh whispered, "Hey dummy, remember we saw Travis on the road?"

"Oh, you're right. You don't think he's there, do you?"

"I don't know. I hope not. It was kind of creepy."

"We'll take a ride down there in a minute just to make sure." They finished the dishes quickly then snuck out to ride down by the barn. Andrea leaned over a little as they rode and said, "It's not that I don't want Philip to know. I just know how he is."

"I understand. Let's just see what's going on first, then if he needs to know, you can tell him."

Ana had been away from the house for about twenty minutes, and if she walked, she would have gotten to the barn about five minutes ago. Andrea was driving her car, and as they pulled down the road, they saw a truck parked in the tree line just past the drive to the stables. Andrea stopped before they got too close to the truck. "What should we do?" Andrea asked.

"Go in through the pasture. It will allow us to see him and what's going on from the back of the barn." They drove slowly down the dirt road. "It looks like he's texting on his phone."

"Yeah, wonder who?" Andrea said, insinuating it was Ana by her tone. Charleigh raised her eyebrows. She knew Andrea was probably right. They saw Diane's car as they pulled to the far side of the main barn. "Wonder how long she's been there?"

"You should know, you have the telepathic connection. Stop the car, let's sit here and watch. We already know Diane is there, so Ana is fine," Charleigh said.

"Good point," Andrea said as she turned off the car. Travis got out and slammed the truck door. You could barely see his face, but you could make out what he was doing. He looked like he was on the phone and was pacing outside his truck. Suddenly, he threw his phone on the ground. It looked like he opened a cooler in the back of his truck.

"Looks like he's a little pissed off," Charleigh said.

"Look, he's leaving," Andrea said. Travis backed up and pulled down the road without passing the entrance to the stables.

"What should we do now?" Charleigh asked.

"We're going in there," Andrea said as she pointed to the main barn and started the car.

"Oh hell, here we go."

"Char, when you have a teenage daughter, and you are stalking her outside of some building, I'm going to remind you of this." They pulled up and could hear Diane talking to Ana. They walked toward the noise.

"Well, you shouldn't have answered his text," Diane said, scolding Ana.

"He said if I didn't call him, he was going to come over here," Ana tried to explain.

"The only thing I heard was you say you're not allowed. That's when I knew who you were talking to."

"Exactly, I was telling him not to come here. You don't trust me either. God-a-mighty, when are you going to listen to me? I don't want anything to do with him. Do you think I'm stupid? Mom would kill me, and Dad thinks I'm a whore already," Ana ranted. Diane and Ana had no idea Char and Andrea were there.

At Ana's words, Andrea and Charleigh locked eyes. "That's your cue," Charleigh whispered as she started to move into the light towards them.

They heard Diane say, "Ana, I hope you're not lying." She paused as she handed a shovel to Ana. Andrea walked into the room and propped herself against the door, crossing her right foot over her left and crossing her arms. Charleigh stayed out of view. Diane and Ana looked very surprised by Andrea's presence.

"Oh, freaking great," Ana said under her breath. "I'm not looking at my phone." Ana handed Diane the phone and walked off. "I've got stuff to do." Ana walked past them into the farthest stall.

Charleigh walked out, picked up a pitchfork, and followed Ana. "Hey, baby girl, you need some help?" Charleigh asked and winked. Ana looked up at her, worry in her eyes. "It's ok, Ana. Let's get the dung done." Charleigh smiled. Ana smiled back, and they emptied the stall together.

Diane and Andrea discussed what had just transpired. Andrea said, "I don't think she knew he was over there on that road, at least not by this text."

Diane agreed. "Well, I don't know why he's hanging around, but it needs to stop." Andrea agreed and sat down in a rocking chair. "I think she's telling the truth, Andrea. I don't think she wants to be involved with him any longer."

"I know, Di. I don't want her down here alone, though. What if that freak shows up here? I don't have a good feeling about him. He was clearly angry on the phone, and then it looked like he was getting something out of a cooler, I'm assuming alcohol."

"Yeah, I will come down here with her, and I'm going to tell Jeffrey to keep an eye out for him in the area."

"He'll shoot him."

"Exactly. That's what I want him to do if he comes near her," Diane said, and Andrea laughed. They walked down to where Ana and Charleigh were. "Hey, girls, about done?" Diane asked. Ana nodded.

"Come on, let's go back to the house. Charleigh has a favorite game she loves to play when she comes over," Andrea said.

Charleigh yelled, "Heck yeah, girls' night!" and started dancing, grabbing Andrea's hands, spinning her around, and dipped her. Ana laughed and walked up to Diane, slapping her hard on the butt, then running steps away from her. Diane spun around smiling, chased her, grabbed her by the shoulders, and kissed her all over her face. Ana laughed.

"Stop it, yuck," Ana said playfully. Ana jumped in Diane's car. "Come on, I'm driving," Ana said, and Charleigh jumped in. "We're going through the woods. She has more clearance than mom."

Andrea and Diane got in Andrea's car and headed back up the road. Diane rolled down the window and reached over, honking the horn at Ana. "Hey, be careful. Don't get my truck dirty and hurry up. I don't want to come after you," Diane yelled.

The rest of the evening until after ten, they played card games and laughed at Charleigh telling funny stories about Andrea. Diane and Andrea talked about when they were in college. Ana went to bed that night, happy. Charleigh had her own room, but she slept with Ana. They laid in the darkness and talked for what felt like hours.

The next morning Andrea decided she should tell Phillip about Travis being on the road near the stables. She was worried for Ana's safety, and until someone else was hired to be there, she didn't want Ana there alone. "Do you think she'll meet up with him?" Phillip asked.

"No, but I feel like he would show up if he could," Andrea answered. "Why else would he be on that road twice yesterday?"

"Yes, you're probably right. Maybe I should call and see if Jeffrey can have someone do the stables, and Ana can take someone if she wants to go riding or whatever. I don't want her down there alone either."

"So that means she can audition for the play?"

"Yes, it does. I will talk to her."

Ana and Charleigh were sleeping. It was only 8 a.m. Ana texted Brittani around noon. "Hey, I'm off horse duty," Ana wrote. "Want to come over? We can do a read through."

"Are you sure your mom won't be mad," Brittani asked.

"I'm sure. It already been cleared by administration," Ana said, laughing. "I can come tomorrow, is that ok?" Brittani asked.

"Sure," Ana said. Tomorrow was Sunday, so Brittani would come over after evening youth church service.

"Hey, you should go with me to church. I mean, do you go to church?" Brittani asked.

"We haven't, but I did in the U.S. let me ask. I mean, who says you can't go to church? That would be against some ethical rule, right?" Ana said.

Later, Andrea was reading papers from work when Ana came into the den. "Hey Mom, can I go to church with Brittani?" Ana asked.

"Brittani goes to church?" Andrea asked.

"Mom, all have sinned and fall short of the glory of God," Ana replied, quoting Romans 3:23.

"Wow, listen to you quote scripture. I can drop you off. Is she coming here for dinner?" Andrea asked.

"Yes, thank you, Mom." Ana wore jeans to church. Her mom dropped her off for the youth service at 5:30. The church, Waterlife, was a modern Christian church. It had a small congregation. Andrea was skeptical of megachurches and found them fake, in her opinion. Ana had been raised Baptist in faith. Andrea and Phillip had attended a catholic church. Although, they hadn't gone in a few years. She thought maybe they should try to start going again for Ana and Drake. It's not that she didn't enjoy going to church, she'd just gotten tired of the typical church drama, and with Phillip's title, it seemed to be exaggerated.

Ana and Brittani sat beside each other in a large room with twentyish chairs placed in a circle. The youth leader, James, was a slender guy, around thirty-five years old. He was well dressed and seemed very secure in himself. He and his wife Heather lead the youth and young adult classes. Brittani and her family had been attending Waterlife for two years. Youth members filled the chairs with only one or two empty seats. Brittani introduced Ana to the group, and a teenage girl asked, "Are you the baby that was missing for like ever? Yeah, aren't you Duke Hutchinson's daughter?"

Ana didn't really know how to act. She'd never been asked that in public before. "Yeah, I guess." Ana's face flushed.

"So, you're Anastasia Hutchinson. I remember that story from a long time ago. Wow, I'm so happy you made it home to your parents," James said, not knowing if the last part of his comment made sense.

"So you have two families? How did you find out?" a boy in the class asked.

Ana was getting nervous and didn't want to delve into the story of how she was reunited with her family. James sensed her anxiety and said, "We are so glad Anastasia is here with us, but let's not make her uncomfortable. As far as those questions, one day when we get to know her, she may tell us her story, but until then, we need to respect her privacy."

Ana was relieved they weren't still sitting there waiting for her to answer. As soon as James stopped talking, two girls to Ana's right began whispering, making Ana feel very insecure. James played an inspirational video and music he had for the lesson. Then the group had discussion. The message was about true friends. Specifically how to be a true friend, meaning someone who builds others' spirits and faith in Christ. James spoke about how not to be a flesh-feeding friend who only contributes to the wants and desires of the flesh and doesn't stimulate the spirit. Ana had heard the term 'flesh' throughout sermons many times. Ana had had flesh-feeding friends all her life, yet she really only had a few true friends. She thought of Jude and Natilee and her friend from childhood, Krissie, and her cousin Nicole. The class ended, and James and Heather both thanked Ana for coming and said she was welcome anytime. Brittani drove Ana home for dinner.

"You're staying, right?" Ana asked.

Brittani turned off the car and answered, "Yes."

When Ana and Brittani walked into the house, Nellie was in the kitchen. "Hello, how are you two this evening?" Nellie asked.

Ana said, "Great, thank you."

"Dinner is ready, so don't go too far. Your dad is already out on the patio. He must be hungry." Ana walked out on the patio; Phillip was looking at his iPad.

He took off his glasses and laid them on the table, and said., "Hello, how was service?"

"Fine," Ana replied. Andrea soon joined the group, and they had dinner. Brittani was comfortable after Andrea asked them about the play. Andrea was interested in the production, and she was eager for Ana to feel like she belonged.

Andrea looked at Brittani, "Where do you plan on going to college?"

"I'm seriously thinking about St. Catherine's. They have a wide variety of interesting programs."

"Oh, really? What do you think you will choose," asked Ana.

"I think it's between education and psychology degree. My mom's a teacher. I love watching the minds of little children as they learn." Brittani said, shrugging her shoulders. Ana grinned and kicked Brittani under the table. Ana knew Brittani was lying to impress her parents.

"Have you thought about any majors that may interest you?" Phillip asked.

"I always wanted to be an army nurse, but that isn't going to happen, so who knows. I like medical stuff. I would love to be a doctor, but I don't have the grades. I love that movie where Brad Pitt cuts out his brother's heart and brings it home in a box when he died in the war. I always told Jude I was going to do that for him if he was killed, and he would say he didn't think it would make it through customs," Ana said, laughing. The others laughed at Ana.

"You can be a nurse Ana," said Phillip.

"Yeah, but I can't jump out of helio's, and crap like the soldiers do," Ana said.

"You know war isn't fun, it's not like on T.V. I would rather be on my own soil, working behind a desk every day, than to be fighting," Phillip went on to say. Ana looked confused like she was missing something.

"Ana, your dad was in the British Air force for eight years. He deployed to Saudi Arabia during Desert Storm," Andrea said quietly.

"Oh, that explains it," Ana said.

Ana and Brittani took the dishes to the kitchen, and then they headed upstairs to the family room. They spent the rest of the evening reading through the play and talking about Corbin from class. "You know he likes you," Brittani said, laughing.

"He doesn't even know me; clearly nobody does after the questions I was asked at Waterlife."

"Oh god, I know. I thought you were going to freak out. It has to feel crazy to know that kidnappers raised you, and you lived through hell while Andrea and Phillip were searching for you. Not to mention your dad is a Duke. You're lucky, right?" Brittany asked.

"Lucky isn't the right word. I don't know how to describe it. I have always felt blessed that I had the ability to rise above my situation. Back at the Academy, I felt like I had finally reached a place where I couldn't be touched by the Peterson's. I felt free and secure, although, now I think back, I realize I didn't have any stability, except for what I could provide for myself, and that wasn't much." Ana said, staring off in thought.

"Wow, that's deep. You're going to do great in your audition. Just channel up some of that," Brittani said, making Ana smile.

At nine o'clock, Jude called. He informed her that his graduation and pinning would be in six weeks. He expressed to her he was saddened she wouldn't be there. Ana wouldn't have been graduating with Jude anyway, but that didn't matter. Ana wanted to be there.

Jude asked. "Do you think you could come?"

"I don't think so, Jude. I'll have to ask to be sure," Ana replied. Ana thought at least school would be over. That was one thing she had going for her. They talked more about his plans and about Natilee's boyfriend, Ryan.

"I just want to see you again. I know it can't be forever, but maybe one day it can. I will be in training for roughly a year, so who knows what we will be doing in year?" he said.

"I'll be here, finishing high school or maybe at St. Catherine's College, if I'm lucky. Jude, my life is so much different now." Ana said.

"Yeah, I can see that…Ana, are you dating anyone?" he asked.

"No, are you?" Ana asked.

"No, I'm not, and I have to go to the formal at the end of the year. If you were here, you could go with me." He said happily, creating that vision in her head. Ana smiled and wished with her whole heart she could go with him. She would love to see him in his fancy uniform and tie.

"I would love to go, Jude. You know that I want to be with you." Ana said, then realized how it sounded.

"I want you too, Ana, more than you know," he said in a low voice.

"I will try very hard to convince my mother to let me come to see your pinning, I promise," Ana promised, but had doubts her parents would even consider giving her permission. They ended the call, and her heart ached a little. She felt like she was losing something she never truly experienced.

CHAPTER TWELVE

Jude, Please

Andrea walked down the hall to the kitchen. It was seven a.m. on Saturday morning, and she was the first person up in the Hutchinson household. Drake was home for the weekend. His door was shut. Phillip was still asleep in their bed. She had done this every morning for years. She checked on Drake then looked into Anastasia's nursery as she walked toward the stairs. The rocking chair that used to sit by the window had been moved. It was now in her bedroom by the window. And for the last six months, she had passed Ana's room to see her lying there in her bed, a pair of shoes scattered somewhere near the bed and usually her iPad or phone on the floor. This morning she saw a book bag in the corner, splayed open, and a laptop shut on the desk. In the past, Andrea had never shut the door to Anastasia's nursery, and it was always referred to as her room. Even before, when it was so empty and only inhabited by a few pictures and a rocking chair. Maybe subconsciously, she had feared that if she shut the door or called the room anything else, she had lost the hope of ever finding her lost baby girl. What used to be a sad reminder was now a new joy. She stopped and peered into her room, whispering, "Thank you, God," because she knew it was a miracle, a true miracle, her child had been found. Andrea had nothing but positive aspirations for Ana. She could see so much potential and life in her, and she could feel how happy Ana made her just with her presence. Ana did not view herself in the same way. She'd always had to hide her emotions in order to overcome. Andrea knew Anastasia's childhood had been rough, but she would never know the extent of the neglect and abuse Ana had endured. Andrea believed that God gave her back Anastasia for a reason, and that reason was to save her from something. What, she didn't understand, but that didn't matter. She was her mother, and she would go to the end of the earth for her even if Ana opposed. She did not desire to give her a lavish lifestyle and unrealistic praise. Ana's life had been a journey for sure, and her journey continued. It would be easy to ignore the reality that Ana had such a past. Past influences, past loves, and past emotions may carry over into her current life. She had the nature part down, she was genetically blessed, but the Peterson's had forever ruined the nurture influence on her life, at least until now. It hurt Andrea that Ana never knew how much she was loved as a child, never knew that her mother yearned for her. Andrea would sometimes hear Anastasia talk in her sleep. The first time it happened, Ana had been in their home only a week. It was near midnight, and Andrea was in bed working on her computer. She heard a voice and went to Ana's door. Andrea called Ana's name, but she didn't answer, so she walked to her bedside. Ana was asleep but talking, with tears running down her cheeks. She looked hot, and her brow was furrowed like she was uncomfortable. Andrea tried to wake her gently with no success. As she watched, Ana continued to talk and cry in broken words. Andrea sat on the side of her bed and put her hands on her arms. She tried to calm her. When this didn't work, she began to talk to her, "Ana, it's ok, I'm here, Ana." She didn't know if Ana could hear her or if she would recognize her voice. Ana sat up in bed and screamed,

"Momma," like someone was hurting her, then woke up. Andrea didn't think she was screaming for her. She knew she was likely screaming for Mrs. Peterson. All she knew was that whatever was happening was not good. When she woke, Ana looked relieved, and reached up for Andrea and said, "Mom? Mom, I was so scared." Andrea reassured her, hushed her, and held her until she fell back asleep. Ana didn't recall the dream the next day. Andrea realized then that the beautiful seventeen-year-old girl she saw as perfection had been hurt and left scarred. Andrea promised she would hold her until the hurt went away and the scars faded. She had just found her, and she would never leave her alone again.

Ana went to school that week and auditioned for theater on Thursday. She was chosen to read again on Friday. The show premiered sometime near the last week of school in mid-May. She hesitated even auditioning because she wanted to go back to the academy and see Jude graduate, which was the same week as the show. On Friday night, she got a call from Brittani that the parts had been posted online. Ana nervously checked the website and saw that she had, in fact, gotten the lead female role. She was happy but sad at the same time. She knew if she took the part, she definitely couldn't leave England to go see Jude in Virginia. Brittani was very excited for Ana, and she, too, had gotten a role in the play. Ana didn't know whether to tell her mother for fear she would expect her to take the role without even considering going to see Jude. Play practice began on Saturday afternoon at two o'clock. Ana had talked to Jude but had neglected to tell him about her being chosen for the role. The graduation ceremony and the play party were the same night as the final show. Ana couldn't tell her mom about her role yet, but if she found out, that wouldn't be good for Ana. Ana wanted to get a feel for what her mother might say if she asked her to go back to the U.S to see Jude, but she didn't want to divulge the truth about the play.

Andrea was already up morning when Ana woke at eight. Ana found her drinking coffee at the kitchen table, reading something on her iPad. Ana sat down with her own cup of coffee and asked, "Is there any way I could go to Virginia to see Jude graduate?"

Andrea looked at her and chose her words carefully. "That would depend on what the trip entailed and what your end of semester grades are."

"It would just be to see him graduate and then to go to the celebration afterward. I guess you could call it like a dinner then dance type thing."

"When is it?" Andrea asked.

"May tenth."

Andrea picked up her coffee and took a sip. She would have to talk to Phillip, but she felt it shouldn't be a problem. Of course, they would need to stay a few days at least to make the distance worth it. "Have you asked your dad?"

"No, I wanted to see what you would say."

"You have to ask your dad, and then we might talk about it."

"I could fly out on the Wednesday before the last day of school and be back on Saturday, or whenever you say you want me back home." Ana was trying to convince her mother. "I could stay with Natilee. Her parents will be there also."

Andrea laughed a little. "Ana, you will not be traveling to the United States by yourself. You're seventeen, are you crazy?"

"Well, are you going with me?"

"If we allow you to go, yes, I will be with you. Going alone would never fly with me, and with your dad, that idea would sink like a rock." Andrea shook her head.

"Well, is there a chance you would let me? I need a realistic answer."

"Right now, today, you need to know?" Andrea was curious why she needed a decision today. Ana looked like that wasn't the way she wanted the conversation to go.

"I'll ask Dad," Ana replied, then walked to the pantry for cereal. Ana sat down with her mom and ate. They didn't really have any plans today, but Ana knew she needed to be at the school at two o'clock if she wanted anything to do with the production. Drake was home, so she hoped she could spend some time with him doing something fun. She hasn't ridden all week and wondered if he would go with her. Ever since the Travis appearance on the road near the stables, her parents hadn't wanted her to visit the stables alone. It did get her out of working at the stables, but it limited her time there also. She had gotten a few texts from Travis, but she had ignored them. She didn't feel like it would be beneficial to keep in touch at all. She finished her breakfast and asked her mother if she could ride with Brittani to play practice.

"When will you know who got what parts?" Andrea asked her.

"Soon," Ana replied.

"I'll take you to the theatre. I need to stop by my office anyway and catch up on some work."

Phillip was home for the weekend and was playing golf in the afternoon with a friend, so Ana knew she should ask him soon before her mom talked to him. He was in the garage fiddling with some parts and some tools he had on a workbench. "Hey, Dad?" Ana said.

"Yes, dear."

"Am I off restriction?"

"I think you have until next weekend."

"Dad, you said I was on restriction until you said so, so you can make it when you want it." Ana smiled, thinking he had forgotten what he had said.

"Yes, I remember, next weekend it is."

"Dad?"

"Yes, Ana."

"You remember my friend Jude? He's graduating in six weeks, and I was wondering if I could go? I mean, if I have supervision." Ana stood staring at him, waiting on him to respond.

"For how long?"

"I was thinking maybe three or four days."

"Have you asked your mother?"

"Yes, she said to ask you."

"Well, if you have asked her, then let us discuss it, and we will let you know."

"Can you discuss it soon, so I can tell him if I can come?" she asked.

"We will talk about it before dinner," he said, trying to be open-minded to her request. He didn't want Ana going back to the U.S., but he realized she had close friends, and this was important to her. Her mother or Diane would have to go, of course, if she was permitted to go. Ana seemed happy they were going to consider her request and accepted the timeframe. Maybe she had matured some after the Travis ordeal.

Ana called Jude to tell him that her parents were at least considering a trip to see him graduate. After they hung up, Jude snapped a picture of himself smiling with big teeth, showing off his chest in his bathroom mirror. He had just had a haircut. She replied back with a selfie sitting outside on the covered porch. "You're so pretty," he replied.

"Thanks, you're pretty sexy with that haircut," she answered. Then he sent a picture of himself posing shirtless, flexing his muscles, almost laughing. Ana loved seeing him on her snaps. When her notification chimed, she was automatically excited. She replied mostly with selfies and texts but tried not to get too carried away with Snapchat. Her mom dropped her off at the theatre, and Ana waved goodbye. She dreaded talking to the director and hoped she wouldn't be mad and never consider her for another role. Although, it really didn't matter because she might be at St. Catherine's College next year if she could get all her credits from high school to transfer. When Ana walked in, the whole class started clapping. Ana thought it was a joke because she was a few minutes late, but it wasn't. Ana was embarrassed and sat down quickly. The director, Beth, said, "They are congratulating you on your leading role," and smiled.

Ana smiled back and said, "Thank you," in a meek voice. She wished she could disappear. How was she going to turn the role down after this? Ana listened as the director discussed the play practice schedule and the production dates. May 8th, 9th and 10th were the show dates, and Ana knew Jude's graduation was May 11th. There was no way she could get there in time. Ana was present for the meeting but wasn't mentally there. She was trying not to freak out, and her mind was spinning. Maybe she could miss the tenth and make it to his graduation, but she knew that would be wrong. She looked at the casting list in her hand. Under her name was listed an understudy, Lillie King. Ana looked at Lillie King, trying to justify what she was contemplating. At that time, it was the only solution that would allow her to please Jude, herself, her classmates, and her mother. She could just not show up for the last performance, and Lillie could take her place. It would be deceitful to conceal the details of the show dates from her mom, and there was no way in hell her mom would let her skip out on the last performance knowingly. She needed her mom to accompany her to the U.S., and there was no way she would go if she knew Ana was purposely skipping out. On the other hand, she thought maybe she could tell her mom the truth, that she would rather see Jude than be in the play. But she felt like her mom would not approve, then might not allow her to go see Jude at all. If she could keep the dates from them, she could have her parents come to the play the first or second night, then they could get on a plane the next day, and Ana could pretend she never missed it. But would it work? She needed advice, but she didn't trust her brother to keep this secret. She texted Brittani, "Hey, we have to talk." She met Brittani after the class, explained her dilemma and her possible solution.

"Do you think it will work? I mean, the play will be advertised, and if she sees the dates, you're screwed," Brittani said, being honest with her friend.

"I know, but if she stays away from the school, maybe she won't see anything, and maybe if she does, I can say the dates were changed," Ana said on a whim.

"Girl, you sure you want to do this?"

"I want to be in the play, and I want to see Jude. I have a replacement Brittani, Lilly. If I tell my mom I auditioned and then turned it down because of Jude, she'll get all disappointed and tell me I can't go. You know it's true."

"Yeah, I guess you're right."

"What if she finds out while you're in the U.S. or when you get home?" Brittani asked.

"I don't know. Maybe by then, it won't matter," Ana answered.

"What's she going to do to ground me? Ok, I can handle that," Ana said, making fun of her mother's effort to discipline her.

Brittani laughed. "Well, I need to enjoy seeing you while I can, because when she finds out you lied, you might be sent off like your brother." Brittani took Ana home. "Bye, friend, text me later." Ana shut the door and waved. She walked into the house where nobody seemed to be home. She walked up to her room and started googling airline tickets trying to think how she would get what she wanted without her mother finding out she was being manipulated.

CHAPTER THIRTEEN

The Plan

Drake had gone with his dad down to the stables. Ana wasn't home, and his dad wanted him to help check on the horses. Drake and Phillip rode home in the ATV. "Hey, son, what are you going to do this summer?" Phillip asked.

"I don't know. I guess I'll be here," Drake replied.

"How is school?"

"Fine, just ready for this year to be over. Hey Dad, look. Whose vehicle is that?" Drake had seen a blue truck pulled down off the road.

"I don't know?" Phillip said as he slowed. It was Travis's truck, and Drake recognized it once he got closer. From the road, you could see the truck, but they were unable to see much inside.

"Dad, that looks like Travis's truck." Drake wished it wasn't true.

"Really? What the bloody hell is he doing here?" Phillip turned in the direction of the truck and started to get out of the ATV.

"Dad, don't get out. You don't know. He may have a gun."

"Drake, don't be stupid," Phillip said, but he considered that Drake might be right.

"I think he's crazy if he's sitting here, so he could be crazy enough to have a gun," Drake said, sounding like he may be on to something. Phillip turned the ATV around, and they left. Drake didn't see any movement in the truck, but he had an eerie feeling that was hard to describe. "Are you going to tell Ana?" Drake asked.

"I don't want to scare her, but I think we should." Phillip pulled up to the back of the house, Ana was home, and Andrea was pulling in. "Hey, babe," Phillip said as she walked into the house.

"Hi, what have you two been doing?" Andrea asked.

"We just rode down to check on the horses," Phillip replied.

"Yeah, Mom, we saw Travis's truck parked on that back road out of sight," Drake said.

Andrea looked perplexed. "Really, I wonder what he is doing down there?"

"I don't know, but I didn't approach the truck, so I don't know if he was in it," Phillip said.

"That is weird. Do you think he's hunting?" Andrea asked.

"Yeah, sure is. Hunting tail," Drake said sarcastically.

"Drake, we don't need that. Ana is not involved with him anymore." Andrea said.

"Well, then he needs to go somewhere else. That is just weird," Drake said.

"I agree," Andrea said. They walked into the house and found Ana sitting in a chair talking to someone on FaceTime.

"Hello, Ana. Who are you talking to?" asked Phillip.

"It's Jude, Dad. Say hello." Phillip stepped into view, said hello, waved, and smiled.

"Hello, Sir, nice to meet you. I mean, virtually anyhow," Jude said, smiling. Phillip said "hello," and waved at Jude on the screen.

Phillip went to help Andrea with some bags she needed to be carried in. Ana finished up her call with Jude and started reading her script. "Ana, did you get the part you wanted," Drake asked.

"Yeah, I did," Ana said.

"That is great news. Great job, Ana," said Phillip.

Andrea walked in the door. "Did you say she got the part?" She looked very excited.

"Yeah, I got it," Ana said, smiling.

"That is wonderful. We should celebrate," Andrea said to them. Nellie joined them in the kitchen, and she and Andrea began discussing dinner plans. Andrea and Nellie started cooking while the kids and Phillip sat out on the patio.

"Hey Dad, remember you and mom are supposed to discuss me going to Jude's graduation," Ana reminded him.

"Oh yeah, that is right." He got up to join Andrea and Nellie in the kitchen.

"Good luck," Drake said.

"What do you mean by that? I'm almost an adult, so I could go on my own." Ana looked at him like he was stupid.

"I'm just saying there is no way. Mom is going to let you go by yourself to the U.S. to see a guy."

"Yeah, I know that dummy. She's coming with me."

"Still, I'll be surprised if they let you go."

"Well, you don't know everything, so I hope you're wrong," Ana said and smirked.

"Travis Ana, remember him? Yeah, that wasn't too long ago, and I know they haven't forgotten."

"Drake, I don't need to be reminded, and it isn't like you haven't ever done anything wrong."

"Well, I didn't get Dad called by some asshole he works with to tell him you're screwing some college kid." Drake was getting frustrated with his sister.

"Drake, why do you have to be such an ass? You know I didn't do that."

"I'm just saying it's not going to happen!"

"Shut up, Drake!" Ana said, almost shouting.

Andrea stepped out on the patio. She had overheard them from inside, and they looked like they were both frustrated. "What is going on out here?" She was waiting for an answer. "Speak." She looked at Ana and Drake, and they both started yelling at the same time.

"She's being bitchy, and I'm just trying to tell her," Drake said angrily.

"He's being an ass because he thinks he knows it all," Ana said with echoed anger.

Andrea stepped between the two, who were now standing, facing each other. Other than the fact that Drake was a few inches taller than Ana, they could have been twins. Andrea pushed them apart. "Stop it now, both of you shut up and sit down. Keep it up, and both of you will get your mouth washed out with soap," Andrea said, yelling over them. They both stopped. Drake was still mad, but he just stared at Ana. "Do we want to go there?" She looked at Ana, who was still focused on Drake and clearly furious.

"Your language is terrible." Ana huffed, turned around, and walked into the house.

Drake shook his blonde hair out of his face and said, "What?" and shrugged.

"What was that about?"

"Nothing important."

"Let's go; dinner is ready." Andrea softly slapped his shoulder. He gave her an annoyed look. She pointed at him then motioned back at her eyes with a look that said, I'm watching you. Andrea found Ana getting glasses out of the cupboard. "Ana, why were you yelling at your brother?"

"Nothing, it was stupid, Mom. Sorry," Ana said as she looked at Drake.

"Yeah, what she said," Drake said as he sat down.

Phillip responded, "Well, we know where they get their tempers from," as he looked at Andrea and smiled.

"Shut it, I had nothing to do with that," Andrea said, smiling. They all sat down to eat dinner.

"So, what is this play about Anastasia?" Phillip asked her.

"It was written by a classmate. It's like a twist on Cinderella, but modern. It's hard to describe. That's the best way I know how."

"Ok, that will be interesting. I'm excited to see you perform," Phillip said.

"When are the performances?" Andrea asked.

"They're around the first week of May, I think, the 7th or 8th,"

"Drake, will you be out of school then?" Phillip asked.

"Yes, I get out the week before," Drake replied.

They were finishing dinner when Ana asked, "Have you thought about the graduation?"

"We haven't. Do you want to discuss it now?" Andrea asked. Phillip and Andrea sat down at the island while Ana was clearing the table.

Phillip said, "Ana, I'm going. To be honest, I'm definitely not excited about you going all the way to the U.S."

"Yeah, I know, Dad, but this is for his graduation. We were in the program together. It's very important to both of us," Ana explained.

"I would be with her, of course," Andrea chimed in, "I guess it depends on your behavior and grades."

"My grades are great, and I'm so busy now I can hardly think about anything besides the play." Ana was hoping this would convince them.

"Yes, but the play isn't the same time we are planning on going, is it?" her mother asked.

"I don't think so." Ana hoped to move on quickly from that subject.

"If it is, Ana, you will have to see Jude another time because you've already made a commitment to the play," Andrea said.

Ana nodded as she made herself busy rinsing the dishes. "So I can go?" Ana asked hesitantly.

"Yes, you can go. But I can change my mind at any time depending on your behavior," Andrea warned.

"Yes, ma'am." Ana was elated with the news. She immediately went to call Jude to tell him.

Drake was in the den and overheard his parents talking. "Phillip, of course, I will watch her. Why do you think? I wouldn't allow her to go alone," Andrea said.

"Diane said she really likes this boy," Phillip replied.

"Yes, I know she does, but I do feel we need to let her have some friends from home. Phillip, her identity has been erased. All of her past wasn't bad, and she needs someone to connect with."

"Have you read those papers I gave you? Ana was in a terrible environment. Do you know the FBI busted her dad for trafficking drugs from the west coast to North Carolina? Did you know Ana was twelve and was holding a box of methamphetamines that was delivered? That her mom had her carry the box, and minutes later, the mobile home they were living in was swarmed with federal officers? Social services took Ana because her mother was in custody and wouldn't let Ana go back until the home had been cleaned from top to bottom. Ana saw her so-called father arrested when he pulled in the driveway, and Ana watched as the cops basically strip-searched her mother. I read this from an encounter with a guidance counselor who let Ana sit in her office when she showed up to school upset and was seen walking away from school. What I'm telling you is that she does not need to remember that life, Andrea. She is our daughter, and I don't want her to remember those events or feel those feelings ever again."

"Yes, dear, I have read that file, but I try to avoid thinking about those things. Phillip, it hurts me to think about that happening to her."

"I know it does, I feel the same, but the information given does show us some of what her life was like."

"Do you know how angry I am at that woman for taking my baby away from me and then damaging her?" Andrea was almost yelling and near tears.

"I'm sorry, dear. I didn't mean to upset you."

"Well, Jude is a good memory. She deserves a good memory, Philip. I want to give her that."

"I know, and you are a good mother. Don't second guess yourself. She needs you, and I am so proud of you. I know this had to be difficult." Philip hugged her into him. Drake had listened to the whole conversation and now felt a little different about his sister.

Ana spent the next five weeks busy with school, play practice, and spending time on the weekends at the stables. She felt apprehensive. She knew in her gut she was lying. Every time her mom mentioned the play or her performance, she had a sick feeling in her stomach. She tried to avoid the subject, but it always came up. Her parents were interested in her life, and that was something she was not used to. A few weeks before the play,

Andrea had taken her on a shopping trip to buy a dress for the party following Jude's graduation. Ana felt awkward getting undressed in front of her mother. "Ana, open the door. Quit being silly. You have nothing I have never seen," her mother said. Ana knew she was right and thought, she is my mom. It shouldn't be weird, and let it go. They spent the whole day out shopping with Charleigh.

"I'm excited for you, Ana. I remember my first formal; it was so fun. We danced like we knew how," Charleigh said.

"I don't know if Jude will dance, but maybe," Ana said.

"Well, you have to make him. No man dances to anything besides a slow song unless they've been drinking. Well, that is my experience," Andrea said.

"True. You get Dylan drunk, and he thinks he can move, but all he does is hump the air. One time, when we were dating, we were at a party, and he was really drunk. He started to dance, and I had to hold him up by his belt. I almost dropped him multiple times. That was the same night he got sick. Oh my god, I will never forget it. He evidently needed to puke, his friend told me, and I gagged him. Look at my finger. They are like Edward Scissorhands. I touched his tonsils. That's when I knew I was in love," Charleigh said, laughing.

"Really?" Ana asked.

"No, it's not lovely watching someone hurl. I was kidding. We dated for a long while before we were married. I met him when he was seventeen. We knew when we had been dating about a month or so. We would get married. I don't know how we knew, but we did."

"Ana, don't be hanging around friends like Charleigh. They will lead you to do bad things," Andrea said, joking with her friend.

"That's bull crap. I was a good kid. Then I grew up and realized I shouldn't have been so good." Charleigh laughed.

"I'm kidding, honey, chill out," Andrea said to Charleigh.

"So, tell me about this guy. Did you date in school? Were you serious?" Charleigh asked.

"No, we were close friends. The attraction was there, but we were both too scared to act on it until the day I had to leave with Aunt Diane," Ana replied.

"Diane said you two were very into each other. She said she had to make you get in the car," Andrea said.

"Do y'all share everything?" Ana asked, annoyed and embarrassed.

"Yes," said Charleigh laughing.

"But that was it until we went out the night before we left," Ana said.

"You went out with him before you left to come home?" Andrea asked, surprised.

"No, it wasn't a date or at least didn't start that way. You know Mom, it was when we got stuck, and Aunt Diane had to come find me," Ana said, trying to jog her memory.

"Oh, the night you didn't call until after curfew, and you had been drinking. You were stuck with a boy. Yes, I remember," Andrea recalled.

"Yeah, Aunt Diane accused me of having sex with Jude because my jeans were unbuttoned, crazy huh?" Ana said.

"Really?" Charleigh asked.

"She may have left out that part," Andrea said.

"Oh." Ana shut up. Andrea was glad she had not agreed to let her go alone to the U.S now more than ever. They rode home talking and laughing.

The play was at the end of the week, and Ana was so excited. Drake would be home tonight, and they would all eat dinner together. Her exams would start on Tuesday, and the play was on Thursday. Ana would pass all of her exams but was constantly reminded of her guilt for the lie she was maintaining. Ana believed in God. She had been saved at eight years old one Sunday morning when her grandmother had taken her to church. She remembered the plush red velvet-like material on the chair where she had laid her head to pray. To think of that now felt odd. How could an eight-year-old girl have such a heavy heart that she felt the need to surrender it to the Lord? Ana had been blessed with a conscience, a very sensitive one.

She was very unsuccessful at lying and was emotionally stricken when she did something wrong. Lying to her mom was causing an ulcer, or at least it felt that way. She didn't know when it had begun, but she did remember being four years old sitting in a bedroom looking up at two child-like angels placed on a wall. To Ana, those angels were watching her; they followed her wherever she went. Ana had been in some risky situations as a child, some she would never remember and some she shouldn't. Ana had had a grandmother and an aunt and uncle who had loved her all throughout her childhood. However, when her mother or father didn't benefit, Ana would not be allowed to see them. Ana's grandmother had instilled in her the value of doing the right thing and knowing what was right and wrong. In fact, Ana had been taught her entire life to do better than her parents. Ana did not hate the Petersons, and she could say that she had loved them, but not like a child should love its parents. It just wasn't there, and Ana felt guilty many times for not having those feelings. Ana's mother and father had not shared the same morals and values Ana had. Her mother was raised in church and had known God at one time but strayed away as a teen and hadn't found her way back while Ana had known her. Her father did not have a religious or spiritual bone in his body. She had seen sides of him that would make you think he was Satan himself. She had seen traits from both of her parents that had scared her into obeying their commands. Ana had separated herself from them years ago. She didn't think it was her doing but felt that God had pulled her away from them for a reason. Ana was tender-hearted. She loved to please those she loved, and to not do so was absolute mental torture for her. In time she would get over it, but Ana always apologized even if she wasn't the only guilty party.

On Tuesday evening, her mother made her a special meal. "Pasta is all carbs, but good brain food," her mother said as she prepared the Italian dish.

"Thanks, mom," Ana said as she took a plate from her mother. She ate in the kitchen with her mother, Drake, and Nellie. Her mother even made cookies, and they drank milk with them in the den.

"I know you're so excited for these exams to be over and the play, so we can fly to see Jude. You have a busy week," her mother said.

"I'm so ready for this week to be over, even the play, I am kind of nervous," Ana admitted.

"I would be," Drake said.

"You will be awesome, I know it. I heard one of my friends talking. Her daughter is your understudy. She said she is so excited to see you perform that the part was made for you, and that says a lot," her mother said.

"Really? I figured she would want me to break a leg, literally, so her daughter could take my role." Ana was now feeling even worse than before. She went to bed early that night. She talked to Brittany and told her what her mother had said.

"Oh girl, yeah, that is bad. This lie is going to kill you. You're miserable," Brittany said.

Andrea came in and kissed her goodnight. "Try to stay off your phone. You need your rest."

"Ok," Ana said, closing her eyes.

Andrea woke up at two a.m. and heard Ana in her room making crying noises. She went in and turned on the light. Ana was hot with sweat on her brow and arms. When Andrea touched her, she could feel how damp she was. Her brow was furrowed, and she was twisting in the bed like she was trying to get out of someone's hold. "Momma, I just want to--" Ana said, or that was all Andrea could make out.

Andrea tried to calm her. She put her hands on her arms and talked to her. "Anastasia, it's mom. I'm here. You're ok." Andrea held onto her.

"Mom, Jude doesn't know," Ana mumbled. Andrea realized then this dream was from the present.

"Ana, what doesn't he know?" her mother asked. Ana didn't answer but continued to flail. Andrea put a blanket over her and held it tight around her, securing her.

"It's ok, sleep dear." Ana finally stopped fighting. She appeared to be asleep, so Andrea pulled her blanket off and pulled her pajama top up over her head. She changed her into a dry shirt without Ana even waking. She couldn't leave her to sleep in a wet shirt. The next morning Ana woke up tired. She walked downstairs in her pajamas.

"You ok?" her mother asked.

"I'm really tired today, and I don't remember what I dreamed, but it was crazy," Ana said, pouring her coffee.

"You were having a vivid dream for sure and fighting in your sleep."

Ana looked confused. "I was?"

"Yes, do you remember me being in your room?"

"No, not at all. That is weird. Did you change my shirt?"

"Yes, you had sweated through the one you had on."

"Wow, I've never done that before."

"Yes, you have, dear. You have night terrors and talk in your sleep."

"Really, since when?" Ana asked, thinking her mother was lying.

"Since you've been here. You've had a few, at least four."

"What do I say in my dreams?"

"It's always different. Last night you said something about Jude not knowing something."

"Hmmm..."

"Yeah, what does he not know?" her mom asked.

Ana knew exactly what he didn't know. He didn't know she was planning to skip out on the final performance either. "I have no idea. Crazy, but I don't remember anything." At least that part was true.

CHAPTER FOURTEEN

The Production

The night before the premiere, Andrea and Diane stopped by to watch the final scenes of the play rehearsed. Ana didn't know they were there until the house lights came on. She looked out and saw her mom and Diane smiling and whispering to each other. The director asked Ana to stay on stage to rehearse her solo with her male co-star Byron. Andrea had no idea Ana was singing in the play and had never heard her sing other than in the car. Andrea's and Diane's presence made Ana extremely nervous, and she stalled on the first verse. Ana clasped her hands together and twisted her foot, trying to get it together. "She's nervous. We are making her nervous," Andrea said to Diane, considering leaving the theatre.

"Sit still. We won't be the only people here tomorrow, and she will have to deal with it then. Better to get it over with now," Diane said. The music started over, and Ana quietly began the first verse. After the first few words, she began to regain her composure. Byron looked at her. He was her lover in the play. Assuming his role and trying to ease her nerves, he pulled her hands apart, put them in his, and pulled her closer. Ana didn't see Byron. She saw Jude. She sang like she and Byron were the only people in the room. The scene ended in a kiss, and they gave each other a peck on the cheek that lasted longer than any of the others. The lights went down.

"That's it, great job. Whatever you did differently, Ana, keep doing that. Finally, you look like a couple instead of individuals," said the director. Byron smiled big and hugged Ana.

"You ok? I hope that was ok," he asked.

"Yeah, it was fine. I was in another world there for a minute."

"Well, whoever you pretended I was, keep it up," Byron said, laughing. Ana turned and left the stage to see her family.

"That was very good, dear. I'm sorry if we made you nervous," Andrea said.

"Yes, I had no idea you could sing," Diane said.

"I sang in chorus in middle school, but that's it," Ana replied. Andrea told Ana she and Diane were going home, and Diane wanted to see the dress she had bought for the party. "Ok, I should be there soon."

A classmate came up to Ana and asked, "Here is the final production of the program. Will you review it.?" Ana looked down and saw the dates of the production in bold, size twenty, Times New Roman font. Ana flipped the book over quickly and tried to act normal. She leaned over to hug her mother and aunt goodbye, holding the book behind her. They didn't seem too suspicious, but Andrea could tell Ana was acting different.

As they walked to the car, Andrea said, "I wonder what that was about. Why was Ana acting so weird?"

"I don't know. It was like she saw a ghost all of a sudden," Diane responded. They drove home, each lost in their own thoughts.

Ana arrived home an hour later. They were in her room when she walked in. "Hey love, I'm packing some of your things. I know you haven't had much time," Andrea said.

"Ok," Ana replied.

"Ana, I love this dress. You're going to look so beautiful. Too bad your mother and I won't be so dashing," Diane said. Diane and Andrea were both accompanying her to Jude's graduation and party. All parents and guests of the graduate were invited to both the graduation ceremony and dinner party after. From Ana's experience, it was very formal, at least for the graduates and their companions. Jude's parents had invited Andrea and Phillip, but Diane was going to take his place. Ana was relieved. She wasn't excited to have her dad around her boyfriend or the guy she was interested in being her boyfriend. Especially if she was going to be dancing with him, they talked about the play and about the trip, discussing details like shopping and spending time in Annapolis. Ana took a shower, and they were still in her room when she came out in her pajamas. Andrea was so proud of Ana and her performance.

"Ana, you did so well. I am so glad you got the part. The director is very pleased. He told me multiple times how happy he is to have you in the production," Andrea commented.

"Thanks, Mom, but Lillie is just as good as me," Ana said, trying to soften the blow they would feel later.

"Who is Lillie?" Diane asked.

"She's my understudy."

"She isn't as good, or she would have the role and not be the alternate, dear," Andrea said. Ana went downstairs, leaving them zipping her bags in her room.

"I don't know what is up with her, but you're right, something is," Diane said.

Andrea just looked at her, then stared at the floor, thinking. "I don't know, but I hope it's just nerves about the play," Diane said goodbye as she left out the front door. Ana was in the kitchen on her phone, texting Brittani.

Britt, I'm an idiot.

You're into it deep, huh.

Yep, IDK what to do.

Ana walked out on the patio for some air, leaving the door open. She felt like she was smothering, and she vomited in the grass. This sometimes happened when she was emotionally distraught. Ana was a terrible pucker and could not control the volume or force of her purging. Ana was bent over with her eyes closed, trying to catch her breath and not look at the vomit.

Andrea walked into the kitchen, but Ana wasn't there. The patio door was open, and she heard her outside. It sounded like she was sick. Andrea stepped outside and said, "Are you ok? Did you eat something that upset your stomach?"

Ana stood up, and Andrea handed her a towel to wipe her face. "No, I'm fine. I think it's just my nerves," blaming the upcoming play jitters for her vomiting." They walked back into the house.

"Are you sure there isn't something going on? You have acted really weird all evening," Andrea asked. Ana's phone beeped. "Brittani is texting you." Andrea read the short text and slid the phone to Ana. Andrea could tell Ana was upset but didn't know how to help her.

Ana's guilt was so heavy on her. She was crumbling underneath it. She walked up to her room, leaned on her bed, and said to herself, "I'm so stupid. How am I going to do this?" Ana wanted to tell her mother so badly, but she knew if she did, her chances of getting to see Jude was close to none. Andrea stopped by her room on her way to bed. She saw Ana leaned over her bed and wondered what she was doing. Andrea opened the door more, and Ana stood up quickly.

"Are you sure you're ok? Do you need to talk about something? I feel like you're miserable, and I can't help you if I don't know how, dear. Is it Jude or school?" Andrea asked, throwing out everything she could think of.

"No, I'm good, Mom, thank you." They said goodnight to each other, and Andrea kissed Ana's forehead. Ana felt like Judas like she was betraying Jesus. That thought almost made her scream out her confession, but she had to keep her mouth shut.

The next day was the first performance of the play. Ana left for school the next morning like always. She texted Jude all day. They talked about the party and planned their time together. Jude knew about Ana's role in the play, and he encouraged her daily. They texted so much Ana would often feel phantom vibrations from her phone.

Ana was very anxious about the show, and she could feel butterflies fluttering in her stomach. She felt like she had to pee a million times. Andrea and Charleigh came backstage to see her before the performance. Ana looked so good in her makeup and costume. Although she was so nervous, she was almost shaking. "Hey honey, how are you?" Andrea asked.

"Oh my god, Mom. I am so nervous. I could puke," Ana confessed.

"You will be fine. You just need a shot," Charleigh said, trying to be funny.

“Exactly right,” Ana said, smiling.

“Once you get on stage and begin, you will be fine,” Charleigh reassured her.

“You’ve got this. I am so proud of you.” Andrea said as she leaned over and hugged her goodbye. They waited for Phillip and Drake before they found their seats. Ana had almost forgotten about the programs until she looked up and saw one in front of her. Ana knew it was too late, so she just hoped her mother wouldn't pay attention. The curtain opened, and she went on stage. The lights were bright, but Byron found her, and that reassured her she was in the right place. After she began speaking, her nerves eased, and before she knew it, she was effortlessly performing her role. The first half was over quickly. It seemed like. During intermission, she peeked out to see her family, but they were not in their seats. For a minute, she worried they had never come at all. She shook her head, reminding herself that that was not her old life. Ana felt happy realizing that her old life was gone, and her new life was filled with people who loved and wanted her. Then she felt bad about lying, but it was time to go on stage, and she blocked those thoughts out of her mind.

Andrea and Charleigh waited on Drake and Phillip outside the theatre. Andrea had seen many people she knew and truthfully wished she could go in a side door. Luckily, it hadn’t been a big story when Ana had reappeared in their lives, and Andrea did not wish for any attention now. She thought most people probably didn’t even know why she was there, or maybe they did. Susan, a past coworker, asked what part Drake had in the play. Andrea didn't want to answer, so she just said, “You will see.”

Charleigh heard this and whispered, “Are you crazy? Now they will think Drake has turned into a transvestite,” and she laughed.

“Oh no, I didn’t think of that,” Andrea said, laughing also. Drake and Phillip joined them, and they went in as a family.

An usher met Phillip at the door and said, “Duke Hutchinson, will you please follow me to your seat?” Andrea looked up at Char, who was making fun of Phillip. They were seated in the center and up high enough to see perfectly. Diane and Jeffrey had already arrived and were waiting on them. She didn’t know why, but their section was roped off. Phillip was very nice, thanked the young man, and they all sat. Drake saw a few friends from school and waved.

"Mom, I'm going to go speak to Derek. I will be back," Drake said.

"Hurry, I want you over here before it starts."

Phillip murmured about how he was still hungry after only having a snack before they drove over to the theatre. The house lights turned down, and Drake came over. The play began, and Ana was in the first scene and almost every scene after. It seemed like the first half flew by to Andrea. Ana was so easy to watch, and her fellow actor was good as well. At intermission, Andrea and Charleigh went to get Phillip a snack. Somebody handed them a program, and they quickly made it back to their seats. Phillip was happy his food had appeared, and Drake was busy texting his friends. Andrea ate a spicy nacho chip and started to drink some water. Her mouth was full of water when she picked up the program to read it. May 8th, 9th, and 10th. Andrea spit out her drink and started to choke loudly. Charleigh got up, ready to do some type of life-saving maneuver. Andrea had a hard time communicating for a few seconds, and Phillip asked if she was ok. The whole auditorium looked up at her. She regained her composure and told Phillip she was fine. But she was not fine. She was shocked. She thought the play was only for two nights because that's what Ana had told her. They were leaving to go out of town on the tenth.

The second half of the play started. Andrea couldn't comprehend what was going on until Ana came on stage. She kept trying to convince herself that Ana didn't know that she was mistakenly misinformed, that Ana had not been paying attention. But Andrea knew better. Looking up at Ana, her heart grew warm. She wanted to praise her, but at the same time, she wanted to pull her off stage by her hair. Andrea watched her sing and was reminded how much of a girl she still was. She looked so soft and innocent on stage. Andrea tried not to treat her like a child, although sometimes she acted like one. Andrea was upset about Ana's betrayal, but she didn't want to ruin the event for everyone. It was the final scene, Ana was holding hands with her stage partner, and they kissed affectionately. Andrea's memory flashed back to Travis, and then she thought Jude. Drake looked over at her, raised his eyebrows, and smiled. Andrea whispered, "Hush." she knew he would say something smart and patronizing.

Phillip chimed in, "Wow, she must get that from her mom." Andrea rolled her eyes. They met Ana in the hallway, where the actors were greeting the audience. Drake gave her roses, and Ana seemed very happy. Andrea hugged her daughter and congratulated her on a job well done.

As Ana was chatting with Drake and Phillip, Andrea stared at Ana, trying to evaluate if Ana had any indication of her deceit. Charleigh said, "What is wrong with you? You look like you're having a stroke," and laughed.

"Shut up, I'll tell you later," Andrea whispered. Andrea told Phillip goodbye and pulled Charleigh outside to tell her about her discovery.

"So you think she lied to you? She's planning to skip the last night of the show so she could make her trip to see her boyfriend? That is sneaky, sounds like something I would do. But give her a break. You never know. Maybe she didn't know the dates," Charleigh said, giving Ana the benefit of the doubt. Andrea gave Charleigh, you've got to be kidding me, look.

"Ok yeah, she knew," Andrea said, "and it is something you would do, but it is stupid."

"What are you going to do?" Charleigh asked.

"I don't know. I really want to tear her head off, considering the whole theatre thought I was dying up there choking on my drink."

Charleigh laughed. "Yeah, I almost pissed my pants laughing at you. Your face was all red, and the vein in your forehead poked out. Then, you spit the drink out of your nose. Oh god, can you do that again?"

They got into their own cars and drove home. On the way, Charleigh called her. "You know, you should wait until after tomorrow's performance at least. I think she might confess."

"I might. I'm afraid if I tell her I discovered her lie, the next two performances may not be so good." Charleigh agreed and hung up. Andrea arrived home and went to eat a snack in the kitchen. Ana showed up around an hour later. She looked tired and hungry. She ate, and they all went to bed. Ana had two exams the next day, so sleep was important. Andrea kissed her on the head like always, and Ana returned her gesture. No sign of a confession to Andrea.

The next morning went as planned, except Andrea drove Ana to school so she could drive her home from the play. "I'll take you today. Then I can drive you home from the play tonight. Unless there is some type of end of production party or something, you're going to." Andrea was trying to pull Ana toward a confession.

"No, that's fine Mom, I'll ride with you." Andrea was getting more upset by the minute, and the worse part was it seemed like Ana didn't care. But Ana didn't know that her mother knew about her lie. School went as planned, Ana finished her exams and went to the theatre after school. Andrea went to the play that night, but Drake and Phillip had their own plans. Andrea sat in the theatre, watching Ana, and wondering how she had looked when she was two. What words did she say first? It still seemed so surreal that the beautiful teenager in front of her was her daughter. To look at mother and daughter, you would have no questions about their biological relationship. Andrea had no doubts as to whether Ana was her daughter or not. She knew that in her heart. Although the time they lost haunted her, and she felt cheated and that she had somehow let her daughter down. Parental guilt is a terrible thing and something that can't be avoided. It doesn't discriminate. Ana bowed, and the house gave a standing ovation. Ana was tired and hurried to the car. She breathed out a sigh of relief when she fastened her seat belt. "Hey, Mom," Ana said.

"You did well tonight, love. Sad, huh?" Andrea was fishing for a question.

Ana caught the hook and left it lying. "Thanks."

Andrea drove, her eyes focused on the road, but her mind was on Ana's lie. Ana just looked out the window, still unaware of her mother's knowledge of her deception. She thought she would go home and finish packing her bags to go see Jude. When they were ten minutes from home, Ana's phone alerted. It was Jude. So happy, can't wait to see your face. Andrea could read the name on the text. Ana replied with something similar. There were bubbles, and Jude replied with a Snapchat. Ana quickly opened her Snapchat. It was a picture of him posed like he was kissing with pursed lips. Ana laughed out loud. Andrea was becoming more and more irritated with Ana's absence of integrity. "What is so funny?" Andrea asked nicely.

"It's Jude. He's excited about our visit," Ana said, playing down her actual snap. Andrea didn't respond but tightened her grip on the steering wheel. She didn't know how much longer she could wait for Ana to confess. Charleigh texted her. Hey, you ok, Momma? Andrea let the words sink in. She wasn't ok. She was angry and hurt. She pulled over to the side of the road. "Mom, what are you doing?" Ana asked. Andrea parked the car. She was so mad she was shaking. Ana was confused and was getting nervous.

She didn't understand her mother's behavior. Andrea looked down at her hands on the steering wheel and attempted to compose herself. Ana looked over at her as she stared at the empty road in front of them, her hands gripped tight on the steering wheel. Ana sat silent, staring at her mother, not knowing what would happen next but hoping she hadn't been found out. Ana's phone alerted; it was Jude again on Snapchat. Ana hesitated before she opened the Snap. It was a picture of him with his service uniform behind him.

Andrea looked over at Ana, saw the picture, and said, "Tell him you're not coming."

Ana looked shocked. "Mom, what do you mean?"

Andrea reached inside her car door, pulled out the play program, and handed it to Ana. Ana took it from her mother and read the dates. She immediately turned her face to the passenger window attempting to avoid her mother. Andrea felt disrespected and said loudly, "I cannot believe how deceitful you have been. So tell me, were you just going to get on a plane tomorrow with me and leave all your classmates disappointed? Do you know how stupid I felt when I read the program and saw the dates of the production?"

Ana didn't know what to say, but she quickly realized she should have confessed. That would have been better than what she felt now. Ana didn't say anything. She just looked out the window. Andrea's patience was diminishing. "I'm sorry, Mom. I knew you would be mad, and I wanted to tell you, but I knew you wouldn't let me go, and I really wanted to go." Ana fidgeted with her fingers.

"Well, you are definitely not going now, young lady."

"Can we talk about it?"

Andrea pulled back onto the road. "You have had plenty of time to talk over the last few days. I thought we were past the lying, Anastasia."

"I know, and I planned on turning the part down, then I didn't, and I just let it keep going. I wanted to tell you, but I knew you would be upset and wouldn't let me go."

They pulled into the garage. Ana was right. Andrea wouldn't have let her go if she knew she had committed herself to the play. "Nellie has our dinner in the kitchen," Andrea said.

Ana felt numb. "I don't want dinner," she said and started up the stairs.

"You're eating dinner. It is not an option." Ana came back downstairs, dropping her bag at the bottom of the steps. The bag dropped loudly, and Andrea snapped her gaze to Ana with a look that showed her intolerance to Ana's attitude.

Nellie asked, "How was it?"

"It was fine," Ana replied.

"Are you ready for your trip tomorrow?" Nellie had no idea about recent events.

Ana looked up at her, and tears welled in her eyes. "I'm not going."

Andrea was at the refrigerator and turned around. "Because she has a show tomorrow night, I was unaware of."

"Was it a last-minute change or something?" Nellie asked, oblivious to Ana's scheme.

"No, Ana has been scheming this plan for the past month. She thought it would be ok to just leave her friends hanging so she could go see her boyfriend." Ana didn't say anything in her defense. "I found out last night in front of the whole world at the theatre. I was in shock when I read that program." Ana started to get up from the table. "Excuse me?"

"May I be excused from the table," Ana asked, looking up from her chair.

"Yes, I will be up to talk to you before bed." Ana got up from the table, placed her bowl on the counter, and left the kitchen without another word. Andrea watched her go shaking her head. Nellie picked up Ana's bowl and walked to the sink.

"Oh lord Andrea, what are you going to do?" Nellie asked.

"I don't know. I really don't know," Andrea said, putting her head in her hands.

In her room, Ana called Brittani and started to explain how her mother had discovered her lie. "What is she going to do?" asked Brittani.

"I don't know, but she isn't letting me go anywhere. I don't want to tell Jude."

"What are you going to do?"

"I want to go. I want to get on a plane and leave."

"Ana, are you nuts? You can't do that. They will hunt you down."

"I don't even care right now. I'm so mad."

"Yeah, I know you're pissed. Are you going to do the show tomorrow?"

"Not if I'm leaving."

"You're not serious?"

"Why not? What do I have to lose? I know the information to change my ticket. It's saved on the computer in the office."

"I don't think you can fly underage without permission from a parent." Brittani was trying to discourage her.

"Well, then I will have to see, won't I?" Ana got off the phone and got ready for bed. She was angry, not just at her mother but at herself and the whole situation. She didn't know what she wanted, but she knew she wanted to see Jude. Andrea came into her room when she was brushing her teeth.

"Ana, did you tell Jude we weren't coming?"

"No, I don't want to. So, you're really not going to let me go after we bought my dress, and we have hotel and airline tickets?"

"Why would I let you go? You deliberately lied for the last month and a half. You had plenty of opportunities to tell me. Evidently, you are so infatuated with Jude you would do anything, no matter the consequences."

"That's not how it is. I wanted to tell you, but I knew you would make me do the right thing, and I wouldn't get to go." Ana was angry.

"You said it. The right thing is to finish what you started. You are not going, and that is final. You are finishing the play."

"You don't understand," Ana said, rolling her eyes.

"Understand what, that you want to spend time with a guy?"

"You don't get it. He isn't just a guy. He's awesome, and he's leaving, and I may never see him again." Ana turned around and started to cry.

"Ana, you did this to yourself. Did you really think you would get away with it, that I wouldn't find out?" her mother asked.

"I don't know," Ana admitted.

"That was very selfish behavior."

"Maybe, but you're being selfish. You're the one not letting me go, and I think it's because you know I would rather be with him."

"Well, let me clear that up for you. I am not allowing you to go because you lied and schemed this whole situation up, and that is wrong. And I am not selfish. You are my child, you live here, and you will stay here. I do not care where you would rather be." Andrea leaned toward her.

"You can't control me," Ana shouted.

"Yes, I can, and I will, young lady!" Andrea shouted back at her. "Give me your phone."

Ana handed it to her. "Here, you can have it, here's my laptop and iPad too. I'm sure that's what is coming next."

"Ana, I am warning you." Ana sat on her bed and pouted but didn't say anything. "Go to bed. You have school tomorrow. Do not leave this house. I mean it." Andrea slammed the door behind her. Ana was angry, and she did want to leave. She wanted to go back to the Academy, and to Jude, and to her life when she felt free. Now, she felt like she was trapped. She sat in her window that night and looked out at the field below her. She could see part of the stables below. She wished she could go there, get on a horse, and ride as fast as she could away from here. There was a light on at the main stable. They always left it on for the horses. It had been two hours since her mom had slammed her door, so she had to be asleep by now. Ana thought she could sneak out to go see the horses and be back before anyone would know. She heard her mom say not to leave, but she really wasn't leaving. She would be back. Ana went to her door and opened it. She saw the light from her mom's room was off. She dressed, grabbed her slip-on boots, and snuck down the stairs closing the doors softly behind her. Once outside, she let her eyes adjust. She didn't have her phone as a flashlight, so she used her night vision. This reminded her of when she did land navigation at night at the academy. The moon was bright, so it was easy. She walked down to the barn and opened the doors. The mare walked up to her, and Ana petted her face gently then placed her head up to the horses. She loved the smell of them and how peaceful they were. She needed their peace right now. She walked to the last stall to see her dad's horse, Shotsley, and something caught her eye out the stall window. She wasn't sure, but she could see something in the distance beyond the fence. Ana stood still, hidden in the darkness of the stall.

The horse whinnied, Ana whispered to her, "What is it, girl?" Ana asked. She knew horses had keen senses. She backed up, her hands on Shotsley's neck. She saw something walking in front of what looked like a vehicle. The interior light was on in the vehicle. She wanted to leave but didn't want to leave the security of the stables. She waited. If she would have had her phone, she would have called her dad or Jeffery. This was not a good idea. I shouldn't be here. She thought. After what seemed like a long time, she saw the lights of a vehicle drive away very slowly. She attached a rope to Shotsley's halter and jumped on her back. She left the barn on the black horse riding swiftly to her house. She jumped off at the house and looked back, no lights. She sighed a sigh of relief and un-tied the rope. She patted the horse and took the rope with her back in the house, carefully.

The next morning Ana overslept, and her mom came in to wake her. "Ana, get up. You're going to be late." Ana was tired, and school seemed so wrong. Either way, she got up and dressed. As she went down the stairs, she heard her mother say, "You can eat this in the car," as she handed her a bagel and a bottle of water.

"Thanks," Ana replied as she shoved the bagel in her mouth.

Andrea cranked her car, and Ana knocked on her window. Andrea rolled the window down. "What?" she asked.

"Can I have my keys?" Ana asked, holding her food and bookbag.

"Ha, no way. Get in. I'm taking you to school. I would hate for you to miss anything."

"Really, Mom?" Andrea ignored her and honked the horn.

Ana looked at her mom and threw her hands up, and said, "Oh my God, really?" Ana plopped down in the seat and put her bag on the floorboard.

"Can I have my phone?" Ana asked.

"Yes, but you have to call Jude and tell him you're not coming. It isn't right to tell him."

"What do I say? Sorry, Jude, my mom won't let me come even though she told me I could, and we bought a dress for the party. How stupid is that?" Ana crossed her arms and huffed.

Andrea thought, is this ever going to end? Is this how daughters treat their mothers?

"Anastasia, tell him the truth."

"Mom, that sounds like I'm a child. I don't see why we can't go. Who cares about the play? I have an understudy. She knows the part."

"You don't do that. You made a commitment, and you're going to fulfill your obligation."

"You should let me make my own choices. It is my life." Ana stared out the window at a kid standing on the sidewalk waiting on the school bus.

"Ana, I know you probably did not have parents that told you what to do or not do. I know you did what you wanted. But I am your mother, and If you make bad choices, young lady, it's my job to correct you and teach you that your actions have consequences and to make wise choices."

"I hate it when you call me that, don't call me that," Ana said.

"So now you're angry, and you're going to pout," Andrea said as she parked the car at school.

Ana wiped her eyes. That comment made her angry, and yes, Ana was a pouter. "I don't know why I don't get on a plane and go anyway," Ana said as if it were a threat.

"Because you know I would come get you and bring you home. And, your father and I would be very upset, to say the least."

"You make me so mad. I don't know why I even care." Ana was breathing away her tears, trying to calm herself.

"Because you know I am right, and you care because I'm your mother. I love you, and you love me." Andrea turned to her and pulled her close to hug her.

"This is my fault. I really screwed this up. But now Jude is going to be crushed." Ana sobbed with big tears streaming down her face. Andrea wiped Ana's tears away with her thumbs, and she smiled. Ana smiled back. It was true, Ana did love her more than she ever thought was possible, and she couldn't really explain why other than the obvious.

Andrea didn't think she was wrong with how she raised her children, although she did have moments when her anger got out of control. She remembered slapping Ana in the face and how Ana reacted. Andrea was so mad. She could remember the anger on her face. She remembered leaving Ana at the kitchen table crying with a red cheek. She got in her car, shaking as she tried to calm herself. For a minute, Andrea reminded herself of her mother. Andrea had been slapped in the face many times growing up, and she remembered how humiliated she felt. On the day she slapped Ana, Andrea had cried all the way into work. Not because Ana was wrong, but because of her actions as a parent. Today, Andrea went to work with plans to meet Diane for dinner.

CHAPTER FIFTEEN

Supervision

Ana called Jude at lunch and told him the bad news. She told him she couldn't come because of the play. He sounded like he understood, although she knew he was disappointed. Ana apologized over and over again, but Jude just grew more and more silent on the other end of the phone. Ana performed that night just like the others, but she was very sad. She kept thinking about how she could have been spending the evening with Jude and how happy she would have been with him. Ana gathered her things from the theatre and walked with her mother and aunt to the car. "Ana, you did so well. Thank you again for playing this most important role. I know it was a lot for you being new, but you really put yourself out there," the director said to Ana in the parking lot. He then turned to Diane and Andrea. "I know you must be very proud of her." They both smiled and said that they were. Ana felt that like a kick to the gut. The three of them rode home.

"You did well. You should be proud of that," Diane said to Ana.

"Yeah," Ana said softly. When they walked into the house, Phillip was waiting on them in the foyer. "How was it, ladies?"

Andrea kissed him on the cheek and softly said, "Fine, but I think someone isn't very happy." He looked at Ana and raised his eyebrows. Drake was standing in the kitchen, watching them.

Ana stood with her bag in her hand and asked her father, "May I be excused to my room?"

"Yes," he said. Ana stopped and handed her mother, her iPhone.

"Did you call him?" she asked Ana.

"Yes, ma'am." Ana walked up the steps to her room.

"Mom, what's wrong with her?" Drake asked as he ate cereal.

"She's upset because of her trip."

"So, you didn't let her go because she lied? And you took her car and her phone?"

"No, I didn't take her phone."

"Then why did she give it to you? That was stupid."

Andrea looked at him and shrugged. "Maybe she feels like she doesn't deserve it."

At 9:30 p.m., Andrea went to Ana's room. She was sitting on the floor near her closet. Her arms were around her knees, just staring at the wall. "May I come in?" her mother asked.

"Yes," Ana said, then stood up.

"Your father and I are going out of town tomorrow, but we'll be back by dinner. Would you like to go with us?"

"No, I'm good," Ana replied.

"Hmm, ok. I will let Diane know you will be with her until we get home."

"Won't Nellie or Drake be here?"

"He's going with his friends, and Nellie won't be here all day. We can't leave you unsupervised," her mother said. Usually, Ana would have argued, but she understood her mother's trust in her was gone. Ana nodded and looked down at the floor. "You should go to bed, dear?" Ana walked over to her bed and laid down. Her mother kissed her head and said, "I love you, goodnight."

Ana replied, "I love you." Andrea turned the lights off and left the door cracked. Andrea was disturbed by Ana's behavior. It wasn't like her to pout that long. Andrea worked in her office until almost midnight, then went to the kitchen for a drink. She peeked in on both her kids. Drake was asleep with his TV on as usual. When she looked in on Ana, she wasn't in her bed but laying in a ball near the closet asleep. It puzzled Andrea. She went in, woke her softly, and put her back to bed.

The next day she awoke early. She went to wake Ana, but she wasn't in bed. She was downstairs in the kitchen with Nellie. "Wow, you're up early," her father said. Ana smiled in response.

"You may need some old clothes. Never mind, those are fine. Diane is working in her garden today," her mother said, smiling at her. Ana looked down at her clothes, then at her mom.

"Andrea, I can take Ana over when I leave around ten. It would be no trouble," Nellie offered.

"We will take her, thank you though," Andrea said. When they dropped her off, Andrea said, "Wait, I will walk you in. Here's your phone in case you need us." Andrea walked her in, Diane and Jeff were sitting at the table.

"Have fun. She will be just fine," Diane said to Andrea as she left.

What am I eight? Ana thought but didn't say. Ana said good morning to her aunt and uncle as they finished their breakfast.

"Good morning to you, Ana, come sit and have some tea," her aunt said. "I'm going to be doing some landscaping today if you want to help."

"Castin is coming over around nine. He's going to help me unload some of the stone," Jeffrey informed Diane.

"Oh great, that will save your back," she said.

Jeffrey got up and walked toward the door, "See you, ladies, soon." Ana and Diane waved. Ana drank her tea and ate some fruit.

"Ana, are you ok?" Diane asked.

"Why?" Ana asked.

"Well, your mom said you didn't want to go with them, so I wondered if you were upset."

"Not specifically at them. I just didn't feel like going, that's all."

"I bet you weren't expecting to be here on a Saturday."

"No, and I'm sorry you got stuck supervising me." Ana used air quotes around the word supervising.

"You know it's part of it, and even if you were not being punished, they wouldn't want you home alone. Are you ok, though? I know you're upset about your trip."

"I'll be ok, but I'm upset because I lost my friend." Diane looked confused. "He won't respond to me since I told him I wasn't coming."

"Oh, I am sorry. But maybe he'll come around. Come on. You need different clothes."

"Mom said these were fine."

"Mom doesn't work outside much, does she?" Diane said with a laugh. Ana smiled and followed Diane to Laurel's room. "Here, you can wear some of Laurel's old stuff. It should fit. Here, wear these boots. You can't wear your shoes in the mud." Ana had never been in Laurel's room before. It was a lot like her own. There were pictures of her and a guy on the dresser and one of her and her mother.

"Who is this guy, her boyfriend?" Ana asked.

"No, they never dated. That's Castin. He's one of her good friends," Diane explained. Ana thought he was handsome.

"Where is Laurel, Aunt Diane?"

"She's at college. She's been there about a year and a half now."

"Why didn't you send her to St. Mary's?"

"We did, and then she got into some trouble and had to go away for a while. She came back home after that and is now studying at a college about four hours from here. She is doing well now."

"Are you close to her, like we are?"

"I think we were at one time, and maybe will be again. It's an age thing, I think." Diane put her arm around Ana.

"I don't ever want to be far from you. I love you."

"Sweet Ana, if you leave me, I will come find you. I love you like you are my own." This made Ana happy.

They went outside, and Diane showed Ana what the plans were. Ana put her phone in the back pocket of her jeans and played music while she worked. The sun shining around the dew-covered blades of grass was beautiful. "This is the day that the Lord hath made," Ana said to herself, not aware her aunt was close behind her.

"That's correct, seize the day. Doesn't it feel good to be out here with your hands in the dirt?"

Ana laughed at Diane's dorky tone and said, "Yes, it does actually. You sound like a hippie."

"Well, I kind of was a little bit hippie when I was a teenager. As much as I could get by with anyhow."

"Did you smoke weed?" Ana asked.

"Well, just dive right into the hard questions, huh?"

"Well, it isn't a big deal. I know a lot of people that have."

"I did try it a few times, but it was never my thing."

"Did my dad or mom?"

"That's not for me to answer," Diane said. "But, to my knowledge, they were not into it." Diane laughed. It was nine-thirty when Ana saw a vehicle. "That must be Castin to help Jeffrey," Diane said. "I will be back."

Ana pushed her hair out of her eyes. She was on her knees deep in a flower bed when a boy walked up. "Laurel, is that you? Oh, sorry, my bad. I thought you were -- Is Diane or Jeffrey here?" the boy asked her.

"Oh yeah, she'll be right out," Ana said.

"Ok, I'll walk around the house," Castin said, but he couldn't stop looking at her. Ana gave him a shy smile that he returned. Ana rubbed her face and realized there was a smudge of dirt on her cheek. Ana rolled her eyes. The one time she sees a cute guy, and she's knee-deep in the dirt. Ana kept working, and Diane returned.

"Where did he go?" she asked Ana.

"That way, I think I freaked him out."

"Oh, don't be silly." Diane walked around the house. She returned in just a few minutes. "I found them. Come on. I need your help." Ana stood up, and without realizing it, dropped her phone in the dirt. "We have to unload these stones. Castin will lift the big ones. Don't hurt yourself." Ana began carrying the rocks from the truck to the side of the yard. She was a hard worker, and her aunt was impressed, so were Castin and Jeff. It took what felt like an hour to unload them all. "Let's take a break. Ana, come with me to the house. We'll get some snacks ready." Ana didn't say anything. She just followed her aunt.

When they walked away, Castin said to Jeffrey, "Who is that? I thought it was Laurel from a distance."

Jeffrey laughed. "That is Anastasia, our niece."

"Oh, that's her," he said softly. The guys went up to the house to have a snack. Ana helped Diane prepare some finger foods and lemonade.

"Take these out on the patio, please," Diane asked Ana as she handed her two plates.

"Diane, you didn't introduce Castin," Jeffrey said.

"Oh, I'm sorry. Castin, this is Anastasia, Ana, this is Castin," Diane said.

"We have met," Ana replied and smiled.

After a short time resting, Diane said, "Well, it's still early, and we have a lot to do. Come on, Ana." Ana followed her away from the patio.

"She doesn't talk much," Castin said to Jeffrey.

"She does if you get to know her," Jeffrey replied.

Ana went back to the flower bed and saw her phone on the ground. She picked it up and had missed a phone call from her mom almost two hours ago. "Mom called," Ana said.

"You better call her back. She will be worried," Diane said.

"Why will she worry? I'm here?"

"Because mothers do that, they worry."

Ana called her mom. "Hey," Ana said.

"Are you ok? I called nearly two hours ago," her mother said.

"I'm fine. I just dropped my phone when we went to help Castin with the rock. Sorry."

"Ok, well, I was just checking in. You seemed a little off this morning, and I was worried when you didn't answer."

"I'm good. It's almost time for lunch, then it will be nap time, then recess," Ana said sarcastically.

"It sounds like you're enjoying yourself. I'm glad you're taking this well. See you when we get home." Ana hung up the phone and shook her head.

"What's wrong?" Diane asked.

"Nothing, I think mom thinks I'm a basket case."

"Nah, she just worries about you. Castin, are you heading out?"

"No, I think I will stick around and help Jeffrey a while if that's ok?" he said.

Diane was curious as to why he was staying, then realized she had a pretty niece in her garden. "Sure," Diane said. Ana smiled at Diane. Ana worked with Diane, and Castin worked with Jeffrey. Occasionally their paths crossed, and Castin took every opportunity to fetch what Diane or Ana needed, so he could talk to Ana. They all had lunch on the patio.

Jeffrey had to go into town. Then he was going down to the barn. "Castin, meet me at the barn in thirty minutes," Jeffrey said.

"Yes, Sir," Castin said, sitting on the patio with Ana. "Do you like it here?" he asked Ana.

"Yes, I do."

"What's your favorite part?"

"The horses."

"Do you ride?"

"Yeah. Do you?" Ana asked him.

"Yes, we should ride sometime," Castin suggested.

"Yeah, maybe." Ana was thinking that wouldn't be happening anytime soon. Diane was in the house on the phone. "Aunt Diane, may I walk to the barn with Castin?" Ana asked aware her aunt knew Jeffrey would be there also.

Diane said, "Sure," clearly engrossed in the phone call. They walked to the barn and were almost there when Diane rode up on the ATV.

Ana thought it figured she would show up. She didn't trust her either. They worked with the horses, and Ana enjoyed talking to Castin. Andrea called Diane and Ana heard her say they would bring her home. "Ana, your parents want you home. I told her we would bring you," Diane said.

"I can walk her or take her on your ATV if you want," Castin said eagerly.

Diane looked at Ana, knowing that wasn't a good idea. "That may not go over well," Ana said.

"Oh, ok," Castin said, feeling awkward and sorry for asking.

"Come on, Ana. Castin can drive us both," Diane said.

"Ok, that's great," Castin said, smiling. He drove them to Ana's. Diane and Ana went in, and Castin said he would stay on the ATV. Ana thanked him softly.

When they walked in, Andrea said, "Wow, you have been working. You are filthy."

"I'll go shower," Ana said. She leaned over and kissed Diane's cheek before going upstairs. Diane patted her of the butt as she went up the stairs.

"How was she today?" Andrea asked.

"She was ok, but she's upset because Jude has unfriended her."

"Is that Castin Summer's on your ATV?" Andrea asked.

"Yes, he helped us today. Don't worry. I didn't let them out of my sight."

"Yeah, that's all she needs is another boy in her life."

"Yes, I know. He wanted to bring her home, but Ana declined the offer before I could refuse."

"Really? That doesn't seem like her."

"She isn't stupid, Andy. She lost her best friend from home because of her own actions, and she knows you have no trust in her."

"Did she say something to you about me not trusting her?"

"No, but you won't leave her alone in her own house. I think she gets it."

"Well, do you blame me? You did the same to Laurel," Andrea said defensively.

"I don't blame you. You are her mother. You have to protect her." Diane smiled then hugged her. "Parenting isn't easy."

They said goodbye, and Diane left with Castin. Andrea waited for her daughter. Then they had dinner together as a family. Ana was tired, so she didn't say much at dinner. "Did you talk to Jude today?" her mother asked as they finished their meal.

Phillip looked at Ana. "No," Ana said.

"What are your plans tomorrow?" her mom asked, trying to change the subject.

"I haven't made any."

"Maybe we can do something fun as a family." her mother suggested.

The next morning the family went boating at a lake. It was so nice to get out of the house. Drake brought a friend along named Janna, although she was younger. Ana just chilled, reading a book. Andrea hung close to Ana, as always. "I saw Castin last night," Andrea said.

"Yeah, he's a nice guy," Ana said, looking through her sunglasses.

"I heard he wanted to walk you home." She smiled at Ana.

"Yeah, we walked to the barn together, so I figured that's why he thought it would be ok. Don't worry mom. Aunt Diane was behind us on the ATV. I was supervised."

"Oh, I didn't say anything. Have you talked to Brittani?"

"Not today. They had something planned." Andrea didn't like seeing Ana so down. She would check her phone, then throw it on the boat seat like she wasn't getting the response she desired.

"Hey Ana, do you want to come with Drake and me later? We are going to a music festival about an hour from here," Janna asked.

Ana thought about it but didn't want to be the third wheel. "My friend is coming over later, but thanks," she lied to Janna. Drake was clearly attracted to Janna. He would sit close to her and smile at her often. Ana just watched and wondered how it would be if she had a boyfriend. She wondered if she could bring him on the boat and to the house.

When they got back to shore, Ana went to the bathroom. "Mom, I'm going with Janna, remember? I'll be home by eleven," Drake said.

"Did you ask your sister if she wanted to go?" his mom asked.

"Yeah, she said she has a friend coming over." Drake shrugged and walked to his car. Drake knew it was probably a lie, but he didn't want Ana tagging along on his date any more than she wanted to go.

Brittani called the next day and told Ana about a party for the cast of the play. "You have to come. Everyone will be expecting you," Brittani said.

Ana knew it was a long shot, but she had to ask. She was desperate to do something besides think about how much she hurt Jude. Andrea was in the kitchen. Ana approached her. "Mom, may I go with Brittani to a cast party tonight?" Ana asked.

Her mom was arranging flowers in a vase. "Tonight? It's Monday."

"It's summer, Mom. Never mind, I should have just told her no when she asked." Ana walked away.

"Wait a minute. You're making me out to be a tyrant. Where is it?" she asked.

"Jake Summer's house," Ana answered.

"Will there be adults there?"

"His parents will be there."

"Isn't he younger?" her mother asked.

"Yeah, but that is where it is. I don't know him," Ana said.

"I can go?" Ana asked, surprised.

"Yes, but home by eleven, phone on, and no drinking and driving. I would say no drinking, but that is unrealistic. Use good judgment."

CHAPTER SIXTEEN

The Party

Brittani knew Ana was upset and wanted to get her mind off of Jude. When they got in the car, she handed Ana a beer. Ana said, "Thank you, I need about two more of these."

Brittani laughed. "There will be plenty over at Jake's house. Ana, you need to relax. You've been working your ass off. You were amazing in the production. Wow, you and Byron really were into it, huh?"

Ana laughed. "Yeah, I was pretending he was Jude." Brittani drove towards Ana's house. "Hey, where are we going?" Ana asked.

"Jake lives near you, duh," Brittani answered.

"Really? I didn't know. Wait, his parents know my aunt and uncle pretty good, right?"

"Yeah, I think so. I think Jake's brother used to be good friends with their daughter."

"Huh," Ana responded.

"Where is Laurel anyway?" Brittani asked.

"At college, that's all I know."

"Laurel was a wild child," Brittani said smiling, "and you kind of look like her."

"Well, maybe I am like her," Ana said as she finished her beer. They passed the stables. It was empty with no cars. Ana looked for the area where she had seen the lights a couple of nights before. When they passed by, it looked like someone had parked and thrown empty beer bottles out of their vehicle. Ana thought that was weird, but she didn't mention it to Brittani.

When they got to the party, Ana was greeted by Jake's mom, his older brother Castin. Ana looked at Brittani. "Hey, Ana," Castin said and smiled. Brittani gave Ana a questioning look. Ana hadn't realized Jake was Castin's brother, but she was sure glad he was. Castin was cute, tall, and kind of thick but not fat, and he had blondish-brown hair. He had a really pretty smile, and he seemed like a good guy. One that would take you home when you were drunk without expecting a favor in return. Jake was outside on the patio, and there were already quite a few people there. He had a fire going in the fire pit, and guys were standing around with red cups, obviously drinking. "How do you know Castin?" she asked Ana.

"I met him at my aunt's house the other day. We carried rocks together."

"You did what?"

"We helped my aunt with her landscaping," Ana explained.

"Oh, ok, well here. You want a drink?" Brittani asked.

"Ah yeah. They're all drinking, I assume?' Ana pointed out at the crowd of teens.

"Yes, the Summers' don't care. They just don't want people driving home. A lot of kids sleep over in their basement or camp in the field behind their house."

"Really? My mom would never allow that."

"Yeah, mine either, but boys are different, I guess."

"Yeah, I guess it doesn't look bad if they get drunk and have sex with different girls." They went downstairs and poured themselves a beer. Soon they were mingling with the other cast members. Around eight o'clock, some other teens started playing a drinking game called "Never have I ever."

"So, you drink if you haven't done it, right?" Ana asked.

"Yea," Brittani answered. They were sitting around the fire. The group was a mix of guys and girls sitting on blankets. They all had beer or some kind of alcohol.

Jake started. "Never have I ever stole something." Ana drank. Then it was, never have I ever kissed someone at school. Ana drank.

Brittani said, "No silly, you kissed Byron in the play." The next one was, never have I ever kissed a friend. Ana didn't drink.

"Never have I ever had sex," a girl shouted out. Ana drank, so did Brittani, and everyone else watched. The girls just looked at each other, feeling somewhat embarrassed. "Oh, what good girls," the same girl said.

"Shut up, Elizabeth, you're just a whore," Brittani said.

"Oh, really?" Elizabeth said.

Castin came over to Brittani and Ana, "Come on, girls, this game is stupid."

"Yeah, Brittani, cool it. You're going to get us in a fight," Ana said. Castin walked the girls to the basement, where a group of kids was funneling beers. "You want to try?" Ana asked Brittani. Ana and Brittani drank two beers easily. Ana said, "Yeah, one more, I guess, but remember, I'm on probation. I'm already buzzed." Brittani agreed, so they stood around and talked to different people and played games with the boys.

It was getting close to Ana's curfew, and Brittani said, "I really want to stay."

"Me too," Ana agreed.

"Call your mom."

"No way, she won't let me."

"She let you come here, and you didn't think that would happen."

"True," Ana said. Ana walked out of sight and called her mom. "Mom, everyone here is sleeping over. Can I sleep over as well?"

"Ana, I am sorry. I can't allow you to sleep over."

"That's what I thought."

"Is Brittani staying?" her mother asked.

"I'm not sure."

"Ok, be home at eleven."

Ana went to look for Brittani but couldn't find her. Castin walked up, and they started talking. "You know, my house is right over there," Ana said.

"I know, we have a trail to your house through the forest," Castin said, "We should walk it sometime?"

"Yeah, we should." Ana got another beer, and they sat down on an old bench looking out towards Ana's house. There were people all around them, but to Ana, it was only them. Ana thought he was very attractive and mature. Ana was feeling the alcohol, and she was enjoying the feeling. "Thanks for saving us from that girl."

"Sure, that game is stupid. I just wanted to get you away from the crowd," he said, smiling.

"Well, it worked. We should have played truth or dare."

"Yeah," he agreed playfully, "we could play. Do you want to?"

"Truth or dare?" Ana asked him.

"Truth," he replied, "Is it true I really want to kiss you?"

"That isn't how you play. You ask me a question, silly," Ana laughed. "Come on, I better check on Brittani." They walked into the dark basement. It was empty. Everyone was outside.

Ana said, "Dare."

"Huh," he answered.

"I dare you to kiss me," Ana said. Castin closed the door and kissed her quickly. "That was awesome. Will you do it again?" Ana was feeling playful. He kissed her again and wrapped his arms around her this time, and she did the same. It was hot, and Ana didn't want to stop. The door opened, and the light flicked on. It was Jake.

"Sorry to interrupt," he said.

Brittani walked down the steps. "There you are. You ok?"

"Yeah, sure," Ana answered. They all walked around to the front of the house.

"Oh god, Ana, is that Travis?" Brittani asked.

"Yeah, it is. I've got to get out of here," Ana said, beginning to panic.

"What's wrong? Do you want me to ask him to leave? I will," Castin said.

"Yes, I mean, no. I can't be around him. My parents don't trust him. But it's ok, I've got to be home soon anyway," Ana replied. "Brittani, you ready?"

"Ana, I want to stay. My mom thinks I am staying with you," Brittani said. "Well, I can't stay. Can you take me home? I don't want to call my mom," Ana said. "Never mind, you can't drive, neither can I. Hey Castin, is that trail long through the forest?"

"No, I'll take you on my ATV. Should be there in ten or twenty minutes," he said.

"Well, it's near ten now, let's go."

"Be careful, let me know when you get home," Brittani said.

"I'll keep her safe," Castin said.

"We should have plenty of time, right?" Ana asked.

"Oh yeah, I know this trail like the back of my hand." He cranked the ATV, and Ana jumped on. She grabbed him around the waist, and they took off. Ana was glad to be getting away from the party and wanted to spend some more time with Castin. He rode slowly up the trail. They rode for a few minutes through the wood. Then he stopped at a clearing that overlooked her and her aunt's houses.

"This is beautiful," Ana said as she got off. The moon was bright, so she could see their houses clearly. She could even see the lights on in her parent's room. Ana was drunk, but she took another sip of her beer anyway. She sat on an old wooden picnic table. "I can't believe I've never been here."

"Yeah, it is nice," he replied. He turned off the ATV and came to stand in front of her. "Truth."

"Yes?" Ana asked.

"Is it true you want me to kiss you again?"

"Yes, so true." Ana laughed, then reached up, grabbed his collar, and pulled him down to kiss her. He cradled her head, and she held onto his body. He felt solid and firm in her arms. "Are you a creep?" Ana asked him.

He laughed. "I hope you know that by now. I won't hurt you, Ana." She kissed his cheek, and he nuzzled her neck. "Are you ready to go home?"

She looked at her phone. "It's only ten-fifteen. We have time to do whatever if you want. I mean, I can see my house." He leaned between her legs on the table and kissed her. She laid back on the table, and he leaned over on top of her. Ana was aroused, and she felt free with him. She knew this wasn't behavior her mother would approve of. Then she thought about that game and how everyone had had sex, but she and Brittani, everybody does it. Ana thought. Ana didn't want to stop. She was very much in the moment. He pulled her shirt over to one side and kissed her chest. She pulled her shirt and bra up for him, and he massaged her breast with his hands and then mouth, suckling her small breast. Her nipple was tender, and his mouth made it hard. "You're beautiful," he said, seeing her white skin in the moonlight beneath him. Ana unbuttoned her jeans, and he looked into her eyes. The moonlight shone bright, and they could see each other easily. "Are you sure?" he asked gently.

"Yes, as long as you don't hurt me," she said. He pulled her jeans off, then her panties. He gently placed his finger inside of her then bent down, putting his mouth between her legs. Her legs were stiff, barely letting him in, but as his tongue touched her and she relaxed. He kissed her thighs then moved higher. When he got to her clitoris, he vibrated his tongue rapidly against it. "Oh, god," she said, then clenched his head between her legs, feeling his hair on her thighs. She moaned. "Castin, put it in me." He stood up and placed his penis at her opening.

"This could hurt," he said.

"It's ok," she said, feeling desperate for him. He gently pushed inside with his fingers first. She gasped, then he kissed her and put his penis inside her. She grimaced, and he stopped. "It's ok."

"Are you sure?" he asked again.

"Yes, keep going." He penetrated her, and she felt him deep inside her. She could feel herself widening around him. It hurt at first, then she felt herself pulsate and shiver all over. He grabbed her around the waist.

"Oh, Ana," he said as he flipped her over on the table. Ana was so into the sex she didn't mind. He put his fingers slowly into her again. "Does that feel good?" Ana was feeling everything and was enjoying it.

"Yes," she answered. With one push, he was inside her again, large and in charge. He pulled her to him as he went deeper. Ana felt all of him and wanted him more. "Oh, it feels so good," she said. He pulled her hair gently, and he exploded into her hard with three deep thrusts. Ana was so weak she laid back on the table, feeling hot fluid on her legs.

He leaned over and kissed her. "Let me help you. He took off his shirt and wiped her."

"Thank you." She leaned over, buttoned her pants, and looked at her phone. It was ten forty-five.

"Are you ok?" he asked, concerned.

"Yeah, I am," Ana said. Castin stood against the trees, his body illuminated with moonlight. Suddenly they heard something behind them, and Castin turned around quickly. A dark figure jumped on Castin, and Ana screamed.

"Ana, run," Castin said in the struggle. Ana heard a thud, and Castin was lying on the ground. Castin grabbed for the person but couldn't reach them. Ana ran for her life and didn't look back.

Andrea was watching TV in the living room when she looked down at her watch. 11:01 was what it read. Where was Ana? She scrolled on her phone, and her location showed she was behind the Summers' house, in between their property and the Summers'. I could ride over there, she thought. No,

I don't want to go storming over there. I need to give her a few more minutes. Andrea texted her, where are you? You ok? 11:10, no response.

Andrea called Diane. "Ana isn't home or answering my texts. She was supposed to be here at eleven."

"Where is she?" Diane asked.

"Jake Summers house, they had a party. Brittani was going to bring her home."

"Well, she's probably drinking because you know they allow that over there."

"Oh, I didn't know that. I'm going over there. Do you want to go?" Suddenly Andrea's phone rang, it was from Ana. "Hello," Andrea said. She didn't hear anything. Then it hung up. "Weird, she just called, but she didn't speak," she told Diane, "I'm going, now. Something is wrong."

"Hold on. I'll go too." Andrea picked Diane up in her car within four minutes. "Do you think she's just too drunk?" Diane asked, hoping that might be the case.

"I don't know. God, I am a terrible parent, I shouldn't have let her go," Andrea said. Diane called Jeffrey and sent him a picture of Ana's last location.

"You can't do this. You have to let her do things. She can't be a child forever." They pulled into the Summers' drive, and the road was full of cars. Teenagers were scattered all over the yard, talking, laughing, and drinking. Diane and Andrea pushed through the crowd to get into the house. Unfortunately, they didn't know anyone inside. They went into the back yard and saw Brittani standing by the fire.

"There's Brittani," Andrea said. Brittani wasn't paying attention, so she didn't recognize the voice calling her name.

"Yeah, what?" she responded as she turned around to see Andrea. Andrea ignored the rude response.

"Where is Ana?" Andrea asked with Diane beside her.

"She went home," Brittani said. Brittani had had a lot of alcohol and was drunk.

"When?" asked Diane.

"A while ago, she should be home by now."

"Who took her home?" Andrea asked.

"She went through the woods, Castin took her on his ATV." Andrea exchanged looks with Diane.

Meredith Summers came outside. "What's wrong?" she asked Diane.

"Ana was not home by curfew. She isn't here, so, where is she?" Diane demanded.

"Was she drinking?" asked Andrea.

Jake stood behind Brittani. "Yeah, the last time I saw her, she was with Castin making out in the basement," he said.

Brittani turned around and said, "Shut the hell up, Jake." Andrea looked at Diane with dread on her face.

"Ask Castin. He probably took her home," said Susan.

"He did. They went through the woods on an ATV," Diane confirmed.

"When did she leave?" Andrea asked.

"It was like right at ten because she freaked out about Travis," Brittani said.

"Travis was here? Where is he? Did he leave?" Diane asked.

"I don't know, but I haven't seen him since," Brittani answered.

"Castin is a good kid," said Diane to Andrea.

"Where is he then, Diane?" Andrea shouted. Meredith sent Jake and his friends to hunt for Castin around the house. Five minutes later, they came back with no Castin.

"Mom, his four-wheeler is gone, but I don't know where," Jake said. Meredith looked frantic and embarrassed in front of Diane and Andrea.

"Let's go to the barn. Maybe they stopped there," said Diane. She called Jeffrey on her way to fill him in, and he beat them to the barn.

"Nobody's here," Jeffrey said. "I'm going to the trail they should have been on." Diane quickly ran after him, telling him about Travis. They got on the

ATV and headed for the tree line. As they neared the trees and path, the headlights shone on Castin.

"Oh my god, look, it's Castin," Diane said. He was screaming, and his head was bleeding.

"He took Ana. He took her! Jeff, he took her! We have to go after him," he said, panting.

Jeffrey shook Castin. "Who took her Castin? Who?" he shouted at him.

"Travis, it was Travis."

"Did he take your ATV?" Jeff asked.

"No, I wrecked it trying to catch him. He was on foot, but I saw his truck."

"Get on the ATV," Diane said.

Castin saw Ana's mother sitting on the ATV. "Oh my god Mrs. Hutchingson, I am so sorry. I am so sorry." He sobbed and held his head. Jeffrey called the police and then Phillip.

The police and an ambulance arrived. The ambulance took Castin in for an evaluation. His parents got there before the ambulance took him. Andrea was in the car at the stables waiting on Diane. "Where are the detectives? Why are they not searching? Damn it, Diane, he will kill her. Please, we have to go look for her," Andrea cried.

"We're going, Jeffrey called Phillip, they will find her. Oh my god, please let them find her," Diane pleaded.

Ana ran hard but was unfamiliar with the terrain. She ran over the creek bank and fell hard, striking her head on a rock. She felt her phone in her back pocket, she reached for it and dialed her mom's number. She heard her mom answer, but she couldn't hear her. Ana could hear him coming. She put down the phone and laid there in pain, hoping whoever it was would think she was dead. Arms grabbed her and threw her into the air. She fought and kicked as she was being carried. She screamed, but no one heard her. She was thrown into a truck, and the door slammed behind her. He pulled her hands behind her and bound them with tape. She tried to open her eyes, but her head was hurting, and she was dizzy. Opening her eyes made it worse. She could feel blood running down the back of her head. She'd caught a glimpse of her attacker but didn't recognize him. She screamed again, a shirt was tied around her eyes, and her mouth was taped shut. She bit him when he tried to tape her mouth, and he pushed her head hard against the window. She was hot and disoriented, and she couldn't hear well out of her left ear. He started the truck and drove away. Ana kicked at him, but he just slapped her legs away. He pushed her up against the door, and her head hit the window again. They drove for a short distance and stopped. He opened the door, and Ana almost fell out of the truck, but he caught her and threw her over his shoulder.

Andrea was back at home, trying to make sense of the whole night. The police had just finished asking her questions. She wanted to leave, and she felt like she was wasting time not doing anything. Castin's mom and dad were with him at the hospital. They, too, were shocked, but at least their son was alive. Charleigh had arrived at the house where Andrea, Philip, Diane, and Jefferey were. and Andrea broke down in tears when she saw her. "I shouldn't have let her go. I should have known better," Andrea shouted. Charleigh didn't say anything, just tried to hold her. Andrea sat down and laid in Charleigh's lap.

"Don't be silly. It sounds like she was on her way home. You didn't do this, and she didn't do this," Charleigh said. Phillip came around the corner. He had just finished talking to the police.

Drake had arrived and ran to his dad. "Dad, where is she? Did you tell them about that truck, Dad? Did you tell them?" Drake was frantic and crying.

"What truck?" asked Andrea.

"We saw a blue truck the other day parked near the barn. It looked very suspicious," answered Drake.

"No, I didn't, but I will," Philip headed back outside toward the police.

Charleigh interrupted, "That's the vehicle Ana, and I passed the other day on the same road. Ana said it was Travis." Andrea looked at Diane.

"Yes, Travis has a blue truck. I saw him driving on the backside of the stable the other week. He was parked there too," Jeffrey chimed in.

"I'm going to Travis's house," Phillip said.

Jeffrey answered, "I'm going too."

"Phillip, find her, please find her," Andrea pleaded. They got in a vehicle and sped away. The police brought Ana's phone to Diane. It was cracked and had blood on it.

"Ma'am, we found this in a creek bed along with this." He showed her a picture of blood that had dripped on a large rock.

"Anything else?" she asked.

"No, we are still searching the area. We did track his truck to the road."

"I'm going to the hospital to talk to Castin. Come on, Charleigh," Andrea said, and Charleigh followed her.

Castin was still in the Emergency room when they arrived. They were sewing up his lacerations as they entered the room. Fortunately, a head CT revealed only a small skull fracture but no bleeding. When Andrea walked in, the police were questioning Castin. Castin recognized Andrea and started talking to her, ignoring the police. "I'm so sorry, Mrs. Hutchinson."

Andrea patted his hand. He looked like he had been struck hard, he had dirt on his knees, and his white undershirt was torn. "Can you tell me anything about tonight, anything about Ana?" Andrea asked.

"What do you remember?" asked the police.

"We stopped at the high point where the picnic area is. We were standing there and heard someone behind us, I turned around, and he jumped me. I told Ana to run."

Andrea looked at Castin. "I need you to tell me the truth. It doesn't matter what you say as long as it is the truth."

Castin replied, "Yes, ma'am."

"Was Ana talking to anyone at the party besides you?"

"She was with Brittani and me mostly. She didn't want to be around Travis."

Andrea quickly asked, "Do you think it was Travis that took her?"

"Yes, it was him. I saw his face. I asked Ana if she wanted me to make him leave, but she said no, she would just stay away from him."

"Who is Travis?" the police officer asked.

"Travis is a guy that Ana had a short relationship with. He's a lot older than her, and when we found out about the relationship, he was fired. He used to work for my sister-in-law at their stables," Andrea answered.

"Why do you think it was him?" asked the officer.

"Because he was watching us, and saw us kiss, and I saw his face..." Castin offered. The police left the room, and Phillip followed them. Andrea and Charleigh stayed in the room with Castin.

"Castin, how drunk was Ana?" Andrea asked.

"She was tipsy but not too drunk. She was talking and functioning like normal."

"Well, that's good news," Andrea replied. Castin kept apologizing to Andrea.

"I know you didn't mean for this to happen, Castin." Castin started to tear up, and he turned his head. "Castin, what's wrong?"

"I'm just really sorry," he said. She felt like he wanted to say more, but he didn't. She knew deep down he hadn't done anything to hurt Ana. She told him to rest and that they would be back when they found Ana. Andrea and Charleigh got in the car and headed home.

CHAPTER SEVENTEEN

The Cave

Ana woke up in a dark place, lying on the ground. Her hands were still behind her, but her eyes were uncovered. Her head was hurting, but she could see clearer now than before. The room wasn't spinning, and she didn't feel nauseous. She was cold because her shirt and pants were torn. There were only small amounts of light that came from behind the door in front of her, but she thought she was alone. Ana tried to remember what they taught her in training at the academy. She had been part of an exercise that taught you how to resist in a hostage situation. Ana spat on the tape and moved her mouth, loosening it. She wiggled her arms and managed to get one hand almost free. She heard a noise, and the door opened. Ana closed her eyes and froze like she was asleep. The captor came close to her, laid his hands on her chest, and stroked her face. Ana wanted to scream, but she knew that would only make things worse. He walked back to the door, and Ana looked up. She turned and tried to see her attacker. She thought she recognized the boots the person was wearing. Ana tried to loosen her hands more and finally managed to get one hand free. She sat on the ground with her hands behind her. When she managed to stand, she felt around the room. The walls were rocky, like in a cave, but the door her captor used was the only way in or out. She heard him coming back. She froze and closed her eyes. He finally spoke, "Ana, wake up." Ana opened her eyes, and he sat her up so she could see him. Ana looked up to see Travis kneeling down in front of her. Ana tried to talk, but it was muffled. "Don't talk, just relax. I'm going to get you cleaned up." Ana struggled as he started to remove her shirt. She loosened her hand and hit him. He grabbed her hand and twisted it behind her back. "Stop moving. I'm trying to be nice to you," he said calmly. He stood her up and tied her arms around a support beam near the wall of the cave.

Ana tried to mumble again, and this time she made sense, "Let me go."

"No, you're staying here. Don't do anything stupid, or you'll regret it." He tore off the tape and pressed his lips to hers, forcing himself against her.

He stood back, and she said, "Travis, what are you doing?"

"I'm keeping you," Travis said. Ana then realized he wasn't in his right mind. He pulled a bottle of whiskey out of his pocket and took a long drink.

"Let me go. What is wrong with you?"

"So you can go back and screw Castin!" he screamed and slapped her face.

Ana shook her head. "Travis, we were never dating. You don't own me."

"Don't move or say a word, or I will kill you." Ana heard him but couldn't believe what she was hearing. Was he for real? What was wrong with him? Ana looked at him and tried to think of ways she knew to get away, what she could say to throw him off. He leaned over, grabbed a rag, and wiped her face again. "That's a good girl," he said as he stroked the rag down her neck.

"Travis, this isn't good. You were a good guy. What happened?" Her voice trembled.

He ripped her shirt to expose her breast. "I was good, and you screwed it all up. You wanted me, but then you rejected me. You pranced around in front of me, and when I got close, your stupid family snapped their fingers, and now my life sucks," he screamed. "You owe me Ana, or whoever the hell you are. You made me think we were together, and then you wouldn't even answer my calls. You're no better than I am." He splashed her with the liquid he was drinking. She was dripping wet all over her breast and cut off her bra with a rusty pocketknife. She was cold, with goosebumps all over her shaking body. He leaned over and licked her chest, then put his mouth on her breast. Ana almost vomited. She gagged. "Get off of me," Ana screamed. Travis slapped her face. Ana tasted fresh blood in her mouth.

"I'm cold. Can I please have a blanket?" she asked.

Travis looked at her and then walked, he said as she grabbed her throat. She didn't respond to him. Ana looked into his eyes, they were so dark, and she could see the demons within him. He looked possessed. He pushed her head back hard and splashed the bucket of dirty water on her chest, drenching her from head to toe. He finally walked out of the room. She clenched her eyes closed and cried. She knew he was going to rape and kill her. She'd seen that demon before in her former father and mother when they were on drugs. No, they never tried to kill her or sexually assault her, but the physical abuse and mental abuse was enough for her to easily recognize that she was dealing with a man serving himself and his needs no matter the cost or however irrational it was to everyone he was determined. She stood there bound, in the dark room, now cold and wet. Her head and her arms and legs hurt. Actually, there wasn't a place she didn't hurt, but that pain meant she was alive, and she would fight. She began to flashback to her childhood. She could see herself not through her own eyes but from the outside looking in. She remembered standing tall during hell week at the academy and how tired and broken she felt. Physically exhausted, yes, but she remembered standing there facing her past and all she was and had been. Many people quit. She was only one of seven females still in her class. She had to reach and grasp what she knew was right and what she had faith in, what she had trust in.

"God, help me," she prayed softly. "God, I want to hurt him because I know he wants to hurt me.". She began to pray with her soul. She didn't say a word or think any certain thoughts or requests, she let go, and all her words of thanks and repentance were communicated effortlessly. Her breathing slowed, and she began to doze in and out of sleep as she crouched on the floor with her head on her knees. The tears stopped and were replaced with anger. As she dozed, she could hear the words, "Never give up, always keep trying, fight till the end," in the voice of her greatest mentor. She could see her, as she had once stood before her, a representation of everything Ana had wanted to be, so strong and brave and respected for all the right reasons.

"Wake up," she heard so loud she thought someone else was in the room. She opened her eyes, but no one was there. She heard her mother's voice, "I will come find you, Ana, I will never let you go." It was like her mother was sitting beside her. Ana shook her head and thought maybe she had a brain injury that was making her hallucinate.

She heard Travis hit something hard, then a scrape across the floor, then all noise stopped. She began to move her hands again and managed to get dirt up around her wrists on the adhesive of the tape. She could feel them loosen little by little, and she was able to again pull one hand free. She stood and slowly walked to the door. Seeing only a crack of light through it, she managed not to fall. As she peered through the crack, she saw him, his gun on the table. He was leaned back in a chair with the bottle of whiskey on the floor beside him. He looked like he was passed out. Ana started to feel her way around the room. She didn't know the dimensions or what obstacles would be in her way, but she needed to search the room for a way out or a potential weapon. She could see the post, and from it, she could judge her distance just in case she had to return quickly. She reached toward the floor and found a few old glass bottles and a softball-sized rock. She could use the glass of the bottle to harm him, but the bottle needed to be broken. Too loud, she thought. She reached down and found what she thought was a rod of some type. There was some sort of stand or table near the door. She knew that because he had placed his bottle on it before when he entered. She heard him move, grabbed the rod, and went back to the pole, pretending to be asleep. He came in and kicked her to wake her up. She barely lifted her head to show him she was conscious but not too alert. She wanted to play off his affection for her, or what he used to have for her. However, his affection was skewed with a dominating force of evil. She began to drool purposefully. He crouched down and picked up her head, examining her. He saw how battered she looked with the dried blood above her eye and swollen face. She hoped it was working but wasn't sure. He picked up her face and wiped her mouth, then stood up and walked out again, closing the door behind him. He came back minutes later with a blanket over his shoulder, his pants undone, carrying the bottle of whiskey. The gun, she assumed, was in his back pocket. He threw the blanket on the floor. Ana knew what was going to happen next, so as he stood in front of her, she waited to take her shot at him. As he reached to get something off the table, she swung at his head. Hitting him hard, he dropped the bottle, and it broke on the floor. As she swung, he was able to reach out and grab her, but she pulled away hard. The rod hit the floor beside her, out of her reach. "So, that's how you want to play?" he said, teasing her. He jerked her to the ground, and she managed to hit him hard in the face. His nose started to bleed. He reached for her hair and pulled her back down to the floor. She tried to move away from him, but he had her pinned by her hips as he straddled her on his knees. She reached out, hoping she could find the rod. Her fingers closed around it, and she swung, catching him off guard, but he ripped it out of her hands and held it to her throat. He threatened her as he choked her. He could easily kill her from his position. "Don't move, or I will kill you," He whispered in her ear.

"Stop, please stop," she pleaded.

"No, you know you want this." He reached down and ripped her underwear to the side. Ana squirmed and screamed loudly. He slammed her head against the stone floor, and Ana blacked out cold. Ana woke up about a minute later with another headache. He was still on her, but she couldn't see him or really feel him, just his weight. She screamed again and suddenly heard a loud noise. It shot a piercing pain through her brain. When she awoke he was gone.

"God, help me," she said out loud praying softly. "God help me, I know he wants to hurt me." Then Ana stopped speaking. With silence and dampness surrounding her, Ana closed her eyes. A feeling of impending doom loomed over her like a death shroud on her shoulders. With the exception of God Almighty reaching down and plucking her from this hell of a cave that embodied her. Anastasia knew she would die. Anastasia pleaded for her life to the only one who could help her, God. Without the uttering of a sound communicated, not through her lips or larynx, but through the deepest part of her, her soul. It was an overwhelming feeling at first to produce the last thoughts, requests she would ever pray, although when she stopped thinking her soul spoke for her and revealed all the emotions and desires of her heart. Thankfulness, and redemption, joy and the desire to live all were communicated effortlessly. At the end her headache stopped and a feeling peace filled her. Her breathing slowed, and she began to doze in and out of sleep, she was now crouched on the floor with her head supported by her knees. During this time of brief rest Ana's mother's face appeared and her eyes were extraordinarily bright angelic almost, she felt around her, the same embrace her dad gave her the first time she met him. She could feel her Aunt Diane's hands on her shoulders as she kissed her head so many times since she had been home. The air shifted in the room, the tiny blonde hairs on her face stood up, she envisioned Shotsley in front of her, Shotsley's felty nose nuzzled to her own, the air warm greatly resembling the horse's earthy breath breathing into her. The tears stopped, she slept.

"Anastasia," she heard so loud and distinct, Ana turned her head actually thinking someone was with her in the room. She opened her eyes quickly but she was alone. Ana could hear her mother's voice deep within her. "I will come for you Ana, I will never let you go." Ana gathered her courage and prepared for the fight of her life.

Made in the USA
Columbia, SC
15 October 2021